THE UNSEEN

THE UNSEEN

A DETECTIVE NOVEL

*BY VALERIO VARESI AND TRANSLATED
BY JOSEPH FARRELL*

PATRICIAN PRESS
MANNINGTREE

First published in Great Britain as a paperback edition by Patrician Press 2022

E-book edition published by Patrician Press 2022

First published in Italian as *Gli Invisibili* by Mondadori Libri 2019

This book has been translated thanks to a translation grant awarded by the Italian Ministry of Foreign Affairs and International Cooperation.

Questo libro è stato tradotto grazie a un contributo alla traduzione assegnato dal Ministero degli Affari Esteri e della Cooperazione Internazionale italiano.

British Library Cataloguing in Publication Data. A catalogue record for this book is available from the British Library.

ISBN paperback edition 978-0-8380598-5-9

ISBN e-book edition 978-1-8380598-8-0

Patrician Press Collective 2022

I

There are some who seek invisibility by choice and others who have no option but to live in the silence, solitude and fearful evasiveness of nocturnal animals. Life is a tapestry weaving everyone into one overall pattern, but these people are loose stitches stretching and weakening the web, making it impossible to reconnect the threads.

Soneri remembered stories of that sort, of people who were incapable, perhaps through shyness, of forming relationships, or who had destroyed them through indifference. Old folk found dead at home after months in a fixed, daily routine, or young people shunned by broken or scattered families, who no longer have a family to which they belong.

The man in front of him was a case in point. According to the mortuary records he was neither old nor young. In his fifties, apparently. Male, robust build, 'white race', as they had written, in keeping with the medical-bureaucratic jargon which contained more than an echo of Fascism. His features had been blurred by his time in the water and perhaps by being pulled about by the currents of the Po on the abrasive sands of the riverbed, sands which had been the man's only tomb. There was no way of knowing how long he had been there before the river in spate had re-exhumed his body. The river is honest, at least in this respect. It always restores everything, even to those who have no idea what to do with it.

And that was exactly the point. The man had been lying in a refrigerated chamber for more than three years and no-one had come forward to reclaim him, now the time had come to bury him. That was the law. In the absence of a name, they would have to assign initials to him. No-one had any idea if it would be appropriate to put a cross or something else above that little pile of dust. Not even that could be permitted to a man like him. He had no-one in the world, and nor would he have anyone on high.

The very idea caused Soneri some anxiety. He could not fathom why they had sent him of all people on a job which should have been the responsibility of the judicial police. It must have been an act of spite by some functionary. He hated all functionaries, with their bureaucratic jargon playing hide-and-seek with common sense. Another small humiliation. The better you are, the harder they batter you over the head. That's the way public administration works, but that had nothing to do with the way he was feeling. He could not get out of his head that the man resting on a slab had the same value as a piece of debris.

Back in his office, he had them bring the complete dossier on the man. The enquiries had been conducted by Inspector Carradori, who had since been transferred to Treviso. On the basis of the division of territorial responsibility, the case should have been handled by the carabinieri, but it had been passed on to the police as initially it was believed that the victim had gone missing in Parma. From that point responsibility for the enquiry had remained somewhat uncertain, with the result that no-one had really given it much thought. The man had been hauled out of the river near the mouth of the Enza on the Emilian banks. The body had marks of trauma in the occipital area, the probable cause of death, and signs of a serious thoracic contusion. The injury to the head could have been caused either by a blow or a fall because, in the forensic pathologist's opinion, the bruise in the thorax was compatible with violent contact with water, as in the case of a person jumping from a bridge, but these were only hypotheses. The autopsy had left open different possibilities – homicide, suicide or accident. Carradori had devoted himself diligently to the case for some time, but had not come up with anything worthwhile before his transfer caused the enquiry to end up in the pending files in the ante-chamber of the archives.

Soneri picked up the dossier again, beginning to feel a sneaking affinity with the dead man and his mystery. He imagined being dead himself. Who would remember him? Angela certainly, but anyone else? Ada, his wife, had passed away too early and the duty to remember her had been left to him. A son who had never been born. Colleagues? Perhaps. Nanetti, Juavara, Musumeci... but for how long? He raised his eyes from the papers and looked out the window. The mist forming over the courtyard was taking the shape of a soft pillow on which to rest those thoughts. If he had chosen to become a police officer, it was because of his determination to find solutions to everything left unsolved. His excessive trust in reason had frequently led to disappointment, but each time he had picked himself up and tried again. He was well aware that a step-by-step ascent towards a solution to the most important questions was nothing more than an ambitious illusion, but that was why he felt such curiosity about this man. He was searching for a meaning to existence, his own and everyone else's. If it happened to take the form of a police enquiry, that was neither here nor there. The life of every man was an enquiry, invariably concluding with a judgement.

He resumed reading. The examination of the fabrics revealed that they had been immmersed in water for three to six weeks. When he was discovered, he was dressed in jeans, shirt, cotton jumper and jacket. In the zipped, inside pocket of the jacket they had found a receipt, a post card with the view of some city and a small, crumpled ticket which must have issued by some underground railway. When these items had been examined, it transpired that the last two were from Toulouse. Enlarged face-on and side-on photographs were attached. Soneri stared at the receipt which the zipped pocket had partially saved from the water. It was still possible to read 'Mot... nave,' and lower down '...vari'. There were also some signs which could scarcely be made out but could have been numbers. At the foot, all that could be deciphered was a truncated word ending in '...issa.' Both the magistrate and Carradori had interpreted the first word as *Motonave*, or launch, and the second as *Stradivari*, referring to the cruise ship which sailed on the Po to the rhythm of a mazurka, but neither had any idea about the final word. According to Carradori, it could have been the final part of 'tariffa fissa', fixed price, and so it would have been part of a boarding card, but Soneri was not convinced and thought the letters referred to something else. He picked up the phone and dialled the number of the company which owned the *Stradivari*. A secretary confirmed that there was no such thing as a fixed price, and each passenger paid according to the port where he got on. Soneri then asked if the launch stopped at Torricella di Sissa, and secretary replied that it certainly did. She went on to add, with some emphasis, that that was one of the most important ports of call.

With that confirmation, Soneri felt that he too was getting somewhere. The body of that man was no longer floating in the current. Soneri knew where he had embarked, so the next thing was to find out where he had got off and had ended in the river, and whether he had fallen from a bridge or from the boat. The latter possibility seemed the less likely. The cruises along the river are made by day and those on board are seated in groups, so it would have been hard for someone to fall into the water or be attacked without anyone noticing. There was more likelihood of a fall from a parapet and a crash onto the gravel on the riverbed. In addition, the doctor had established that in the man's trachea and upper windpipes a small quantity of water had been found, but he had been unable to judge if that water had entered after death while the body was still in the water, or if it was a consequence of a final, feeble struggle. In this latter case, it signified that when he plunged into the water, the man was still alive.

While he was reading the dossier, the phone rang. 'I've got Superintendent Capuozzo for you,' the superintendent's secretary said, to Soneri's annoyance. He could never understand why Capuozzo did not dial the number himself. Rather than an operational centre, the police station was a theatre of vanities where a power struggle was acted out. Part of the script involved being kept waiting on the line. As Soneri pondered the uselessness of this procedure, a deep sigh at the other end announced the superintendent's arrival.

'I know, I know, Soneri, it shouldn't have been been assigned to you but the judicial police had no officers and the mortuary... consider it a personal favour,' he said hurriedly before even uttering a greeting.

'Don't worry,' Soneri replied coldly.

'Listen, as far as I'm concerned, it looks like an open and shut case.'

'To me it looks totally open.'

'What do you mean? Even the magistrate has given up on this one.'

'You don't know who he is, you don't know how he died. Can we really consider it closed?'

Capuozzo paused for a moment. Soneri could have sworn he was cursing to himself.

'I might seem cynical, but no-one has ever come looking for him, no-one has...'

'Except the possible murderer,' Soneri interrupted him.

'That may be, but he might also have killed himself. Carradori was almost convinced of that. Off a bridge, banging his head against a pillar as he fell. He checked up. At that time the waters of the Po were seasonally low, and with low waters the foundations begin to appear.'

'When did we ever close a case on the basis of a hypothesis?'

At the other end of the line, Capuozzo grunted something incomprehensible. 'Want to know what I think? He was a foreigner, one of the many who turn up to catch our catfish in the Po. There are plenty of these people up and down the banks. Maybe things didn't go too well for him, maybe he got out of his depth and that was that. I repeat, you might think I'm a cynic, but how many nameless folk disappear after turning up here among us? The seas are full of them. All right, this guy didn't end up in the sea. He's a fresh water fugitive, but that doesn't change anything.'

'So we just drop the whole thing?'

'That's not what I said,' Capuozzo rushed to clarify. 'This is a confidential conversation, between you and me, understand? I've told you what I think. Anyway, with the limited forces at our disposal... I mean to say, we can't pursue everybody. We don't know much about those who get washed up in the sea, and it's not as if anybody's lining up to reclaim them. They knew from the outset that they wouldn't be back.'

Capuozzo waited for Soneri to reply, but he remained silent.

The Superintendent continued, 'Look, do what you please. If you want to continue with the enquiries, go ahead, but make sure you co-ordinate what you're doing with the carabinieri.' He hung up, giving the impression of a man freeing himself of an inconvenience.

2

Soneri was on the point of leaving the office when the duty officer told him someone wanted to see him.

'Who is it?' he asked.

The officer made a gesture indicating he had no idea. 'He said his name was Ragu Camillo.'

The name meant nothing to him, but Soneri turned back and sat down again at his desk. A few seconds later, he watched as a somewhat dishevelled youth with long black hair and a bushy beard came in. Without embarrassment, neither saying hello nor waiting to be invited, he took a seat.

Soneri shot a questioning, confidential look in his direction.

'You were looking for me, were you not?' said the man.

'Not me, but this place is full of people who are searching for somebody or other.'

The man started rummaging about in his multi-coloured, woollen bag and pulled out a rolled-up newspaper which he flattened out on the desk, pointing to a picture and a brief article at the foot of the page. The headline over it said simply, 'Missing'.

Soneri stared at the photo, looked up at the young man and took it all in. 'So you're this missing person?' he asked, savouring the paradox of the situation. His thoughts went to the unknown man from the Po.

Soneri looked at the top of the page for the date and saw that it was a copy of the Sardinian daily, *La Nuova Sardegna*, from three months previously.

'I never read newspapers. A friend passed it on to me.'

'And you're not in the habit of phoning home?'

'Home!' the young man exclaimed.

'If there's been a report made to the police, it means there must be a home from which you're missing.'

'Read it again. It's a lawyer who's looking for me.' Alongside the article, there was the address of a lawyer's office in Nuoro.

'It seems my father's dead and I've inherited his things. They couldn't locate me, so they're obliged by law to put a notice in the papers to cover their arses.'

Soneri agreed. 'I hope your father left you enough to let you live comfortably. I don't know why they directed you here to the Flying Squad. I'll call a colleague to take a statement.'

He had already lifted his phone to dial the extension when the man said, 'I couldn't give a fuck about the property.'

Soneri made an effort to remain professional, even while he recognised the young man's distress. 'So why are you here?'

'I only wanted to let you know that I'm alive,' Ragu explained angrily. 'I'm one of the unseen, but the unseen do turn up, and in a rage.'

'Don't imagine you're the only ones,' Soneri heard himself saying as he put down the phone. He was puzzled about the man's attitude.

'It seems you lot have never been all that curious.'

Soneri thought of his contemporaries who were satisfied with taking a salary, yoked to an easy job.

'How come you have no-one?' he asked, changing tack.

'The fact that two miserable beings toss you into this world. Normally it's the children who cause problems for their parents, but for me it was the opposite.'

'Why did you come here? You're Sardinian.'

'I wander about. I don't actually have a home. Sometimes, I stay in one.'

Soneri was so taken aback by this that for a moment he thought he might be dealing with a fantasist, like many others he had come across in the past. Some had been so convincing as to make him later feel ridiculous, and for that reason he turned back to the computer and began to type in the youth's name. After a few moments, he received confirmation that he was indeed on the missing person list, but another entry had been logged prior to the lawyer's, in the name of a girl, Tina Canu.

Soneri pointed this out to the youth. 'Who is she?'

Ragu seemed upset. He shook his head, making his hair wave about.

'She was my girlfriend.'

'But you left her?'

'Do I look like the kind of guy who wants a wife and kids? After all I've been through? I got myself together some time back. I don't go screwing at random to create more unhappy souls.'

'I don't believe your folks wanted all this,' said Soneri, trying to provoke him. Ragu seemed to be one of those people who are desperate to speak but are held back by a kind of shame, the result of loneliness and long silences.

'What would you think if your father abandoned you when you were three to the care of an addict mother whose only love was for her next fix? Do you know who saved me? Or maybe I should say who kept me going as one of "life's unfortunates". A social worker whose name I don't even remember, followed by years in an institution run by nuns and then a succession of foster families, who kept me for a bit and then threw in the towel. I was too demanding, too rebellious. Even generosity has its limits before it expires, like a bus pass when all the holes have been punched. Puppy dogs are abandoned; children are handed back.'

'What became of your mother?'

'How should I know? She'll have ended up stretched out under some bridge, or struck down by some illness.'

'You never went looking for her?'

'Do you imagine she came looking for me? I couldn't care less. If you don't give love, you can't expect it.'

'That girl, did she give you love?'

'Tina,' he muttered with a melancholy smile. 'Yes, she did.'

'Well then?'

'You can't really keep a stray dog in your house. He runs off and you take him back, and after a while you both suffer.'

Soneri changed subject. 'As far as the inheritance is concerned, you need a lawyer.'

'I've already told you I couldn't care less. I'll write to this lawyer, but only to tell him that I haven't disappeared. He's free to consider me as one of those who have.'

'In any case, you'll have to appear in person or get a representative. That's the procedure.'

'They can stick their procedure up their arses. Living is now a bureaucratic matter, a signature on waste paper. They register you, stamp you and then file you on a shelf. Humanity is an archive in a registry. Well, count me out. Nobody wants anything to do with people like me, apart from lawyers, judges and the police. We're no good to anybody, end of story.'

Soneri scribbled the telephone number of his partner, Angela Cornelio, on a piece of paper and handed it over to him.

'If you like, you can contact this person. She might be helpful. No obligation.'

Ragu grabbed at the sheet of paper, sending it spinning over the desk, folded it and put it in his bag. Soneri picked up the phone and called his colleague who would have to record everything in the register.

'I can't be bothered with these things any more than you but, as I've told you, it's the routine,' Soneri said. He told the officer the youth would be coming down. Ragu got up and for a moment seemed reluctant to leave. That moment was an expression of gratitude.

Shortly afterwards, Soneri left and saw the duty officer. 'Why did you send him to me?' he asked.

'Aren't you involved with some missing person?'

'Not that one!' he said, heading straight out onto the Bordo della Posta. As he continued on his way, he reflected on the strange coincidence. It occurred to him that Ragu could still demonstrate his existence by giving vent to his rage and kicking out at indifference, while the dead man had the advantage of having no consciousness of these things.

The encounter left him troubled. He phoned Angela to inform her of the possible arrival of a new client.

'Who is he?' she asked.

'A young lad they sent to me by mistake, someone with no family and who went missing.'

'And what am I supposed to do with him?'

'His father died and he is the heir, but he doesn't care about what's been left to him.'

'So he wants to renounce his inheritance?'

'I don't know. He's very confused and I couldn't quite understand. I'm not even sure if he'll come. I gave him your address.'

'So you've been downgraded to the information office?' Angela joked.

'In one sense... This morning I had to go to the mortuary because of someone they'd been keeping in a fridge and had been unclaimed. Someone fished out of the Po. And today the duty officer got mixed up and thought that the missing person I was involved with was this youth, and not a corpse.'

'That was no mix-up. These things never happened by accident.'

'You getting superstitious again?'

'Faced with coincidences like that, yes. And I'm nearly always right. You know how the court environment is packed with superstitious rituals. I've got colleagues with more lucky charms in their pockets than you'd find in a market in Naples.'

'In fact, that man in the refrigerated chamber has unnerved me, but I don't know why.'

'The chick's pecking at the shell to get out.'

Soneri stopped in his tracks. He felt the mist on his face and stood for a moment in silence. 'It's more than a suspicion,' he finally said.

'Then it's an even more serious matter,' Angela replied.

'They'll give him a symbol, you know?'

'I know. I know the law.'

'M89, which stands for Missing 89. They've no imagination at the mortuary. They number them in order.'

'And they put the year he was found alongside the number, so every January they start afresh.'

'There'll be a tiny tombstone on top of a pile of earth: Here Lies

M89,' he went on, walking along Borgo Giacomo Tommasini, looking over Parma under the gentle, restless mist.

'Sometimes it seems to me that you're not cut out for the career you've chosen. You should be enclosed in a shell rather than dressed in a linen suit.'

'What a fine figure I'd cut! The grand gesture is the loser's consolation.' He switched off his phone, lit a cigar and dialled Carradori's number.

'Commissario!' the inspector bawled, as though he were giving New Year greetings. 'You know, you make me nostalgic.'

'Cut it out! Don't act the fool. They've even promoted you up there.'

'Ah yes, so they have, but you know how happy I was in Parma. I even had a circle of... Emilia is more free and easy. Here in the Veneto, it's all more difficult.'

'They make you work, is that it?' Soneri said, letting it be known that the pleasantries were over. 'Anyway, you were in charge of the case of that man who was fished out of the Po, is that right? I mean, that guy no-one claimed, about three years ago.'

'I put my heart and soul into that case,' Carradori confirmed, emphatically.

'I know, I know. I just wanted to understand if you had formed any idea on the case.'

'Unfortunately I didn't manage to get beyond a couple of hypotheses.'

'I have read the dossier. I just wanted to know what you thought.'

'In my view, he was a foreigner, someone from Eastern Europe. Over there, there's no shortage of people fishing for catfish. You know what a lucrative trade it is, don't you?'

'But is it possible that he had no-one? When you were here, was the information circulated to Interpol?'

'Everything possible was done, believe me. Maybe his relatives thought he was having a high old time of it in Italy and had forgotten about them.'

'So after a bit, you gave up?'

'You know how it is. If no-one's putting on pressure, if not even the family come forward, and with all that needs to be done...'

'I know. The dead aren't all equal.'

'Have you seen him? His face was half eaten away, his flesh was boiled. We couldn't even take fingerprints. The best we could do was rough out an identikit, but it was so vague that even if they'd seen him...'

'Yes, I get it,' Soneri murmured, vaguely irritated.

'In the circumstances, what could we do?' As he was speaking, Soneri heard some music in the background, perhaps coming from a café. 'The magistrate had an autopsy done but didn't release the body in case the identity might be uncovered. I worked on the case for weeks, months, but you know how things go. There's a robbery, a drugs ring, an attempted murder, trouble at the football ground... we can't be everywhere.'

'Yes, I know how it is. Things come up. You bang your head against it a couple of times and end up like a fly on a window pane. You get used to the situation, and walk away from it.'

3

Perhaps Angela was right. Only apparently do things happen by chance. The very day Soneri had decided to take up Carradori's half-completed enquiry, a man threw himself into the Po to end it all, only to be overcome by fear and have second thoughts. He started screaming and they pulled him out a kilometre downstream, by then half dead. The spot he had chosen to deliver himself to the current was the same as had many others: a loop in the river at Santa Croce di Polesine, known as Curve 39 by dredging crews. The attachment of would-be suicides to certain points was extremely curious. People who wanted to leave this world still felt such an affection for certain spots that they chose them for their last moment.

That obsession was the main topic of conversation at the nautical club in Torricella. Five people had jumped off at that point

'It's a sheer drop and you get it over with quickly,' explained Ceriani, waving his huge oarsman's hands about.

'Yes, but you obviously have time to repent,' objected Marisa, who did the cleaning, cooking and tended bar at the club.

'If Gorini hadn't heard him shouting... he spent half an hour struggling to get him out, and every time he grabbed hold of the bank the two of them were nearly pulled back in.'

'If he wanted to jump in, I'd have left him,' said the no-nonsense Marisa.

Soneri overheard that conversation in the half-light of the club. The smoke inside added to the mist outside. He liked the place for the rough anarchy of thought that reigned there, not to mention the freedom to smoke in disregard of restrictions. The Po was a free zone, a corner of the world with laws all of its own, with no clauses and sub-clauses. It was the river with its rages, its invasions and retreats, which laid down its laws every time.

'Anyone can change his mind,' said the Viking, so called because he was fair-haired and every spring his skin burned when the first sun peeped through the clouds. 'Remember Casimiro?'

'Casimiro was off his head,' said Marisa.

Ceriani turned towards Soneri. 'You know what he did? It must have been two years ago. He got it into his head that he had cancer and he wanted to die in the river. He took a deck-chair, went up beyond the embankment at the flood plain at Buca dei Francesi and sat down waiting for the river to burst its banks. Two days and two nights he sat there, but the water never came up high enough so all he got was wet feet. He got fed up waiting and decided it wasn't his time. From then on, he has gone round telling everybody that the Po had won him a pardon. He waited for death, but it didn't come, so now he considers himself cured.'

'He's sick in the head,' said Marisa.

In that world of uncertain contours, it was no easier to define the border between the mist and the river water than to mark the boundary between truth and legend. Everything appeared to Soneri like a stage on which reality blended into performance.

'And what about the guy they put into the deep freeze?' he asked.

Ceriani stretched out his arms, but Marisa butted in once again. 'He was one of those who go fishing by night. They're semi-gypsies, with no home or family. The only good thing about them is that they get rid of the catfish.'

'Didn't you just say that you liked catfish,' asked Cefalú with a touch of malice. Sicilian by birth, he was now as much part of the river as the main embankment.

'Look, one of these days I'm going to throw you in head first and watch you sink,' Marisa said, referring to the moving sands of the Po.

'I have a theory,' said the Viking.

Ceriani, who obviously knew what was coming, nodded in agreement.

'Not long before they fished that man out of the river, they found a boat against the breakwater at Stagno, and nobody had any idea whose it was. The carabinieri at Roccabianca contacted all the ports but no-one came forward. Same as with the dead man.'

'Do you think it was his?' asked Soneri.

'Wouldn't you be a bit suspicious? Supposing the boat had turned over on its side and crashed into the bank?'

'That breakwater at Stagno is always a problem. They built it over some tanks the Germans abandoned during their retreat. They're still under there,' said Ceriani.

'By now, they'd be sunk a good twenty metres into the sand' said Cefalú, who sounded sceptical.

'That boat was never a Po boat,' said the Viking.

'Never seen one like it around here,' Ceriani confirmed.

The Viking continued, 'It was a sea craft, the kind you get in the delta but not here. They say it had been put into the water at Cremona and had drifted down with the current. Somebody said they saw it being helped along by a pair of short oars.'

'Saw it where?' asked Soneri.

'At the river port, but we're talking about when they found the boat.'

'Who saw it?'

'Who knows? It was Landini, the commander of the *Stradivari* who told us.'

'The drowned man had a ticket for the riverboat in his pocket and he went on board right here.'

'It was summer, if I remember correctly,' said Marisa, 'the time when they do the cruises, provided the water is high enough. There's no shortage of folk. It's hard to remember. Do you know the date?'

Soneri shook his head.

'In that case...' said Marisa, throwing both her hands in the air to indicate that it was all futile. 'If you ask me, he was one of those...' she said, referring to the fishermen from Eastern Europe.

In the background, the roar of an engine and the metallic beat of a crane could be heard as it hauled the boats ashore before darkness fell. Every so often a van struggled up the towpath after depositing its load at the oil press.

Gradually the discussion drifted to chatter about fish of

unimaginable weight; people who had reported seeing monsters emerging from the water; mullets which leapt over the Ponte del Diavolo at Gramignazzo; hermits who built houses from tree trunks; the skulls and bones of pre-historic animals which appeared in the sands when the water was low; witchcraft and black masses celebrated in the poplar groves and of the disappearance of the sturgeon which for the river men had been the equivalent of the pig for people living off the land. An imprecise and imaginary world took shape, shimmering in a mist which enclosed it like a glass ball.

During a pause in the conversation, Pezzani, president of the nautical club, made his entrance. He noticed Soneri. There were not many new faces in those parts. Marisa made a brief introduction, explaining what had brought the commissario there. She put a couple of glasses of Malvasia down on the table.

'We too made an attempt at a search, but found nothing,' said Pezzani, looking out at the mist. 'No-one should be allowed to depart like that, without a name. It's a question of dignity.'

'That's why I'm here.'

'They'd like to bury him, is that right?'

'They've got to free up the space at the mortuary. There's a limit to everything.'

'Here they all believe he was a foreigner and since no-one's got much time for such people, they didn't take much interest.'

'If finding the name of that man were a wager, I wouldn't risk my money.'

'I admire your tenacity. It does you honour,' said Pezzani.

Voices were heard from under the trees in the piazzale and some figures began to emerge from the mist.

'Here's the cruise ship,' Marisa announced, as she prepared to welcome the passengers. Within a few moments they were all at the bar, enjoying a drink to warm themselves up. The last to make his entrance was the captain, resplendent in his naval uniform with its gilded decorations.

'Here's Landini,' said Pezzani.

'That's the last cruise,' said the captain.

'Not many takers?'

The captain shrugged his shoulders. 'Not enough income to cover the costs,' he admitted looking around at the twenty or so people scattered around the room with drinks in their hands. 'The fact is that the water's so low there's a risk of ramming the prow against a sand bank. They've given up dredging. The river's a trap now.'

Landini was short in stature, as blond as the Viking, with the darting eyes of a ferret.

'The commissario is here about that man in the mortuary,' Pezzani informed him.

The captain's gesture indicated he understood. 'He wasn't the first and he won't be the last,' he said.

'There's a queue,' added Ceriani who had drawn close to hear the latest news about the river. Is that hole at Isola Serafini still operational? They tell me that even the fish can get into it now.

'The eels are pricking about,' sniggered Cefalú, who was famous for his *doubles entendres*.

His many journeys up and down from Cremona had made Landini the river's messenger. He counted a championship in power-boating among his achievements, and knew the Po like the back of his hand.

'A queue?' Soneri repeated, picking up the interrupted conversation.

'Mothers, wives, lovers, you've no idea how many of them have come to look for anyone who goes missing,' said Landini. 'There was one woman who went up and down the Po three times hanging onto the railings, staring into the water. After three days, she thought she saw her son in the river. Her husband had to drag her away from the moorings at San Benedetto.'

'Tell him about the one who threw himself in,' Marisa insisted, bringing over a full bottle of Malvasia.

The captain made a gesture of annoyance, but it was clear he enjoyed being the centre of attention.

'There's no shortage of madmen. It happened at Motta Baluffi. A guy said he had seen his brother who drowned a month earlier but it was only a lamb carried away by the flood.'

'Do you believe our unknown friend committed suicide?'

'If you're asking me, yes. Near here, over by San Secondo, there's a hospital for nervous illnesses, and a whole army of madmen comes from there.'

'When they finish their medical treatment, they take it badly. It's the final straw,' explained Marisa.

'Many of them run off and you find them wandering all over the place,' Ceriani added.

'Are there many French tourists here?' Soneri asked.

'More Germans and Dutch. They have a passion for the river, but there are one or two French people.'

'This one might have been French,' Soneri explained.

'That's why no-one came looking for him.' It was the Viking who spoke.

Landini disagreed and shot a glance at Soneri as if in confirmation. 'Something should have come out. Unfortunately I don't ask for documents from people coming on board, only tickets.'

'He did have a ticket, and he got on board here at Torricella.'

Silence fell and they all looked at one another. This was new information and had caught them off guard. Perhaps it even strengthened previous suspicions or undermined hypotheses, but soon everything faded once again, swallowed up in the mist which grew thicker as evening drew in.

4

'What did they tell you?' smiled Maresciallo Motti from behind a pile of papers. 'People in these parts are odd. They have their own way of thinking about everything. Things move silently, like the waters of the Po, but don't fool yourself that everything is tranquil.'

Shortly before, Soneri had drawn up in front of a pink building, a colour more suited to a nursery than a police station. He had been greeted by the maresciallo himself, and once inside he had been struck by that discordantly homely feel of provincial police offices, where it would have been more natural to find a neatly set table and the smell of soup rather than uniforms and desks.

'They say there's been a suicide. They believe it was one of those men who've been trying to land the catfish.'

The officer agreed, furrowing his brow. 'It's the most probable explanation,' he said, somewhat distractedly, and then fell silent, as though the matter was closed. Curiosity prevailed, 'You're not here for that?'

'The magistrate's decided that the time has expired, so they want to bury him.'

'Well, what else could we do?' asked Motti with outstretched arms.

Soneri felt sucked into a vacuum. The maresciallo mirrored the futility of that unfocused enquiry for which he had no mandate.

The officer went on, 'If not even his family or friends came looking for him, and if he himself had decided to disappear, when all is said and done, surely not giving him a name is a way of respecting his wishes?'

'What if they'd killed him?'

'I can't exclude that, but it seems to me unlikely.'

'In the river, everything is possible.'

'I know, but sometimes you've just got to have the courage to give up, especially when faced with silence. If he'd been from around here, with a network of relatives…'

'You'd still have people banging at the door,' Soneri said.

'You know how it is, with cold cases like this one…'

Soneri detected the innate inertia of the public administration with which he was all too familiar. The laziness of officials, the zeal of secretaries for stamping cards, the dry formality of departmental heads so keen on their own careers – a catalogue of vices forming a dense residue capable of making any movement seize up if it required more than a casual re-run of the routine.

The maresciallo said, 'We can't do everything. Don't imagine we're sitting here twiddling our thumbs. All sorts of things happen on the Po: illegal immigrants, sand dug up and unlawfully removed, goods stolen, criminals on the run, you name it. Until a few years ago, we had colleagues from Cremona on river patrol duty, now they've become a Forest Service and they don't have a single boat, so when something happens they have to hire one.'

'What about that boat found some years back? The seacraft, I mean.'

Motti stared at him with a sad smile. 'Ah, yes. It turned out it had been stolen from the port in Cremona. The owner was called Andalò, a man of some wealth who had a summer villa in Cesenatico and took the boat up there.'

'What was his line of business?'

'He dealt in electronic devices.'

'Doesn't it seem to you strange that a man who wanted to commit suicide would steal a boat?'

'And who says it was him that stole it? It was only a rumour in the town. There was a mystery man and an abandoned boat, and the two were put together. Possible but not definite.'

Once again, everything was slipping away into that shadowy world like the embankments on the river.

The maresciallo went on, 'I'd also prefer to give that man a name. Everybody has that right, but even for those of us who do, does it really change anything? Take me and my men, lost in the winter mist and dissolving in the summer heat. Some days, I have the impression that no-one will ever pull me out of this hole.'

'You too, Motti, are one of the forgotten. In some ways, we all are.'

'He's not the first man with no name. Think of all those skulls we found with the low water in August. The river is honest, but it gives things back when it chooses, and that might be after thousands of years.'

'Which wouldn't make it easy to find a name.'

'And yet he must have had one. They applied one at random to the body which emerged from the ice block,' said Motti.

'Ice and river behave in the same way. When you get down to it, they're both water,' said Soneri, as he took his leave. 'We've done all we could.'

Once outside, he phoned Angela.

She said, 'I appreciate you finding me clients, but in spite of all your efforts, no-one has turned up.'

'Who was supposed to turn up?' he asked, absent-mindedly.

'That youth. Don't you remember sending him to me?'

'Ah yes, of course. He'll come if he wants to, but it's more likely he'll simply disappear.'

'Just like you. Where are you?'

'In the mist.'

'Are you ever out of it?'

'I went to find it in its birth place.'

'The Lower Po valley?'

Soneri did not reply immediately because in his rear-view mirror he saw a blue flashing light, and immediately after a siren blared out.

'Yes, in the valley,' he finally said.

'What's going on? Are you pursuing a criminal until he crashes into an embankment?'

'Could be, especially considering that the bridges around here are nearly all closed and full of cracks,' said Soneri, pressing his foot down on the accelerator and making after the carabinieri car which had now overtaken him.

From the silence between one sentence and the next, Angela

became aware that Soneri's mind was elsewhere as he drove along the verge of the embankment. 'Just as well there's some activity to stop you falling asleep at the wheel in that hole. You can tell me later how your Grand Prix finished up,' she said before hanging up, listening to the background roar of the engine speeding up.

The carabinieri were headed for Sissa, but had to watch their speed in the mist. Finally the town lights came into view, followed by the brightness of the shop windows in the piazza. They stopped in front of a bar. On the far side a crowd had gathered, and from among them a buzz of excited talk could be heard. The maresciallo strode in amongst them and through the gap that formed as people stood back, Soneri saw the door of the bank lying wide open. He guessed what had happened, and looking around the piazza whose outlines were blurred as though they had been corroded by the mist. He thought that in those conditions no-one could have caught up with anyone who had even ten minutes' start.

Soneri saw Pezzani in the crowd and went up over to him. 'When did this happen?' he asked.

'An hour ago. The bank clerks were closing up.'

'How many of them were there?'

'Just one, on a motorbike.'

An ambulance drew up and shortly afterwards they carried out a female employee.

Pezzani said, 'It must have been someone who knew what he was doing, someone familiar with these roads even in a mist as thick as this.'

The officer who had stayed in the vehicle was speaking on the radio to surrounding police stations, telling them to set up road blocks. Inside the bank, the maresciallo interviewed witnesses, and a few moments later came out with a bald man who must have been the branch manager. Both made their way to the car. Motti could then be heard informing HQ. He gave a description of the robber: 'One eighty in height, slim build, face covered by a balaclava, armed with a semi-automatic pistol, made his getaway on a motorbike.' Everyone listened in silence as though in church.

Motti and the manager went into the bar and only then did the murmur start up again. The odd thing was that motorbike. No-one had ever heard of a robbery carried out in that way, as though the driver were going fishing on the riverside.

'Mist allows you to do that sort of thing,' said Pezzani. 'If it all goes wrong, you can throw it into a ditch and make off over the fields. Who's going to catch up with you if you're fast on your feet.'

'You'll see that someone was waiting for him on the outskirts of the town. Wait till they find the motorbike and we'll find out where,' someone said.

A somewhat distinguished-looking gentleman came out from the bank and went into the bar. 'That's Fabio Gallerani,' said a voice from the crowd.

Soneri threw an interrogative glance to Pezzani, who informed him: 'He's the owner of the slaughterhouse. He's also got a salami factory and about a thousand hectares of land,' he added, as though no further explanation was necessary. 'He's got money coming out his ears.'

An elderly man butted in: 'He must have been there depositing money. Gallerani still deals in cash.'

'If the robber got away with it, he's won the lottery.'

Another carabinieri car drew up in the piazza and two officers got out. 'The motorbike's at Torricella, at the quay,' announced the driver.

The maresciallo obviously knew that already from a radio communication, because he carried on talking to the manager without paying much heed. Meantime, an excited interrogation was underway on the piazza.

'Was there a car waiting for him?'

'Not at all. He made his getaway by boat.'

'And nobody heard a thing? Somebody making off in the dark?'

'They didn't notice anything at the port. Maybe he had an outboard motor, like the poachers.'

'Was the boat already there?'

'There's no boat with an outboard motor at Torricella. He must have arrived on one and maybe he had the motorbike on board.'

'He must be a strong man to unload about a hundredweight of stuff from a boat to the bank.'

'A man who knows the Po.'

'With the low water, he could have unloaded it at a beachhead, couldn't he?' said an elderly man, and others agreed.

'This low water is bad luck,' said someone else.

'What I don't get is the fact that Gallerani just happened to be there,' said Pezzani.

'Do you think it was just chance?' asked Soneri.

Pezzani looked around the group, with a doubtful expression. 'It certainly was one almighty coincidence.'

'You think he was depositing his money and the robber already knew?'

'Who knows? You hear so many stories.'

'For example?'

'Didn't you hear what they were saying? He deals in cash. But then, who could have known that?'

'The 'black economy'? Is that what you mean?'

Pezzani made a meaningful gesture. 'If it isn't, what is it? His father before him... everyone knows all about it, but God help anyone who breathes a word. They give work to about two hundred families around here, and nobody is going to stand up to them.'

'To him and his father?'

'No, the old man is dead and he, Fabio, and his brother Rinaldo will inherit the lot.'

One by one the crowd dispersed. Motti said goodbye to the manager and Pezzani moved off. Soneri saw the maresciallo climb into the car and wave a goodbye that seemed almost like an apology.

When the car drove off, he found himself alone on the piazza. It was chilly and a light the colour of aluminium hung over that little world. The bank door was wide open, like a mouth screaming in terror, until the manager with the air of a grave digger came along to close it delicately.

5

Soneri had been reluctant to return to the city. He could not get that image of the open door out of his mind and, as he drove through the mist which was gradually lifting and dissolving in the rain, he asked himself why not? Certain emotions freely establish direct and inexplicable links, and that image reminded him of the woman's corpse who years previously had committed suicide by throwing herself from a fourth floor. He could still see her stretched out on the pavement in the disjointed and dislocated pose of a broken doll, legs wide apart and skirt up around her waist. Then as now he experienced a sense of pity and an urgent need to intervene, and that was the reason for his displeasure on returning to the city. He felt as though he had left behind something uncompleted, something resembling guilt.

At dinner with Angela in the Milord he attempted to chase that thought away by drowning it in the melted butter in which Alceste's potato *tortelli* were awash, but the diversion did not work.

'That's a bad sign,' she laughed. 'If the medicine doesn't make it disappear, that means it's serious.'

'If only I had some pretext for going back,' Soneri complained.

'Didn't you say that you suspected he'd been murdered?'

'That won't do. There're too few of us and the Chief will be against it. He'll say it's too zealous, a waste of time. None of them give a damn about this case.'

'But he sent you there, didn't he?'

'He asked me to look into the case of the unknown corpse as a favour. I knew nothing about the story, even if it was Carradori's in the first place.'

'Exactly the point. He sent you there and you sensed there was something rotten about the whole business.'

'But it really might only be suicide.'

As they chatted, they could hear voices on the TV in the kitchen reporting a new shipwreck of migrants at sea. In the silence, the reporter's words describing what had happened could be clearly made out.

'It's a matter of dignity,' he said.

Angela nodded.

Soneri went on, 'A name, you understand? Just a name to say so and so died, but instead we'll bury M89. Even cats and dogs are given a name.'

They continued eating in silence. The reporter's voice in the background mingled with the noises coming from the kitchen. Suddenly, Angela said, 'It's Sunday tomorrow and you're not on duty.'

Soneri raised his eyes from his plate and they widened, waiting for what was coming next.

'Go there. It's what you want to do.'

'But we were going to…'

'Never mind. Just remember it was my idea.'

Soneri smiled at her. Their deep understanding often took the form of some sacrifice. That was one of the reasons why he loved her.

Back home, while the rain drummed on the window sill, the phone rang. The caller was Pasquariello, head of the Flying Squad. 'Did you go to Sissa today?'

'I came back yesterday evening. What's the matter? Did I forget to pay my bill in the bar?'

'No, I was wondering if you knew anything about a bank robbery?'

'Certainly I do. It had just happened when I arrived. But who told you I was there?'

'Word gets around, my dear colleague!'

'Ah yes, of course. I had forgotten about the Secret Services.'

'Come off it! I was informed by our friends and rivals, the carabinieri.'

'Have you taken up with one of their female officers?'

He heard his colleague snigger. 'With all their belts and shoulder straps, I'd have a hard job undressing her.'

'OK, enough of this chatter. If you've called me at this hour, it means something important has happened.'

Pasquariello cleared his throat. 'This evening we arrested a drug pusher, someone we'd never heard of before, but there's always a great turnover in that line of work. The fact is our friends and rivals in the carabinieri had been following the purchaser because they believed he was a member of a network of dealers, and they learned he was bound for Sissa.'

Soneri turned serious. 'Did they find out where he lives?'

'You're kidding! Probably he shook them off in the mist, and they don't want to admit it to us.'

'Did you put pressure on the guy you did capture?'

'He says he sold his stuff to several people but doesn't remember who, and doesn't know the names of his clients.'

'Maybe the robber is an addict as well as a dealer, someone from the Valley who knows the roads and can cover his tracks. He'll have come to the city to pick up supplies, and knows where to get the best stuff.'

'Could be, but don't imagine that the one we caught is going to tell us anything,' said Pasquariello. 'It's easier to have a conversation with a trout. It's not good for their health, and the organisation is somewhat more pitiless than the police.'

As he hung up, it occurred to Soneri that he should create some pretext for going back to the Po. He tried to justify the move, starting with the arrest made that night, but in any case he had a free weekend so would not need to explain himself to his superiors.

He fell asleep to a gurgling from the gutters. The rain was falling patiently and giving every impression it would be for some time. It was one of those autumnal rainfalls which were as reassuring in their predictability as the slow, inexorable sway of a pendulum.

It was still dark when he awoke, and he remembered having dreamed of the river and its silent flow. He heard again the light beat of the rain, with its familiar rhythms, like those of a woman sleeping beside you.

He was on the road half an hour later. The mist had given way to a gloomy greyness, and from the dark, creamy skies the water came down in irregular bursts, like an old man peeing. He came into Torricella along the raised road which ran above the level of the roofs. Some of the houses at the roadside were so squat they looked like brooding quails, and that all he had to do was stretch out a hand to touch a chimney. As he drew near the port, he noticed a man standing at the side of the road, staring at the river. He was wearing a yellow raincoat with a hood, and seemed heedless of the driving rain which was falling ever more heavily. When he came closer, he recognised Casimiro, known in the village as 'the Madman,' one who knew all there was to be known about the Po. Soneri stopped the car, picked up his umbrella and got out. Immediately he found the man's haughty, grey-blue eyes turned on him, and made out a white moustache with water dripping from both sides.

Soneri said hello and introduced himself. Casimiro did not reply instantly, and then said, 'You're not from here.'

'Is it so obvious?' asked Soneri.

'If a man is walking about with an umbrella, he's not from these parts. Only women carry umbrellas.'

'Be that as it may, it's not entirely useless.'

'This isn't a place for a person who's afraid of water.'

'Do you think it's going to rise higher?' asked Soneri, pointing at the river.

'It will be better soon. There's hardly enough to water a garden.'

Ahead of them stood a strange structure resembling a bizarre rock made of intertwining logs and tree trunks, topped by a banner of rags. Only then did Soneri realise that that was what Casimiro had been looking at.

'Looks like a beaver's been at work,' he said.

The man turned to him with what might have been gratitude. 'It's my work,' he said with a quick smile. 'I make one every year. I live there in summer.'

'And in winter?'

Casimiro made a vague gesture with his hand indicating the village, but did not turn his face towards it. 'Every year it's carried off and when May arrives I remake it,' he said, referring to the Po without naming it. 'Like the birds with their nests.'

It was true that the twigs in the structure made it look like a magpie's nest and yet it had a certain robustness.

'I want to see how long it will resist. Year after year I make some improvements, and this time the river will need to burst its banks and reach the edge of the flood plain if it wants to carry it off.'

A pair of cormorants skimmed over their heads and landed on the structure. The Madman picked up a stone and hurled it at them. 'Bloody beasts,' he yelled. 'Away and shit yourselves.'

'If you're headed for the port, I can give you a lift,' said Soneri.

Casimiro stared at him as though he had been insulted. 'I never go on wheels. I don't trust them. My car doesn't have any. It glides on the water.'

'At least there won't be any traffic problems.'

'Nowadays there's traffic there too. Everybody goes that way. Including the criminals.'

'Are you talking about the one last night?'

Casimiro shrugged his shoulders. 'He's the least of them. I'm talking about the catfish poachers. There's not one beach left free, and it's us who have to move aside.' The man spat on the ground and then wiped his soaked moustache. His face was wet and wind-swept.

'Are you here about the man in the fridge?'

Soneri nodded. 'Do you know anything about him?'

Casimiro seemed to think it over for a bit and then shook his head. 'A terrible story, like so many others.'

'Do you think he was murdered?'

The Madman stretched out his arms. 'Could be. I've seen so many that come here and end up dead, but this is a strange business. There's that boat...'

'Maybe it wasn't his.'

'So whose was it then? No-one on the Po has a boat like that, or at least no-one uses it. They might keep it here because the mooring is cheaper here than at sea.'

'It was stolen, which means the thief didn't know what he was doing.'

'What use was a wide-bottomed boat here? If you've to go against the current, four oars wouldn't be enough, and neither would a tank of fuel for the engine.'

Soneri suddenly found the conversation interesting. The Madman no longer seemed quite so mad.

Casimiro continued, 'If you're here it means that something stinks. You're like one of those carabinieri who go about in plain clothes, without a uniform, I mean.'

'We're related.'

The man stared at him with an intensity mingled with distrust. 'So then, it must be serious.

'It was you who said it was a nasty business.'

'He's dead, isn't he? Isn't it bad when that's the truth?'

'But you don't seem to believe either that he killed himself.'

The man hesitated a moment too long before replying, but then made up his mind: 'Strange, very strange but it could be one of the many cases we'll never get to the bottom of.'

'Like that accident... the boat that had its side smashed in. It ended up against the breakwater at Stagno.'

Casimiro guffawed. 'You see why I say the whole thing is odd? Only a complete idiot could end up crashing at that point.'

'So what's your explanation? The mist?'

Once again, Casimiro spat on the ground, his preamble to any reply. 'If you ask me, I don't believe there was a crash. They took it there. And even the damage...'

'What about the damage?'

'It looked deliberate to me. The force of the current would never explain a hole like that. The only way would be if you had a powerful engine and drove into it, but that doesn't make sense.'

Soneri was thinking over the many gaps in the investigation when

Casimiro added, 'You've got to get some things straight. No-one around here believes it was an accident. Vandalism, perhaps. We've just been talking about what's happening on the Po. It was the first thing that came into everyone's mind. Whether it's got anything to do with the man in the mortuary, I couldn't say.'

'Did you think it had anything to do with him?'

The man hesitated before replying. 'It was just that it suggested something to me.'

Soneri made a gesture inviting him to go on. While waiting, he took a cigar from his pocket and put it in his mouth, without lighting it.

'I see things other people don't see because I live here on the flood plain and in the mist.' Casimiro interrupted himself as though he really had seen something.

'What did it suggest to you?' asked Soneri.

'When they fished him out, I remembered somebody who used to wander around here. Don't ask me why, but I had the impression that it was him.'

'There're so many folk wandering around here. They tell me they come from the hospital.'

'I don't know. I could be wrong. I have seen that man, but he was on foot.'

6

There was no let up in the rain, and the skies once again seemed to descend onto the plain and touch the top of the poplars. In the half-mist which softened the outline of the houses, everything appeared grey. The outlook from the embankment was a mixture of the real and the imaginary, merging into that undefined state which springs from madness or genius. Casimiro too had confessed to seeing things which were unseen by other people. The point was to decide whether or not they should be taken as genuine.

Soneri did not head for the nautical club. His ponderings caused him to make for the Villa Serena Neurological Hospital. Soon he found himself in front of a two-storey building made of cubes, as though someone had thrown together half a dozen giant dice. He saw a courtyard and a garden with benches, the whole enclosed within an outer fence. When he rang the bell, the door opened automatically onto the silent interior and deserted corridors. All that could be heard from the rooms was the occasional voice, the lament or scream of some deranged inmate.

The director was a tall, thin, middle-aged man exuding an air of efficiency. Soneri introduced himself, explaining that he was conducting an inquiry. The director listened in silence, then showed him into a room without asking any further questions. He remained on his feet, leaning on a desk, in either what could have been a confidential or dismissive attitude.

'Let me start by admitting that this might all seem very strange,' Soneri began, slightly embarrassed.

'You're talking about strange things, in a place like this?' smiled the doctor, whose name was Del Gaudio.

'I've been told some of your patients run off and wander about the countryside.'

The doctor turned serious. 'I have been here for six months and nothing of the kind has ever occurred. We always keep the doors and gates locked, as you will have noticed. Some inmates are allowed out, but only in the company of family members. That is also what we advise when they're released but aren't capable of looking after themselves.'

'In the town they said that...'

Del Gaudio interrupted him sharply. 'It might have happened in the past. I'm not responsible for the previous management.' His tone suggested that the subject was a painful one.

'Who was your predecessor?'

'What does it matter? He's dead.'

'Here they're all a little...'

'Mad? Is that what you want to say?' the doctor butted in again. 'No, the hospital has different wards according to the type of illness, but even those without cognitive or sanity problems require authorisation before going out.'

'You have no surgeries or out-patient facilities?'

Del Gaudio waved his finger to signal no. 'Anyone admitted here, even if only for a mild breakdown, will be an in-patient for a couple of days.'

'Is it possible to consult your records to check when people are admitted and released?'

'I could do that, if the request was well-motivated,' said Del Gaudio, plainly ill at ease. 'When are you interested in?'

'Three or four years ago.'

The doctor furrowed his brow and shook his head. 'I found everything in total disorder. I don't know if I can help you.'

Then the door opened and a nurse came in, but when she saw Soneri, she quickly closed it again. Del Gaudio gave a disapproving grimace. 'You see what goes on here? They enter without knocking and never apologise. I have made every effort to introduce a bit of discipline, but it takes time. That's one of the reasons why I would ask you to make your request through the normal channels.'

Soneri made no attempt to conceal his disappointment.

'Can I ask why you want me to consult the archive?' the doctor asked.

'I'm conducting enquiries into a corpse with no name.'

'It will be difficult to trace him if you don't know his name,' the doctor replied sarcastically. 'Are you referring to the man still lying in the mortuary? Are there any suspects?'

'Only some things that don't add up, and that's exactly why I need to have a look at the documents.'

The doctor all of a sudden seemed interested. 'Listen, even if you did search the archives, with the state they're in, you wouldn't come up with anything much. Unfortunately, there's been an almost complete change of staff here over the last couple of years, but there was one man who did work for the hospital from its foundation until a few months ago. He retired quite recently. Perhaps he could be of some use to you. His name's Bosi, Giulio Bosi, I think.'

'Does he live near here?'

'In Colorno,' he replied, rifling through some papers on his desk. He then held out a sheet of paper with the man's address.

Soneri took his leave and went out into the rain. As he got into his car and set off across the Po Valley, he was once again assailed by that unpleasant sensation of going nowhere and of having no mandate. He was following the suggestion of a visionary, perhaps a madman, who swore he had seen a man walking along the banks of the river. His head was buzzing with a swarm of confused conjectures, as varied in form as the gravel on the river bed. He felt pangs of guilt for having given up a weekend with Angela to pursue a phantom.

With these thoughts still on his mind, he drew up in the Piazza di Colorno (in front of a building as wide and solid as certain women seen along the Po).

Bosi lived in a narrow street in the old town, in one section of a two-storey residence. In spite of his advancing years, he still cut an imposing figure. When he greeted him in the kitchen almost occupying one floor, Soneri had the impression of facing one of those oak trees on the plain which stand guard over wells. His wife, on the contrary, was a tiny woman with a cheery face. She immediately produced two glasses and a bottle of *Fortana*.

Bosi listened in silence as Soneri introduced himself. He poured the wine and held up his glass in a kind of toast.

'They tell me you were there at the hospital's foundation,' Soneri began.

'From the first stone. I was a builder at that time, but then they took me on to work with the mental patients.'

'Even though you had no specialist knowledge?'

'It wasn't necessary in those days. The ones with strong arms were more useful to work as labourers or odd-job men. Have you ever seen a madman really put his back into a task? He has the strength of three men.'

'Who was the consultant then?'

'Professor Righetti.'

'The one who died recently?'

'That's right. That was part of the reason why I retired. I could have stayed on, but everything was different there.'

Soneri noted a certain tone of regret. 'Didn't you get on with Del Gaudio?'

Bosi shrugged his shoulders. 'Righetti was from around here. He knew everybody. He spoke to people in dialect, and to us as well. We used to go down the Po in a boat, and we had picnics at the flood plain. Then all that stopped.'

'When Del Gaudio came?'

'Who else? It started with protocols. That's all he had in his head, protocols!'

'Is it true that some inmates got out of the hospital and went wandering about the countryside?'

'Sometimes. They went off for a bit and then they calmed down. We always brought them back unharmed.'

'That's not exactly orthodox practice...'

'Righetti had his own ideas in regard to people who were ill. He loved freedom, drifting on a boat on the Po, not having too many regulations. Just like the river.'

Soneri shook his head, with a smile. 'I'm interested in those who got out. I've always had a weakness for rebels.'

'A good sign,' Bosi agreed. 'What would you like to know about them?'

'Something of their histories, who they were, where they went... I know that some of them made for the Po.'

'Most of them went into the town, to Sissa, but the river did attract them as well. If they went there, the people would get in touch, because Righetti knew them all, so when they saw someone a bit odd turn up, they would phone us.'

'Was there one man who would go walking along the banks?'

'Why are you trying to dig all this up? Why all these questions?'

'Did you hear about that man taken out of the river about three years ago?'

'The one no-one wants?'

'That's him.'

'They say he killed himself. That's why we always rushed to pick up anyone who was seen heading for the river. If they took it into their heads to throw themselves in, there would be a lot of trouble.'

'Nobody knows if he did kill himself,' murmured Soneri. 'I'd like him to have a name.'

'Does it matter that much? We might have a name, but what good does it do us?'

'It does matter,' Soneri stated, remembering a similar reply from Maresciallo Motti.

'Whatever you say, but there were some we had to go and bring back from the river bank.'

'Do you remember their names?'

'How could I?' he said, throwing his hands in the air. 'Have you any idea of how many people I saw in my forty years of service?'

'Think it over. Might that name be written in the hospital's registers?'

Bosi stood in silence, gazing at the floor. He was plainly not a man much given to thinking of the past and Soneri imagined that his memory was probably in the same state as the registers in Villa Serena.

'I do remember one man, but for a strange reason.'

'Strange reasons always make good clues.'

'Someone came to pick him up in a taxi.'

'Who would that have been?'

'You're asking me too much.'

'Was he someone who would run away and go in the direction of the Po?'

'Yes, he was one of those. I even remember his name, Gianni.'

'Could you describe him?'

'Well built, about five foot ten in height, balding.'

'Mental health problems?'

'No. Nervous breakdown, maybe. He spoke correctly, and rolled his 'Rs'. Righetti let him do as he pleased because he trusted him, and in general he came back of his own accord. I used to go and get him when he phoned from the nautical club because it had started raining or because he was unusually worn out.'

'By taxi? In what period?'

'It was summertime, a couple of years ago, but maybe I'm getting mixed up. I've seen so many of them.'

'You've just said that somebody came to fetch him in a taxi. Do you remember if it was a man or a woman?'

'A woman. I'd say she was middle-aged. I gave her a hand to carry the suitcases, and before the car set off she gave the driver the address.'

'And where did she tell him to go?'

'Parma, 15 Viale Duca Alessandro. I remember because I have a relative who lives there. I even said to him, "See you soon, Gianni," and he nodded back.'

'Did you ever meet him again?'

'Not too long after, I was in that neighbourhood but I didn't see him. Nor did my relative remember having seen anyone who resembled him around. Maybe he moved soon afterwards to another district.'

'Would you be able to find the surname of this Gianni?'

Bosi gestured with his chin. 'I'd have to ask, but everything has changed there. And then my memory...'

'The archive,' said Soneri. 'You could consult the registers.'

'Ah well now! You would have to have known Righetti to understand. As a doctor, he was a genius, but as regards orderliness... After so many years in the hospital, I got some idea of the doctors there.'

'And that is?'

'That they're as mad as the inmates, and the madder they are, the better they are. That's why I believe that Del Gaudio, with his mania for protocols and order, is a fool. He'll come a cropper and might even go mad himself, and I mean one of those raving madmen for whom there's no hope.'

'Are you telling me there used to be no order in the institution?'

'Zero. Searching about in that registry was like laying a bet. Someone looking for a document might find it right away, or he might rummage about for a fortnight and not come up with anything. It was all a matter of luck.'

'Del Gaudio demands a warrant.'

'I told you what he's like, but the world isn't like that, especially for the insane, and those outside are more insane than those inside.'

'You couldn't just break the rules? You know everybody in there, and you know your way about.'

'He has a poor opinion of me, but maybe for that reason I wouldn't mind giving you a hand.'

'Who knows, we might just get a break,' Soneri said, rising to his feet.

Bosi showed him out and when he was at the door, he murmured: 'A taxi! I never saw anyone leave the hospital in a taxi.'

7

There was no let up in the rain, which continued to fall relentlessly. Everything was dripping, creating a uniform dampness in the houses and on the ground. The only way to find a dry corner was to slip into a bar in the colonnade or into a half-open doorway giving onto the penumbra of silent houses.

On his way back to the Po, Soneri dialled Musumeci's number. 'Are you in the office?'

'I popped in for a second.'

'I'd like to ask you to do a little job for me. Maybe you could do it on the way home.'

'And what would that be?' the inspector asked, already slightly alarmed

'Nothing complicated, a quick check.'

'On you go,' said Musumeci, resignedly.

'Could you stop off at 15 Duca Alessandro and talk to the people who live there? I'm interested in finding out if a new tenant arrived around three or three and a half years ago.'

'What's his name?'

'That's the problem. I've only got his first name, Gianni. Nor much of a description: five foot ten in height, robust, balding.'

'That's not much to go on!'

'It's not likely a dozen men answering that description turned up,' said Soneri impatiently. 'And I doubt if they'd have missed a new tenant. We're not exactly talking about a boarding house!'

'I'll see what I can do.'

The moment Soneri switched off, his mobile started vibrating. It was Angela announcing, 'Your lad has turned up.'

'Ah, good to see he's using his head. Is he still intent on giving up his inheritance?'

'What inheritance! He's got himself into big trouble, and as he found my number in his pocket, he's called on me to help him out.'

'What's he been up to?'

'He started smashing windows and throwing stones at the carabinieri, so they arrested him.'

'What an idiot!'

'Didn't you know he's involved with these so-called communes?'

'How was I supposed to know? I saw he was in trouble but I didn't go into it.'

'They must have knocked him about a bit, because his face is swollen. You know how it goes.'

'Yes, I know only too well. They never lay a hand on young Fascists. What state did you find him in?'

'In a rage, like a viper. He plays the hard man, but he's naive and frightened as a child.'

'What's he charged with?'

'A long list: resisting arrest, vandalism and bodily harm. Two officers were injured, and in these cases anyone who's rounded up will face charges.'

'Will you accept his defence?'

'I've already done so.'

'Well, that's reassuring.'

'Your concern surprises me.'

'I'm the first to be surprised,' admitted Soneri.

'Maybe he's the son we never had,' murmured Angela, with raw frankness. 'We've reached the age when we can't change this.'

Soneri took her point. He moved over to the side of the road, stopped the car and switched off the engine. In the ensuing silence, Angela's voice brought him back to earth. 'Anyway, I'm not interested in a pet dog.'

'Maybe it's a sense of guilt,' Soneri agreed. 'We've left the next generation one shit of a world.'

'I feel sorry for them, but I'm not responsible. Neither are you, in my opinion.'

'I don't know. We have tried to resist, but when all's said and done we've been guests at the banquet.'

'And what could we do? We've lived our lives attempting to be honest, but if you trudge through mud, you're going to get dirty.'

'Do all you can to get him out as quickly as possible,' said Soneri, bringing the conversation back to Ragu. 'These kids only want to show the world that they're there.'

'Are you making any headway to do the same for the man in the mortuary?'

'I'm doing my best. You and I have got a similar task.'

He drove alongside the embankment up to the flood plain and arrived at the nautical club. He took out his umbrella and decided to take the long way round, along the pebbly path behind the fishermen's cottages which were on raised iron beams to keep them above the flooding level. From where he was standing, they looked like a line of wading birds lying in ambush in low water. At the end of the avenue, there was a path which led at various points into the poplar grove. It was then that he noticed groups of military tents erected on the edge of the flood plain over on the Lombardy side. They looked uninhabited, but a couple of trucks suggested the opposite. Soneri observed them for a few minutes until he saw a man in an oilskin emerge, take a few steps, turn his back on the river and open his fly to do a pee.

As Soneri decided to go back to the club, it occurred to him that the dead man could have been like those men. There were so many of them between Cremona and Ferrara. He turned away from the water and went in. It was Saturday evening and the place was crowded.

'You see how it's come up? Now we really recognise it,' said Pezzani, alluding to the river.

'Holy water,' Marisa added.

'Women enjoy getting moist,' said Cefalú, with one of his crass jokes.

'As soon as they see you, they dry up,' Marisa retorted.

'Were you aware of Righetti coming here when someone from the hospital dropped in?' asked Soneri, interrupting the laughter.

'Only if it was somebody who was off his nut. We kept them here.

With the offer of a glass, they always hung about. They say that even Napoleon would have stopped for a Lambrusco.'

'Did you come across someone called Gianni?'

'Gianni?' Pezzani repeated.

'Yes, I knew him,' said the Viking. 'But he wasn't off his head, not at all. He seemed perfectly balanced. I don't know why he was in there.'

'Once he told me he'd undergone a series of crises, but I don't remember what crises,' said Ceriani.

'He was a well-built man,' said Soneri, and the others agreed.

'He pronounced his 'Rs' like people from Fidenza.' It was Marisa speaking. 'When I said that to him he burst out laughing, but said he had spent time in France.'

'Had he lived in France?' asked Soneri.

'Who knows? I thought he was joking. Those people talk such nonsense.'

Everything seemed confused, uncertain, lacking in clarity.

'You hear so many stories,' said Pezzani, looking around at the others as though inviting them to enter the conversation. Soneri would have sworn they were repeating old, familiar tales, like people listening time after time to a song or a mazurka in a dance hall.

Ceriani turned to the commissario, 'Do you believe in miracles?'

'I shouldn't,' he replied ambiguously. The growing number of empty bottles and the boisterous atmosphere led him to believe that he had been accepted into the company.

'You're wrong there.' said Ceriani, with a giggle. 'Did you know that in Busseto there is a wooden Christ which was discovered in the water at Vidalenzo. It was covered in mud, but it had beautiful, black hair. It seemed as though some young woman had donated it before becoming a nun.'

'Jesus saved from the waters,' Pezzani interrupted, receiving for his troubles a contemptuous look from Ceriani.

'They washed him down as though he had just been taken down from the cross, and found him a place in the Collegiata Church, but obviously he had no wish to be there because the following day he was on the floor alongside the high altar in another church, the

Santissima Annunziata. Nobody has ever been able to explain how he got there.'

'Come off it! The priest took it there. The one in Busseto who preferred the Santissima Annunziata,' was the Viking's explanation.

'If it was the priest, somebody would have seen him,' said Marisa.

'All right then, explain to me why the water has always stopped at the feet of the Madonna of Loreto at Polesine,' retorted Ceriani, referring to another miracle. 'All those floods year after year, but the Madonna never even got her toes wet.'

'And you can still hear the voices of the dead in the submerged graveyard at Tolarolo, can't you?' said Marisa. 'When the Po is low and the tops of the two columns appear, lamentations come from the water.'

The nautical club was a misty theatre in that river zone where everything took on the dimensions of a dream. Coming up from the embankment meant plunging into an insidious vagueness. Soneri reflected that, all things considered, it was not so strange that a psychiatric hospital was sited nearby. He called to mind Bosi's words about the real madmen being outside its walls.

At that point he brought up the subject that really mattered to him: 'Did many of them from Villa Serena come here?'

Quite suddenly silence fell. All that could be heard was Landini working on the deck of his motor launch, preparing to set off when the water rose.

'Seven or eight,' Pezzani finally said, as though he felt that it was up to him to rescue them all from embarrassment.

'Apart from Gianni, who were the others?'

'There was one who fancied Marisa. He wanted to make off with her,' said Cefalú.

She silenced him with a look. 'All he wanted to do was talk. He was no danger,' she said.

'There was another one we caught staring into the current at the dredgers' loop,' said the Viking. 'That time it cost Righetti a fortune, for he had to stand us all our dinner.'

'Gianni was the only one who seemed all right,' said Marisa.

'Which is why they allowed him to move about,' said Ceriani.

'Did he go to other places as well?' asked Soneri.

'All over the place, and when he got fed up he just asked someone in an *osteria* for a lift back, or else he phoned Righetti.'

'Where did they see him most often?' asked Marisa.

'In Pizzo,' said Cefalú, who was now serious but still reeling from Marisa's put-down. 'It's a bit out of the way, a village.'

'Why there?' asked Soneri, becoming more curious.

'Go and see for yourself,' said Pezzani. 'It's got about two dozen houses on either side of the main road.'

'Isn't that where the Gallerani house is?' asked Marisa.

'A bit further on,' said the Viking.

'The Galleranis?,' asked Soneri, remembering the man from the bank the previous evening.

Understanding glances were rapidly exchanged around the table. 'The owners of half the Lower Po Valley,' said Ceriani.

'Are there many of them?' asked Soneri.

'Two brothers, Fabio and Rinaldo, and their families. Old Gualtiero is dead,' explained Marisa.

Soneri felt his mobile vibrate in his pocket, and went outside stopping under the overhanging roof. It was Musumeci. 'I've been to 15 Via Duca Alessandro, but no-one has any recollection of a tenant who answers your description.'

'Did you tell them it was three or four years ago?'

'Of course I did,' said the inspector a little heatedly. 'The only new arrival was a female student from Lecce, one Simona Perrone. Obviously well off, since she bought the flat.'

Soneri made no reply, so Musumeci, unnerved by that silence, started up again: 'I can tell you all those who live there. There are only eight families.'

'No, it doesn't matter,' Soneri reassured him. His mind was elsewhere, so much so that he switched off his phone without even saying goodbye.

He regarded that news as odd, and oddities always had some significance. His work as a policeman had taught him that behaviour tends to be guided by habit, often by the worst of habits such as poking malignantly into other people's business. Enquiries relied on that, and that was why any deviation became a clue.

At that point, remembering he was on duty that Saturday, he called Juvara. 'Could you do a check in the registry for me?

'Why? Are you thinking of moving house?'

'I want to know about someone who has moved house.'

'But aren't you at home?'

Soneri snorted, 'I should be.'

Juvara's naivety was sometimes disarming, but he was unsurpassed on the computer. 'Here's what I want you to do. I want you to find out who sold 15 Via Duca Alessandro which was purchased some years ago by a certain Simona Perrone from Lecce, a student, but I don't know in what subject.'

'I'll see if I can get it online. The registry website doesn't always work well on Saturdays.'

Soneri switched off the phone and went back into the club, where he found Marisa moving all the objects in the room to the tops of tables and shelves. 'What's going on?' he asked.

Marisa did not reply. The men had sat down for a game of cards. The Viking, without raising his eyes, said, 'The river's rising and Civil Protection has ordered the evacuation of the flood plain.'

'So what are we supposed to do?' asked Soneri, clearly worried.

The Viking gave a shrug. 'It won't rise more than half a metre here, so as long as you have a pair of boots you'll be OK, isn't that right, Marisa?'

'The foodstuffs are high enough up,' she said, as though that were the most important thing.

'Stay calm. The Po never springs surprises. It arrives gradually,' said Pezzani.

'How can you be so certain that it'll rise only one half metre?'

'From the poplar grove,' said Ceriani.

Soneri stayed silent waiting for an explanation.

'The snails. They know what's going on,' continued Ceriani, even more cryptically. He seemed to enjoy playing the mystery man, and exchanged occasional glances and little smiles with the others. Soneri's unease grew. That little riverside world grew more inscrutable to him by the minute, until Pezzani intervened to help him out.

'The snails become aware of the rising water and climb up the trunks just far enough to guarantee they won't end up under water. Today they're little more than a half metre off the ground.'

'Snails are better than any Civil Protection. They've been living by the river for thousands of years,' added the Viking.

'They're not half better! The Civil Protection is full of southerners!' sniggered Cefalú.

'And where are you from?' asked Marisa.

By way of answer, the man made a remark in dialect.

'But you're naturalised, like the football players,' joked Ceriani.

Once again, Soneri's mobile vibrated in his pocket. 'Hello, Juvara.'

'Hello, sir. The apartment was sold a little more than three years ago to this Perrone woman...'

'By whom?'

'By Elvira Andalò. Do you want to know the number of rooms and the price?

'No, it doesn't matter.'

'There's a garage and cellar.'

'I told you. It doesn't matter,' said Soneri as he switched off.

8

Andalò. That name haunted him until he was suddenly enlightened. That was the name of the owner of the boat stolen at Cremona and found crushed at the breakwater at Stagno. It all began to add up. Even if it only slightly indicated a link between the dead man and the boat, Soneri had the impression that a pattern was beginning to emerge – a corpse floating on a river. Perhaps that was how they found the nameless man. Soneri picked up his phone. 'Could you do another check for me?'

He heard some confused babble as Juvara ended another conversation in a rush. 'Sorry, I was on another line.'

'Has something happened?' asked Soneri.

'It was some officers from the Digos. There's a demonstration in front of the town hall by people from these communes, and the Digos have arrested some for identification.'

'Am I wasting your time?' asked Soneri, feeling yet again that he was clutching at straws with this obsessive need of his to understand.

'No, sir, not at all.' Juvara, clearly embarrassed, attempted to reassure him.

Soneri knew that his was a solitary struggle, little more than stubbornness, but insistent for all that. He felt that giving up was equivalent to betrayal. 'It's about that woman, the one who sold the apartment in Via Duca Alessandro.'

'Yes, sir.' The inspector did his best to conceal that he was busy and invited him to go on.

'I'd like to know more about her. Is she married, with children, relatives, profession, that sort of thing?'

'Give me a little time,' said Juvara, with the hint of a sigh.

'Take as long as you need,' said Soneri, feeling himself caught up in a time passing as slowly as the current on the Po. He left the club and walked in the rain along the flood plain on the opposite side to the cottages, towards the poplar grove, its trees in geometric order like a detachment of soldiers. He wanted to confirm what he had heard about the snails. When he spotted one, he realised it was at the height indicated by the Viking, as if there was no point in climbing any higher.

He was startled by Casimiro's voice. 'Still got your umbrella? Get rid of it if you want to be taken seriously.'

'Doesn't the colour fit in?' he tried to joke.

'Around here, an umbrella is like a dog in a church.'

Casimiro had mastered a kind of aesthetic of the Po and was guardian of its unwritten laws, which may be why they called him mad.

'The water's coming,' Soneri said.

'Tomorrow around noon,' Casimiro confirmed, as though it was a fixed appointment.

'It won't amount to much. Your construction will withstand it.'

'That's not what I'm worried about.'

'What then?'

Casimiro gave a slight shrug and turned to look into the trees. 'Anyone who's not from here won't understand.'

Some crows flew cawing over the embankment. He observed them as though scrutinising an omen.

'Have you seen something?' asked Soneri, detecting some unease in Casimiro, who assented without speaking. Soneri waited patiently. Everything inside that suspended bubble went at its own pace.

'Footprints.'

'Someone might have gone to check the level of the water.'

The Madman shook his head. 'They weren't made by feet.'

'I've heard this is the time when deer and wild boar make an appearance.'

Once again Casimiro indicated that that was not correct.

'Wolves then?'

'It's a large animal,' he whispered as though he were afraid of being overheard. 'A beast that no-one here has seen except inside the mist.'

Soneri thought of the tales about the river which were told in the club, but Casimiro seemed terrifyingly serious.

'If no-one has ever seen it, how do you know it exists?'

'There are the footprints, and more than one person has seen its outline as it scampered into the water'

'It lives in the water?' said Soneri, trying to keep abreast of the conversation.

'In those dips at the bottom of the river where the eddies are born. It comes out at night or in the mist, and more frequently in spring because it's fond of poplar seeds.'

'So because of the footprints you believe it came out last night?'

'No, this morning, before dawn.'

'What are these footprints like?'

Quite suddenly Casimiro seemed grateful for this questioning. 'Think of a pheasant's feet, only much larger, with three fingers and a kestrel's claws.'

Soneri remained silent and Casimiro stood staring at him. 'You don't believe me, do you? I've always said it's a waste of time telling certain things to people who aren't from these parts.'

'They've never found a beast like that,' said Soneri, trying to justify himself.

'The Po is a district like no other. Is this really the first time somebody has found a beast never seen before? Who could have imagined the catfish?'

'Have you seen this beast?'

'The footprints, yes, more than once, but I told you it only comes out when it's misty or dark. Like other things that happen around here.'

'What are you getting at?'

'Aren't you here because of something terrible?'

Soneri lit his cigar. 'That man who was occasionally seen here by the river,' he said, following up immediately, with a pretence at vagueness, 'the one you described to me... did he ever talk to you?'

'I've spoken to everyone at various times.'

'What did you make of him?'

'He wasn't in any way brainless like the rest of them. A bit odd,' he said, whirling his hand with his fingers pointing upwards. 'Anyway, around here... they say worse things about me.'

'Have you any idea why he came down here?'

'He wasn't the only one. If he came here, it was because he liked the Po. This isn't a place for holiday-makers.'

'Could he have been from these parts?'

'Who knows? The river can give you pleasure for a couple of hours at the most. Ask Landini how many of them take his trips. But to really have it in your blood so that you want to go there, that's a different story.'

'Did he have it in his blood?'

'How could I know? He had a certain knowledge, but then so do the people in the Civil Protection.'

'What do you mean?'

'They know all about river banks and depths, but as for the rest... The Po is another world,' he concluded, drawing a circle in the air with his finger.

'Exactly. People, histories, tales,' agreed Soneri, as though coaxing the man to continue.

A rumble of falling stones from the quarry broke both the silence and the subtle understanding with Casimiro, who shook himself but said only, 'Ah well.'

'Was the man's name Gianni?'

'I have no idea,' he replied quickly. 'He never told me his name.' He seemed to have suddenly reawakened from a dream and realised he was out of place. As he was leaving, Soneri asked him again, 'Do you think he really had the Po in his blood?'

Casimiro turned back, thought it over and then said, 'Maybe he did.'

The rain bounced off Soneri's umbrella, its rhythm blending with the background chorus of raindrops in the poplar grove. He thought it was time to purchase a rainproof jacket like Casimiro's. As he walked back in the direction of the port, Landini was going down to his boat.

'You're all excited about something,' he said.

Soneri gave a faint smile. Even the others considered his presence there unprofessional – a bizarre, unseasonal holiday.

'You getting ready to set off?' he asked

'I'm moving it to Borretto,' he said, indicating the boat with his thumb. 'The moorings are more secure there even if the water won't be very high. Have you come up with anything?'

'Not much,' said Soneri, shaking his head. 'That man could have been someone from around here,' he added, as though giving voice to a thought which had only just crossed his mind.

'Many of those who end it all are like that,' agreed Landini, who was wearing his sailor's uniform and decorations under his oilskin. 'So many stories start with the river and end with the river.'

There was a rumbling noise from the other side of the embankment. Landini stepped back up the track to have a look.

'Manotti's barge. It's been waiting for two weeks with its cargo in its belly.' He signalled to the commissario to follow him. They climbed on board while other boats passed.

'They're all going up to the delta,' observed Soneri.

'On the way up they take the Canal Bianco, because that way they don't have to go against the current and so they cut down on fuel. The water is still and high all year round with no low waters to cause problems.'

They stepped onto the deck which was surrounded by glass walls, an incredibly dry spot even if lashed by the current.

'If you like, we could have something to eat here,' said the captain. 'All I have is some *culatello*, some *coppa* from Piacenza and a little *strolghino*.'

'Can't imagine anything better.'

Night was drawing in over the river, and the rain and the mist made the darkness even more dense. The lights in the club could scarcely be made out, and every so often a small wave made the craft roll gently, the river's way of making its presence felt.

'It takes us by the hand and shakes us about a bit so as to have a better look at us, just as we do with insects.'

'That's a good comparison,' said Soneri.

The captain disappeared down to the galley and re-emerged with a tray of *salume*. 'I have some *Lambrusco* from Reggio, or would you rather have *Fortana*?'

'Let's go for the *Lambrusco*. Do you always dine alone? You don't go to the club?'

'Only occasionally. After a while, you've heard all the stories. From Cremona to Ferrara, some variations are thrown from one bank to the other. The accents change, but the substance is always the same.'

'What do they say about this guy with no name?'

'I don't know much about it.'

'You must have heard something, surely?'

Landini opened the bottle from which some froth escaped before he filled the glasses. 'Do you know what I've picked up? A sense of embarrassment.'

'In regard to this episode?'

The man nodded.

'And what's the reason?'

'I've no idea. There might be so many reasons. Maybe even those who work on the river know nothing about it.'

'But in that case, why this embarrassment?'

'They like to give the impression of knowing everything! Or else...'

'Or else?'

'Do you know how many people come from far off to throw themselves into the Po? It's a graveyard.'

'What if he was murdered?'

Landini stopped to think it over. 'The carabinieri say it's not that. Certainly, they could have killed him somewhere else and thrown him off some bridge into the river. Considering where he was found, I would suggest the Ragazzola bridge.'

'The cause of death is uncertain. There was some water in his lungs, but it's not clear if he was on the point of death or in good health when he went into the Po.'

'What a mess! I don't believe it's possible to clear it up after all this time.'

'At least we could give him a name to bury him with.'

'That's right. Having no name means being worth nothing. The very sand is worth more than that.'

'That's why I'm so obsessed.'

'I thought you wanted to clarify how he died.'

'That comes later. There can be no justice if there's not some recognition first.'

'True enough,' mused the captain. 'My grandfather was deported and he never managed to free himself from that number engraved on his arm. Some people had a skin graft done by a surgeon but the scar was still visible.'

'The scar that can't be erased is inside.'

'Everything is removed when your identity is erased.'

The vessel rolled a bit more heavily and the chug of an engine could be heard. Landini went over to look out the window, and then resumed his seat with a worried look. 'Who could be travelling on the river at this time?' he wondered.

They ate in silence. The *culatello*, slices of solid, well-seasoned meat of just the right thickness, was exquisite.

'As you've noticed, there are always strange things happening on the river,' the captain resumed. 'It looks like a world where everything is always the same, but then things happen which wouldn't occur elsewhere.'

'Is that the reason why there's some embarrassment over what happened to that man?'

Landini thought it over. 'If you ask me, they know nothing about it.'

'Or else they do know something but don't want to talk.'

'I don't believe that anyone from the club is involved,' Landini was quick to add.

'Neither do I, but they might know about someone else who is.'

The captain thought it over for a few seconds, while another boat passed by on the water. He turned towards the darkness outside before answering distractedly, 'That might be so.'

9

The jetty quite suddenly burst into life, and the lamps in the courtyard created a garland of light in the darkness. As the sound of animated chatter rose, Landini and Soneri left their food on the table and went outside. A car drove up, its headlights projecting giant shadows on the walls. A boat spluttered into life as it moved cautiously off.

As they approached the little huddle, Soneri heard Pezzani refer to places and villages along the river. 'What's going on?' asked Landini.

'They've stolen two engines from the mooring at Polesine. It seems the thieves escaped up this way,' said the Viking. 'Two Mercurys, ten thousand euros each.'

The agitation and the outrage seemed as palpable as the mist. 'If they were new, that means they had a spy keeping an eye open for them, an expert who knows what to choose,' said Ceriani.

'They arrived by the river. They know their way about.'

'The same as for the robbery at Sissa: they always come by the river,' the Viking continued.

'You can't blame the river,' Cefalú said. 'It's up to us to remain alert.'

'As long as these foreigners go wandering about...' mumbled a man whom Soneri had never seen before.

Pezzani came in again, 'They come by the river because on the Po no-one can stop them. Everybody knows it's an uncontrollable space. And if you have a small boat you can moor anywhere you like, unload and go on your way. If you're stopped, you can always say you were out on a trip on the river.'

A giant light was switched on to reveal a fluid mixture of mist and rain. Marisa was on the phone at the doorway to the club. 'It happened an hour ago? Nobody knows for certain... they spotted two of those... always the same... the y can't lay a hand on them... let's hope that with this rain they decide to...'

Cefalú was adamant. 'They'll never find them. By now those engines will be on their way to Hungary.'

'Nothing easier,' agreed Ceriani.

'What makes you say that?' asked Pezzani.

'The robberies start in April and end in October, the period when those people are here.'

The Viking agreed: 'That's true enough. And it isn't just robberies.'

'What else?' asked Soneri.

'There's no doubt about it,' said the Viking, looking around to invite the others to back him up. 'The least they do is cut a boat's mooring ropes. If you're lucky, you'll find it at San Benedetto or Revere.'

'Usually they sink them so deep that it's not worthwhile trying to raise them again,' added Cefalú.

'And they go about armed,' said the Viking, coming back in. 'It's a waste of time trying to talk to them. You'd better not try because you're likely to get shot in the back.'

'They stretch nets above water level from one bank to the other with wire cable, so that if you're not careful, they'll take your head off,' explained Ceriani. 'Everything they do is illegal. They sweep up all the fish that come their way, from the catfish to the sheatfish, and then they sell them on.'

'They sell them as food to the fishers who come here for sport, as well as to Sunday day-trippers.'

'Don't they sell them in their own countries?' asked Soneri.

'Once they did, but now they've discovered there are people here who want to buy fish cheaply, and so they cut out transport costs,' said the Viking.

'With all that goes up and down on the Po...' said Pezzani.

'Once it's gutted, all fish is the same,' sniggered Cefalú.

'Some strange characters have turned up in these parts to take over restaurants and *trattorias*, the kind that offer a ten euro, fixed-price menu, know what I mean?' It was again Pezzani who spoke. 'It's a murky business, maybe run by front men. The fact is that over in Ostiglia they came across one guy who was serving carp in a basket, fish he'd bought from these guys,' Pezzani concluded, pointing vaguely in the direction of the river banks.

'He claimed it came from a fish farm,' said Cefalú still sniggering. 'There was all sort of stuff in there.'

Marisa came off the phone. 'And you should see the state they leave the river banks in. From about a hundred kilos of catfish, they leave about eighty on the gravel or in the woods. You can't go near it for the stench and the flies. Thousands of them.'

'Bastards,' said Cefalú, spitting. 'Nobody stops them. They've taken over.'

'I've always said the Po is a lawless place,' said Pezzani.

A flashing blue light shone out in the darkness. 'Here comes the law,' said Ceriani sarcastically.

'There's only two of them in a cheap car and not even a hut to shelter in,' said Marisa, in their defence. 'The other lot are well organised. They've even got electric engines so as not to make any noise.'

The maresciallo got out. 'They escaped, with the current on their side. Did you hear anyone pass by?'

Landini came forward to report, 'Two boats. They weren't going very fast but with this mist... From the sound, I'd have said eighty horsepower Yamaha.' He spoke with the authority of an ex-champion in motor sports.

Motti listened to the information in silence. His sense of inadequacy in a circle of people who lived by the river was plain to see.

'Sooner or later, you're going to have to make up your minds about doing a round-up along both banks,' said the Viking. 'But it would take an entire division.'

'The same as the D'Este Commission the Austrians set up against the *Criminals on the Po*,' said Pezzani.

'That would put pay to all our problems,' said Ceriani. 'Three or four questions and then up against the wall!'

'Eh, if only we could,' retorted the maresciallo.

A rancorous frustration lay just under the surface, and now in that murderous dialogue it seemed on the point of breaking out.

Soneri was distracted by his vibrating phone. 'Sir, I've got the information you asked me to get. I apologise if I'm calling only now, but there's been so much to do today.'

Soneri once again felt peculiar and out of place. He limited his response to a muttered assent, which the inspector took as a reprimand. His reaction was to begin reading his notes coldly. 'Andalò is the husband's surname. Her maiden name is Elvira Gallerani, born in Zibello, 11th February 1950, resident in Parma, 15 Via Italo Pizzi. One daughter, Giovanna, thirty-five years of age, resident in Milan.'

'Thanks. Did you find out anything about siblings or other relatives?'

'No, but I could look into it further.'

'It doesn't matter. You've got too much to do.'

Soneri thought the information over. Possibly it opened up other scenarios, but he could not say which. As he went back to join Landini, he bumped into Motti, who said, 'We don't have the resources, but they all want us to take action. There's me and my colleague Cervone up against gangs of dozens of criminals.'

'I understand,' replied Soneri, whose mind was focused on other matters.

The maresciallo made a kind of salute, and got back into his car. Soneri went back into the club.

'That unnamed dead man of yours, he's another one,' said Marisa, when she caught sight of him. 'Who do you think he is? He's one of them. There are no two ways about it.'

'Who cares?' said Pezzani, annoyed and embittered by the maresciallo's visit.

'And how many more are there?' exclaimed the Viking. 'They're divided into gangs, Hungarians against Slovaks, Czechs against Ukrainians. They squabble over the best fishing grounds, and when they can't come to an agreement, it ends in a fight. And if it should so happen that someone gets killed, what do they do? They toss the body into the Po, and that's it over and done with,' he concluded, making a gesture of washing his hands.

Soneri changed the subject. 'Do the Galleranis have a sister?'

Silence fell. Astonished glances were exchanged, but it was unclear if they were in response to the delicacy or unexpectedness of the question.

'No, no sisters,' said Pezzani.

'Or at least no legitimate ones,' Cefalú insinuated maliciously.

'Do you believe there were any illegitimate children?' asked Soneri.

'The old man was a bit of a playboy,' Cefalú sniggered.

'Do you know an Elvira Gallerani?'

'Elvira...' repeated Marisa, in an effort to place the name.

'Of course, she was a cousin,' said Ceriani. 'The one who went to Parma. She's the daughter of old Gallerani's brother.'

'Has something happened to her?' asked Marisa.

'No, no.' said Soneri. 'It's just that I'd imagined that she might've been the sister and still have some interests around here.'

'Ah, Giacomo's daughter,' said the Viking, with the hint of a smile. Cefalú too gave one of his grins.

Soneri turned to Pezzani with a puzzled look. 'No, no, nothing. Just malice,' he said, cutting off further discussion. 'Compared to his brother, Giacomo was a shy and reserved type. There's nothing more to it.'

Landini butted in. 'Don't you think we've left some work to do?' he said, pointing to the boat whose lighted deck could be seen.

Soneri agreed and made a move to follow the captain, but with a sense of unfinished business.

'What do you think?' he asked once they were on board.

'I understand their frustration. Here everything is finely balanced.'

'No, I'm talking about the Galleranis and this cousin.'

'Well, Giacomo was always under his brother's thumb. He did what he was told, recognised his brother's superiority and accepted a secondary role.'

'Did the two not get an equal share?'

'Anything but! I think Giacomo got about twenty per cent.'

'Was that what their father decided?'

'I don't know about that. In any case, with all the property they have, it was still a tidy sum. Elvira can lounge about if she wants to.'

The lights in the club's courtyard went off, leaving no trace of the excitement of a few moments ago. Everything was once again silent and indistinct. Soneri and Landini ate without speaking, and all the while the current beat against the vessel with increased force.

'The river is rising in the rain which is swelling the waters,' the captain announced. 'I'll have to set off early tomorrow morning, before the current carries down floating rubbish that will damage the hull.'

'Have you ever heard talk about monsters living in the coves along the river?'

Landini smiled. 'You mean the Anguanas, the water nymphs? They say they came down from the Alps because they were desperate to see the sea.'

'Some people believe in them.'

The captain leaned his head to one side. 'Hereabouts you can hear and see all manner of things.'

'Some huge footprints have been sighted, like those of a pheasant, with claws.'

'The crocodile man. Everybody claims to have seen him but nobody can quite describe him. I believe it's a matter of suggestion, like dreaming. When you wake up, the dreams vanish and so they end up imagining things.'

'The mist helps.'

'Everything here is finely poised. There's never anything clear cut. This is a world of amphibians, creatures of land and water.'

They finished eating, keeping the *strolghino*, the sweet salami made with strips of *culatello*, for the last.

'You must never take things that happen here too literally,' the captain warned Soneri. 'Everything is double-edged, like the world seen from the Po or from the river bank.'

10

Soneri woke up to the chime of the bells from San Giovanni Church. He had got home late and for a while felt badly disorientated, but then he settled into his familiar routine. He was going to have dinner with Angela in the Milord. Half an hour later he was ready to go out. He walked in the direction of Via Italo Pizzi, a road which bordered the Cittadella moat, with trees and bushes on either side giving the illusion of being in the country. Before ringing Elvira Gallerani's bell, he glanced at his watch. It was a quarter past ten, a suitable time for a Sunday visit.

Soneri found himself facing a sixty-year-old woman, whose hard features were softened by carefully applied make-up. They introduced themselves and he told her he needed to ask her some questions. They sat down in a living room whose solemn furnishings somehow had the feel of a museum. One shelf had a photograph of a girl with plaits, alongside a boat.

'Your daughter?' asked Soneri.

She nodded. 'You see? The Po is part of the family.'

'It's your family I wanted to talk about,' Soneri explained.

'She's my family,' replied the woman, indicating the photograph. Aware of some embarrassment in the air, she went on 'Before you ask, let me tell you that my husband and I are separated. He lives in Cremona.'

Soneri indicated that he understood. 'In fact, I'm more interested in your cousins.'

'I have no relationship with them. I never see them, and have no interest in seeing them,' she replied firmly.

'Was there a quarrel?'

'Not exactly. Let's say we live at a satisfactory distance from each other.'

'Did you know a certain Gianni who was a patient in the Villa Serena neurological hospital, when Dr Righetti was there?'

Elvira gave a look of surprise. 'Gianni? Gianni who?'

'I don't know his surname. That's one of the reasons I came to see you.'

She shook her head. 'I've no idea who you're talking about.'

'And yet it must have been you who picked up this Gianni when he was released from the hospital. It must have been about three and a half years ago. A witness asserts he heard the address of your former house being given,' Soneri stated firmly.

'I don't know what you're talking about,' she repeated. 'Three and a half years ago? I don't even remember where I was then. What month?'

'Summer time.'

'Then it's impossible. I go to Portugal from June to September, and then come back for the winter months. It's cheaper and the climate's better.'

'But the witness is reliable. He also says you arrived in a taxi.'

The woman burst out laughing. 'And you really believe this nonsense? Just who would take a taxi down the Po Valley to accompany someone to somewhere unknown?'

'Yes, it's odd,' Soneri agreed, 'but for exactly that reason...'

'It's not odd. It's crazy and absurd. I don't own a car, but if I needed one, I'd have hired one, don't you think? It would have cost me less, even if I'm not badly off,' she concluded with a touch of ostentation.'

Soneri sat in silence. He was disappointed and confused in the face of the woman's questioning and scornful stare. He was conscious of something sensual in that challenging glare, all of which made him think that Elvira preserved the indomitable will of youth deep inside her. 'I'm sorry I can't be of greater use to you,' she said, with sudden gentleness. 'That woman wasn't me. Perhaps it was someone who wished to pass herself off as me.'

'So why was the driver given the address of your house?'

'This one?'

'No, 15 Via Duca Alessandro.'

'I haven't lived there for four years.'

'Are you sure your memory isn't misleading you?'

'Quite certain. I received the deeds from the lawyer Tonelli on my daughter's birthday in April four years ago.'

'And the purchaser was Simona Perrone?'

'I see you are well informed,' she said, with a touch of sarcasm.

'Only the broad lines. I didn't know the actual dates.'

'As you see, it couldn't have been me.'

'I wonder in whose interest it was to pretend to be you?'

'Perhaps someone who knew me well, but who wasn't wholly aware of the most recent changes in my life,' she suggested, with a certain ambiguity.

Soneri nodded. 'You don't have even indirect news about your cousins?' he asked.

'No, not for some years. We grew up together but nothing remains of those years,' she replied coldly.

'What about your ex-husband?'

'The indispensable minimum. I know some things through my daughter who goes to visit him every so often. He has another woman, did you know that? Much younger than me, his company secretary. What originality! The boss who takes up with the secretary,' she sneered.

'What company is that?'

'He deals in electronic goods, but with all that he spends...' her voice trailed off, leaving the rest to be guessed.

Soneri got up to leave.

'Should I consider myself a police informer?' she joked.

'Regrettably I'm not in a position to impose any restriction on residence.'

'What do you mean?' she asked, fixing him a seductive look.

'You'll be off to Portugal and I'll not be able to seek any further advice.'

Elvira lowered her eyes and became serious once again, managing to conceal her disappointment. 'These are my contact numbers,' she said, handing over a visiting card to the commissario. 'With modern technology, distances hardly count.'

As Soneri was leaving, she asked him, 'But did something happen to this Gianni? Why did you put all those questions to me?'

'Just a matter of verifying identity.'

She laughed. 'And a police officer went to all that trouble on a Sunday for such a banal question?'

'It's not exactly banal,' said Soneri, as he went down the stairs.

An hour later Soneri crossed the threshold of the Milord. He had taken full advantage of the time on his hands before meeting Angela for lunch to take a stroll through the streets of the still sleeping city. Nighttime and the torpor of autumn Sundays were ideal moments for a silent dialogue with Parma and inducing a dreamy inebriation exposing the grim darkness of his life. The dialogue consisted of suggestions, of snapshots of life and of acute feelings of deep nostalgia as painful as knife wounds, aroused quite suddenly as though by an ambush.

Alceste, as he came out from the kitchen, pacified the tumult still troubling Soneri's spirit. Whether by lack of awareness or resignation, he was a serene man whose smile and talk were the equivalent of a drug. Angela's embrace completed the therapy.

'I thought I would get a whiff of chub or carp from you,' she joked.

'I've been dealing with people who squirm more than fish.'

'Mission unfulfilled?'

'I continually have to deal with other people's memory lapses. Three and a half years are a long time, but there are some people who do know.'

'Not so much as a lead?'

'There is one ex-inmate of a mental hospital in the area who corresponds physically to the man found dead. A certain Gianni, but there's no certainty even about his name.'

'Could it be him?'

Soneri thought it over. 'It could be, but it could equally be one of those fishermen from the East who come to the river for a six-month period. They're extremely violent and have frequent fights.'

'What do you think? Your intuition is usually reliable.'

'If I were to put it in percentages, I would say there's an eighty per cent chance that it's one of those outsiders, but as you know I have a weakness for minorities.'

'The minorities lose out, but they're almost always right, at least in this country.'

'The mistake is not listening to them.'

'So what about this Gianni?' Angela went on, while Soneri was delighted by an irresistible plate of *tortelli di erbette*.

'He's some guy who went for treatment for a mild nervous breakdown and who was often seen wandering about in Torricella and on the banks of the Po. One summer's day about three years ago a woman turned up in a taxi to take him away, and from that day on nothing more is known about him.'

'Is that it? Won't he just have gone about his business?'

'The strange thing is that the woman gave the taxi driver an address which corresponds to that of a certain Elvira Gallerani who is a member of a wealthy family in the Po Valley, in Pizzo to be precise.'

Angela put down her fork to listen carefully, allowing Soneri to continue. 'The lady had sold the apartment a few months earlier, and it turns out she is the ex-wife of a certain Andalò from Cremona.'

'And what does that have to do with anything?'

'It's got to do with the fact that shortly before the appearance of the body, a boat was found half smashed up against the breakwater at Stagno, and according to some witnesses it appears it had been stolen from someone called Andalò at Cremona. In addition, the boat aroused interest because it's a *gozzo*, a sea-going boat of a type that's never seen on the Po.'

'These links are a bit weak, but they do arouse suspicion.'

'It's all I have to go on, so I'll have to content myself.'

'I doubt if it'll get you very far. The bureaucratic machine grinds out paper as it moves on, and it can't permit itself the luxury of allocating a head of the Flying Squad to look into a mere question of identification.'

Soneri thought this over and then replied seriously, 'If necessary, I'll take time off.'

Angela did not reply immediately. She was halfway between admiration and disappointment. Her partner's determination reinforced her esteem of him, but any time taken to pursue his aims was time taken away from their lives together.

That indecision created a silence. Soneri, who was afraid of Angela's reaction, changed the subject. 'What can you tell me about Ragu?'

'He's under house arrest at a friend's place. He's got himself into a right mess.'

'When's the trial?'

'They haven't fixed the date, but it's going to go badly for him. The TV cameras caught him throwing stones more than once.'

'That's the wrong way to be in the right,' commented Soneri.

'But what are these kids supposed to do, except put up a fight against the paper tigers of the revolution they used to hear people chanting about in the fields, while the bosses and financiers were cheerfully fucking us?' Angela burst out.

'Today's revolutionaries with no ideas are scarcely any better. Ignorant and self-deluding, they're the worst of all. At most they aspire to replace those who've got their snouts in the trough.'

'This is an excellent trough,' said Angela, indicating the restaurant while Alceste was serving the dishes. 'What do you plan to do?' she asked, returning to the question of the unknown man.

'I'll speak directly to the examining magistrate and will do my best to be convincing. Signora Falchieri is in charge, and you can discuss things with her.'

'If they've left the case suspended for over three years, the least they can do is allow you a couple of weeks, surely?'

'That's my hope. No man should be simply wiped out like that.'

Angela felt that Soneri was eager to go on. 'Is there something else?' she asked, without doubting the answer.

'I don't know. Just a feeling. A suspicion.'

'Suspicions are clues waiting to be proved.'

'Why did this Gianni go for treatment for a mild nervous breakdown in an out of the way clinic lost in mist?'

'The mysteries of the Health Service bureaucracy.'

'Or else he himself wanted to go there. Nearly everyone there comes from the Po Valley. It's the local hospital.'

'If it had been someone local who disappeared, something would have already come to the surface.'

'Well, someone has come to the surface,' smiled Soneri. It took a few seconds before Angela laughed at the unintentional joke.

'In fact,' he said, becoming serious once again, 'nothing in this whole story quite adds up. Whichever way you turn, you run into something.'

'Should I be jealous of this Elvira?'

'Only if I were ten years older. She's a good catch. She must have a stack of money.'

'There're some who have a great life just getting bored and waiting to ensnare some principled servant of the state, and others who don't have enough to live on, like poor Ragu.'

'A very single-minded lady, of terrifying solidity.'

'Being solid like that also means being pitiless.'

This last remark of Angela's made a deep impression on Soneri. They were the last people in the restaurant. When they went out, afternoon was fading into the precocious darkness of the autumn. Angela announced she had work to do and both were weighed down by the approaching goodbye as though it were a final farewell. Ever since boyhood, Soneri had loathed post-prandial Sundays. Everything always ended that way, with the momentary euphoria of the holiday giving way to anxiety about encroaching life. A continual repetition of the passage from childhood to awareness, the autumn to which both he and Angela were heading. They said goodbye, with a kiss, a brief whisper and a quick hug in the darkness of a doorway.

I I

Signora Falchieri, the magistrate, looked at him with her usual expression, a mixture of perplexity and irony, before turning to stare at a random point on the wall, as if making out the sea in her home town, with seagulls in flight, the hubbub of the market place and the smell of fish.

'So you think we should dig up this old story?'

Soneri nodded in agreement.

'In fact, we never dealt with it properly. And I have entertained similar scruples as well.'

'No-one should be treated that way.'

She began to reflect, her wandering eyes seemingly anxious to scan far horizons, leaving the commissario by contrast fixed on the mists and his customary myopic panorama.

She started up again. 'It's quite true that sometimes this work is cynical. Each and every day a load of documents suffocates you and makes you forget that you're dealing with other people's lives. Do you know one of the reasons for the law's delays? It's very simple. Several of my colleagues are bone-lazy.'

Soneri made no reply, but they exchanged glances which summed everything up.

'Carry on with it, but you'll have to work fast. A lot of them think I'm a fantasist, but I can also be a realist.'

Soneri gave an understanding nod, and as he went out he felt that dreamy gaze of hers fall on him. He drove in the direction of the Po Valley with the rain making silent patterns on the windscreen. He received a phone call from Bosi. 'He's called Caputo, Giovanni Caputo,' Bosi said with no preliminaries.

'I'm on my way,' said Soneri, switching off at once.

Twenty minutes later he parked in the piazza at Colorno. As he crossed the hump-backed bridge, he stopped to observe the water in the River Parma which was almost up to the arches and was flowing above the top of the houses and alongside the Palace stables, whose walls were already soaked.

Bosi, seated at the corner of a table in the kitchen, greeted him. His wife emerged, wearing a heavy house-coat, under which a night-gown could be glimpsed. Everything in that house suggested dignified poverty, perhaps the consequence of many missed opportunities,

'Caputo, you say?'

'Yes, Giovanni, but everyone called him Gianni.'

'It couldn't be someone else?' Soneri asked.

'I had the same doubts myself, but I've made some checks. It so happens that he was called by a name which is slightly different from the one on the documents.'

'But Caputo?'

'It's not a name from these parts. I'd say it's from the south of Italy,' he agreed.

'A southerner who likes the Po and the mist,' laughed Soneri.

'People move about, so family names don't mean anything anymore.'

Soneri agreed.

'We're all a mixture,' said Bosi.

'Did you ever talk to this Gianni? Did he have a southern accent?'

'Not at all.'

'Where was it from?'

'I couldn't say. It was strange, as though there was one layer on top of another, so that you couldn't make it out.'

'Here in the Valley there're more foreigners than locals,' Bosi's wife said, giving the commissario time to work his way through a tangle of hypotheses.

'Did the hospital take people from outside as well?' he finally asked.

'Yes. If there were no spare beds in the city, they sent them to us.'

'Could a person make an explicit request to be sent to Villa Serena?'

Bosi smiled. 'With Righetti, anything was possible. He did deal directly with some people.'

'Was this the case with Caputo?'

'Who knows?'

'What's your opinion?'

'Could be. The card I found gave only surname and first name. It didn't even say where he was from.'

'No other details about identity?'

'None whatsoever.'

'Was that normal practice?'

'Far from it, but knowing Righetti... I've told you what kind of man he was. He could've even made some changes to the card.'

'What do you mean? He falsified?'

Bosi remained silent for a moment, until he chose to speak. 'Anyway, he's dead.' He shrugged his shoulders. 'For some patients who didn't want it revealed that they were patients there, he filled in an index card with false names.'

'Did you only have to ask, or did he take money?'

'That I don't know. In many cases, we're talking about friends, perhaps well-off people, so I can't exclude that they greased his palms. Understand?' he said, rubbing his hands together.

'So Caputo's card could be forged?'

'Could be,' Bosi admitted.

'I never did like that Righetti,' Bosi's wife interrupted. 'Women, cars...you couldn't trust him.'

'He was good at his work,' her husband protested, showing the admiration of the faint-hearted for reckless spirits.

Soneri, on the other hand, was floundering between reality and fiction, quite normal in that transient, yielding, fluvial universe where nothing was solid and everything seemed to be sinking: mist, sand, clay and water. Appearance was always double-edged. Objects and their disappearance merging, and Soneri felt that if one or other came out on top, was as much down to chance, like the throw of a dice.

He was on his way back to Torricella when he had a flash of

inspiration. He stopped the car in front of the town hall and went into the registry. The young lady gave him a smile that did not conceal her concern over a request from a police officer.

'Giovanni Caputo, did you say?' she asked, just to be sure, as though the very sound of that name made it unlikely she would trace it, and in fact, after some inputting on the keyboard, she shook her head. 'No-one of that name in this registry.'

'Obviously, because he's dead. I wanted to know if there was any trace of this individual, such as a birth or marriage certificate.'

'Unfortunately, a while ago there was a complete breakdown of the digital archive which totally wiped the memory, and we're still trying to reconfigure the data.'

'Don't you have index cards?'

'Yes, but they were stored in a building in Coltaro, and the flood five years ago left them all illegible.'

The Po in its eternal flow had carried off all memory of the town and of the lives of its inhabitants.

'If you like, I could contact the other registries in the Union of Po Towns to see if they know anything about this Caputo,' she offered.

Soneri agreed, but after some brief work on the keyboard, she said, 'No, it appears not.'

'With these things you can connect with everything, and still draw a blank,' Soneri concluded.

He got back into his car and drove through the town. In the piazza he noticed a shop selling equipment for fishing and hunting. He wanted to buy a waterproof jacket with a hood like the one the Madman wore. He chose a yellow one and put it on before going out in the rain. He closed his umbrella and threw it into the boot of the car. In a restaurant, he had some *spalla cotta* and a glass of *Fortana* before setting off for Torricella. He decided the yellow jacket was better than an umbrella. It would prevent him from smoking his cigar, so his health would improve.

'Now you do look as though you belong here,' said Casimiro, emerging from under a poplar tree.

'Have I gone up in your estimation?'

'Anyone who comes to the Po with an umbrella is either someone with nothing to do or else he's a lord and master. In either case, he gets on your nerves.'

Soneri listened to that declaration, the water running off his hood.

'If you've got work to do, how are you going to manage with only one free hand? Tell me how you could unhook the mooring or pull a boat ashore if you've got to hold an umbrella at the same time?'

'I've got two free hands now but since the Po is rising, I could still do with an extra one,' he laughed.

'If that's all, you could keep them both in your pocket.'

Soneri threw him a puzzled look.

'There's not much doing,' said Casimiro. 'Even the snails overestimated what seems to be happening.'

A car pulled up in front of the club. Pezzani got out and rushed in without looking in their direction.

'Something seems to be up if the president turns up for work at this time,' said Casimiro in an indifferent tone.

Soneri moved away and went into the club.

'I was looking for you,' said Pezzani. 'Have you heard about the man found at death's door?'

'Where?'

'Three kilometres from here. He was lying among the bales of hay in a farm outhouse. One of those people from the East.'

'Settling scores among themselves,' said Marisa from behind the bar.

'With these brawls and the robberies, the maresciallo has his hands full,' said the president.

'They're one and the same thing,' said Marisa.

'This might be the answer you're looking for,' said Pezzani, taking no heed of what the other two were saying. 'You see what these people are like? One squabble after another. If I were you, I wouldn't waste any more time. They themselves didn't bother about a colleague left lying in the fridge, so why should you?'

'They're staying mum because somebody's got a bad conscience,' Marisa said.

Soneri made no reply, but changed subject and asked, 'Has either of you ever heard of a certain Caputo?'

The two looked at each other, stuck out their chins and shook their heads. 'Never heard the name,' said Pezzani.

Soneri kept his eyes on their startled and dismayed faces, then looked away, at which point he noticed the motor launch. Landini had not moved off.

'How come he's still here?' he asked, pointing down to the pier.

'I was just going to check up,' replied Pezzani.

'I called you precisely because it seemed odd to me,' said Marisa, referring to the president.

They went down to the river. Further upstream, among the cottages, they heard someone working with a winch, followed by a torrent of curses which bounced off the water to the opposite bank. Soneri and Pezzani picked up the gangway, moved it into position and climbed on board over the railing. They called out for the captain several times, shouting louder and louder. When they received no answer, Pezzani turned to the commissario with a worried look.

'Could he have gone into town?'

'I doubt it. He's on foot.'

Pezzani started to yell, trying at the same time to force the hatch. A dinghy passed at top speed, making waves which shook the ship.

'Let's go and get a crowbar and force the door open,' Pezzani said, as he made off.

Soneri did not follow him. He remained on the deck, soaked by the rain which continued to fall relentlessly, and after a little he became aware of a shadow moving about as though drunk in the semi-darkness on the other side of the windows. He knocked on the glass and the figure straightened up as it approached. Landini was flushed, and staring about vaguely. He was swaying so heavily on his feet that he had to sit down as soon as he opened the door. Soneri went over to examine him as though he were a doctor.

'Chloroform,' he announced, as he smelt the captain's breath. 'They've drugged you.'

Landini stared at him, bemused. 'I've got a sore head,' he said.

Soneri left him there to search about the empty dining room from where passengers could admire the river. The window on the far side from the club was broken. 'They broke the window to make their entrance,' he explained, as he came over to Landini, who had not moved and was looking about in bewilderment.

'So that's why I was feeling chilly.'

Pezzani re-appeared and seemed almost disappointed to see the door open and the captain dishevelled, with his uniform unbuttoned as though he had been ousted in a mutiny.

'I didn't notice a thing,' he said in self-justification, somewhat guiltily.

'They cut the window with a diamond and then attached some tape to deaden the noise,' said Soneri, who had seen that system used for dozens of robberies.

'They'll have stripped everything,' Landini groaned, still dazed, as he rose to his feet to go and check.

'Fortunately, you're a heavy sleeper. If you'd woken up and found them here, it might have gone badly for you,' said Pezzani.

'He could hardly have woken up,' said Soneri, coming into the tiny room where the air was heavy with a pungent scent of narcotics.

Landini started rifling through all his drawers. He went off to check in the adjacent rooms and came back, looking surprised.

'Well, then?' asked Pezzani.

'They haven't taken anything,' he replied, sounding almost disappointed.

'That's good news,' said Pezzani, attempting to offer reassurance.

Soneri shook his head.

'Not even the takings from the last cruise,' said Landini, confused by the hangover from the chloroform and the sheer oddness of the situation.

'So all you have to do is repair the broken window,' Pezzani concluded, with phoney relief.

The captain agreed, unconvinced.

As they went out, Pezzani asked, 'What do you make of it?'

'A bad situation,' was all he would say.

'It's certainly very strange.'

'Here everything is ambiguous,' said Soneri, with a gesture taking in everything around them.

12

'Do you think it was intimidation?' asked Maresciallo Motti.

Soneri thought about it. 'At best, a warning.'

'These people run risks only for money, the robbery in Sissa, the engine theft in Polesine...'

'Articles of some value, but what could they've been stolen here? Small change.'

'That's not certain.'

'What about the guy who was beaten up?' asked Soneri.

'They were settling scores, or so it seems. Maybe two gangs fighting over fishing in the Ciucion inlet. Or else a squabble over a woman.'

'Who was the victim?'

'A Hungarian, who's now in hospital, but he won't speak. He makes out he doesn't understand Italian,' Motti went on. 'We found him half frozen and numbed.'

'Did they dump him off after beating him up?'

'He would never have got where he was by himself. And he was next to a graveyard. You know what that means in underworld symbolism.'

'Did you say there might be a woman mixed up with this?'

'It's a hypothesis. There's a single woman who's been seen going out with these East Europeans. However, the peasants round here are not great talkers.'

'No, they're hardheaded folk, a bit savage. They size you up and a police uniform isn't a great help.'

'We didn't find anything on him. They'd taken the lot. We're doing a fingerprint check and on the name he gave us the one time he opened his mouth.'

'And you think leaving him beside a graveyard was a kind of warning?'

'In the language of this lot it was. I've got some experience now.'

'Where is the graveyard?'

'Just follow the signs. This isn't exactly New York. Take the street on the left off the piazza. It's called Via del Pizzo. Once Pizzo was a village, but it's been swallowed up by the Po. They rebuilt it further away from the riverbank. All that's left is the street, not the town.'

'It's the same up and down the river. Walking makes the destination evaporate,' reflected Soneri.

Motti stared at him without understanding. 'We've already gone over the ground inch by inch, outhouses, fields and graveyard,' he said, with a touch of annoyance.

'I have no intention of going there,' said Soneri, making the gesture of fending off a blow.

'I was only trying to save you the trouble.'

'It's forbidden to get mixed up with carabinieri affairs, nor would I attempt to,' proclaimed Soneri, smiling as he rose to his feet.

A few minutes later he was on Via del Pizzo. It was quite true that he had no wish to get involved in brawls, thefts and bank robberies. His walk in the rain made him appreciate his new jacket, giving him the feeling of being inside a shell. He saw the farm outhouse and the bales of hay appear before him, with the high wall of the cemetery a little further on. He heard the sound of wailing from behind the half-opened gate. Instinctively, he broke into a run along the avenue. The wailing turned into sobs which rebounded off the arched walls, until the varying notes formed one deafening echo. Soneri finally made out the figure of a woman kneeling in front of a freshly closed-off tomb in a burial wall. The moment she saw him, she stopped weeping, overcome by a sudden reserve, changing tone to a gurgle which sounded like a growl. Soneri turned off to one side and exited through a portico in the direction of those tombs soaked by the water from the skies and from the river when it overflowed to give the dead something to drink. Near the boundary wall, there were the pauper graves, some marked only by a wooden cross and plastic flowers. He reflected that there was a proletariat even among the dead, but the man who was occupying Soneri's attention had not found a place even there. At one of the graves, on the pile of earth long since overgrown by grass, someone had placed a large vase of flowers, now withered, together with a large plant resembling a bonsai cactus. The vase seemed so totally disproportionate that it obscured the crucifix. He bent down to look more closely and it was then that he noticed on the discoloured, cracked wood a little card with a name: Carmela Caputo. Soneri sprang back and stood stock still in astonishment. The woman who had been weeping passed along the pathway while he remained alone among the dead, one of whom seemed to be offering him a lead.

He remembered that in the club they had spoken of the ghost town of Tolarolo near Roccabianca. All that remained of that town, swallowed up long since by the river, were two columns at the entrance to the cemetery, and on certain nights the dead could be heard talking. A little later, when Soneri ran into the Madman on the path alongside the river, he spoke to him about that story.

'It's true. The dead do speak to us,' Soneri said.

'I've always said so.'

They were standing in front of his construction.

'They told me about a certain Carmela Caputo.'

'And?'

'Did you know her?'

'Now that you tell me she was called Carmela, I do remember her. She must have died a number of years ago. Carmela... they all used to call her Napoli.'

'Why Napoli?'

'Around here, to keep everything simple, they call everyone from the South of Italy Napoli.'

'What can you tell me about her?'

'Not very much. I might have seen her about ten times in all. She lived further inland,' he said, indicating the plain.

'Did she work in these parts?'

'I think she was with the Galleranis. Nearly everyone here works for them. They own half the valley.'

'Did you ever speak to her?'

'No, with women… I've never had many dealings with them and I never wanted to get married.'

'Why was that? You don't like them?'

'They're all right, but you've got to be careful. I've got too much respect, because women are delicate.'

'You look to me the type who would respect them.'

Casimiro turned away, shaking off the rain water off. 'Well, I don't know about that. Do you see where I live?' he said, pointing to the makeshift construction. 'Do you think a woman could adapt to living in that? And with somebody like me?'

'There are many who're much worse. They beat women up.'

'There are things you're free to do when you're on your own but couldn't do any more. I don't know,' he cut off in embarrassment.

'If it's a question of freedom, you're quite right,' Soneri agreed, while Casimiro seemed to fumble for words.

'For example, I fart. How could I do that in front of a woman? Or burp? And I'm none too clean, but farting really is something I just couldn't do, and that's quite important. Am I supposed to stay all swollen up until she goes out? My grandfather used to say – while the arse can blow, the body's healthy, stop the one and the corpse is deathly.'

'Dante quoted someone or other who made his arse a trumpet.'

'I don't know Dante, but I do know it would be a torture for me. You see, I just can't do it.'

Soneri turned back to the subject on his mind. 'This Carmela, did she have any relatives here?'

'Can't help you there. I didn't even know her surname was Caputo,' replied Casimiro. 'Are you married?'

'Almost.'

'And do you fart when your wife is there?'

'They say a harmonious couple can do so without embarrassment or protest.'

'I could never do it. But, you see, that's the rule for staying together.'

'Like so many other things. And it's not exactly the most important.'

'But for me...' Casimiro interrupted himself, and once again Soneri waited. A word from him would have stopped that semi-confession. 'I've never had a bathroom in the house. A woman needs a bathroom.'

Soneri indicated the poplar grove visible in the half-light, as though to say that there was space there, the biggest bathroom imaginable.

'No, not there,' the Madman disagreed, as though it were a vital correction. 'I take the boat out early in the morning. It's really beautiful to do it when it's still a bit dark but not too dark, such that you can scarcely see.'

Soneri smiled. 'Isn't it a bit uncomfortable?'

'I've bored a hole in the overhang in the stern, and I sit down there. I do my job while the birds sing on the Po in the morning.'

Soneri felt it his duty to humour his innocuous craziness. 'Have you ever seen those footprints?'

Casimiro moved close and lowered his voice. 'The monster came to sow his evil plant.'

'What plant?'

'They call it American *zucchini*, something never seen here. It even grows in winter in spite of the ice. It climbs and suffocates everything in its way, like one of those fine-mesh fishing nets. They come and take photographs of it, just for fun. They say that it's an enchanted wood because it's beautiful to look at, but they're deluded. They don't know that it will swallow them too, and that it will cover the river so that no-one will be able to navigate it anymore.'

'And it's the monster who's sowing it? The crocodile man?'

'Who else could it be? I've found his footprints in the woods among the willows, and one morning I saw a great movement in the waters in front of the Internati island. It wasn't some whirlpool spinning you round thousands of times like you were on a spit. It was him diving down, I'm sure of it.'

'You should rip out this American zucchini,' said Soneri, trying to provoke him.

'I'm not mad! It would soon get its own back. It would wait till you went by on a boat and drag you in. I wouldn't like to think that's how it happened for that nameless corpse,' he whispered in a more confidential tone.

'You don't think he was a foreigner?'

'They go fishing in the Po, but they know nothing. For them it's just another river.'

'So the monster only considers those who live on it?'

'The ones who have some feeling for the river. The others don't see it, and if by chance it pulls them down, they'd say it was an accident, but I know how some of them are going to end up.'

'You mean some drownings that seemed accidents?'

Casimiro nodded. 'There are some who instigate them and others who pray for them,' he said before adding quietly, 'You've no idea what goes on at the flood plain at night time.'

'I'm the same as your foreigners. I don't know anything.'

'They light fires and practise certain rites that look like the Mass.'

'Is there one precise spot?'

'It all depends. There's more than one. All you need is a deep flood plain where there's a lot of woodland. I've seen them in the Barnon inlet.'

'Did you see what was going on?'

'Not completely. It's dangerous to get too close. They want to stay concealed, known only to their affiliates. They don't like other people sticking their noses in.'

'Are you sure there were no children? There're some people who meet up for the chance to abuse them.'

'No, in the morning you can see the remains of the fires and strange signs on the grass, as well as the footprints, because he likes to emerge from the water to greet his faithful.'

'Are they people from here?'

'Of course! They must know the river. They come from all the nearby towns, including on the other side,' Casimiro explained, pointing over to the Lombardy side.

'And they're not afraid when he goes out in his boat?'

'He withdraws in the morning. It's at nights that he jumps out, and that's why no-one sees him. At first light, he goes back underwater and heads off to sleep in the ditch at Stagno or beside the the railway bridge pillars where there's deep water. If only Venanzio, the Po's deep-sea diver...'

'I didn't know there was a diver.'

'He cleared all the mines from the bridges between Cremona and Ferrara. When they were retreating, the Germans wanted to blow them all up but they didn't manage it in time. Once when he was underwater in the Stagno ditch, he saw it, and there and then he gave up the job. They pulled him out more dead than alive with fright.'

'So the people here, are they afraid?'

'None of them want to admit it, but they are. The only ones that aren't afraid are the foreigners, but that's because they don't know anything about it. If they did, they'd be scared too. That's why I wanted to tell you everything.'

'Should I be scared as well?'

Casimiro looked hard at the commissario. 'Yes, the same as everyone else, and especially because you're so curious.'

13

Soneri went back to the same official in Sissa, and asked her to look up Carmela Caputo, but once again he drew a blank. The woman reported that they had handed the work over to an agency specialising in deciphering flood-damaged documents.

'Call back in about a month, and perhaps we'll have the entire registry,' she told him.

The difference in the perception of time between his line of work and bureaucracy was astounding. It was enough to enter the office of any administrator or prefect to get the impression of wading in water. In a month's time, that man would be buried or cremated with his accumulation of life and loves along with him. Only one single set of initials, S89, in a corner of some dispassionate archive to remember him by.

He pulled out his mobile and called Bosi. The only way to attempt a reconstruction was to let him recall random episodes of his life, as in the varied mosaic of a family album.

'Carmela? I seem to remember a woman of that name,' stuttered the man who seemed to be waking up from an afternoon nap. 'Just a minute. Let me think. What a lot of things escape you!' he cursed as he floundered among the flotsam of a memory, flooded like the town's archive. 'I think she had some connection with the Galleranis. She was from Naples, if I'm not mistaken. It was about thirty or more years ago.'

'With the Galleranis?'

'She might have worked for them, but I don't remember where. They have so many things on the go.'

'The same surname as that Gianni, so you see...'

'Oh yes, there must be some link. She was the only Caputo around here.'

'Could he be her son?'

'Could well be,' Bosi confirmed.

Soneri was about to ring off when Bosi said, 'You could ask Don Amilcare. He's an elderly priest and I believe he knows a lot about Torricella.'

'Is that the church at Sissa?'

'Yes, that's the one. The priests are the only people who resist time, and the only ones who have retained some memory. Go there.'

Soneri passed by the club first. The cruise ship was still there with the gangplank lowered. He crossed over it and knocked. Landini seemed a bit more himself. 'I still have a tremendously sore head,' he lamented.

'Have you any idea why it happened?'

'None at all,' replied the captain, rubbing his forehead. 'Maybe it's because of something they think I might have seen.'

'Do you know what?'

Landini shook his head. 'I travel a lot on the river and keep my eyes open, but there's nothing that comes to mind.'

'So often that's how it goes. Unintended witnesses, one of the most unfortunate situations.'

'But a witness to what?'

'Possibly to people organising strange nocturnal gatherings?'

'Have you been talking to Casimiro?'

Soneri agreed.

'You mustn't pay too much heed. He's a bit crazy. He comes from a family of savages. His father lived on the Internati island and used to build castles with branches. Casimiro learned from him. The house caught fire once and he was burned alive inside it.'

'And where was the Madman?'

'At school, but he lived with his mother in Torricella.'

The ship was rocking more than usual, accompanied by the monotonous sound of rain on the roof.

'See how the river's rising?' asked Landini. 'It swells and pushes.'

Soneri looked out. The water was choppy and had turned an asphalt colour as it poured downstream with greater urgency.

'Now that I think of it, the only vaguely odd episode I came across was some time ago, but I don't remember exactly when.'

'Was it the same as last night?'

'No. I was passing by Polesine and I noticed there were three or four houseboats in the inlet, the sort you would hire for fishing or for spending a week relaxing on the water. It seemed a bit strange. Normally these things are kept apart. Anyone who goes fishing keeps clear of competitors, and someone there for a bit of romance doesn't want anyone else nosing about.'

'And what was odd?'

'I was afraid something had happened, so I moved alongside and I saw a certain movement.'

'What do you mean, movement?'

'I don't know, but something didn't seem right. Excited, that's the word. It was dark and I couldn't see too well. Yes, that's it, the fact that it was dark...'

'So what did you do?'

'I refocused the lamp on the prow to see better, but just then they closed the houseboat door. That seemed even stranger to me.'

'Were you alone on board?'

'Yes, I was taking the vessel back to Boretto.'

'Try to remember when this happened.'

'I'd have to consult the logbook. Offhand, I can't remember and this pain in my head is stopping me from reasoning at all.'

Soneri left the ship and walked up to the front of the club without going in. He got into his car and set off for Santa Maria Assunta Church. He rang the bell at the parish house, but no-one answered. He tried again and after a while the door half-opened and a priest, introducing himself as Don Amilcare, appeared.

'I've got the flu, but if it's urgent, you can go and see Don Fernando at Trecasali,' he said in a hoarse voice.

'I'm a police officer,' announced Soneri.

The priest must have judged that to be of sufficient urgency, because after a few seconds he unlocked the door.

Soneri found himself facing a small, slightly hunchbacked, wrinkled man, wrapped in a full-length house-coat which dragged along the floor. He had a woollen scarf round his neck.

'So what's going on?' he asked, plainly irritated.

'I'd like some information on a woman who lived here some time ago,' Soneri explained.

'Ever since the flood carried off the entire Council archives, they all come to me,' the priest complained, 'but all I have are records of births, marriages and deaths. If you need something more, complain to those semi-Communists at the town hall.'

'That's the first time I've heard them called 'semi-Communists'. Do you think they're an improvement?'

'What improvement! The Communists were more much serious than this lot, and they made the Council work.'

'Do you remember a certain Carmela Caputo?'

Don Amilcare coughed, looked startled and became thoughtful. 'All I have on her are funeral records.'

'When did she die?'

'It was the Year of the Eucharist, so twenty years ago.'

'Was she a regular churchgoer?'

'Not regular, but she was devout. She never failed to turn up for the procession of Our Lady of Fatima at Zibello on 13th May. You know about the miracle?'

Soneri shook his head.

'On that day, in 1944, a bomb fell on Piazza Garibaldi when it was packed with people but it didn't explode. It was a miracle of Our Lady of Fatima, and from then on it's been celebrated with a procession. But there is another miracle. From that year to this, it has never rained on the evening of 13th May. Even on the worst days, the stars come out at dusk. It's been that way for seventy years.'

'For the love of God and his Blessed Mother,' Soneri joked, but the priest did not take the remark well, and turned a disapproving look on him.

'This's the truth,' he said petulantly.

'Do you know if she had a son, called Gianni or Giovanni?'

'I'd have to look it up in the records. I don't remember. He certainly didn't come to catechism classes here. I still remember the ones I taught.'

'Where could I find some trace of this person?'

'If she received the sacraments as I think she did, the diocese will have the papers. Carmela some times spoke to me about the Salesians at San Benedetto. Maybe they know something. For over two thousand years the Church has maintained contact with her people. Cities and States come and go, but the Church is always the same.'

'What do you remember about Carmela?'

'A young woman from the South of Italy. They called her Napoli, but I don't know if she came from that city. Nor do I know why she ended up here.'

'Did she work for the Galleranis?'

'Yes, as a servant, I think.'

'So in Pizzo.'

'The family is certainly from Pizzo. They used to live in the village that the Po swept away. It was only later that they built their villa where it is now.'

'As far as you know, was she married?'

The priest gave a little cough before replying. 'I don't think so,' he replied, as though he was choking. 'But she attended the church in Trecasali more often. Ask Don Fernando.'

'And who should I ask for at the diocese?'

'What a lot of questions!' the priest expostulated with some irritation. 'Ask for Monsignor Gorini.' Immediately after that, he looked at Soneri and asked almost imploringly, 'Has something serious happened?'

'A man has died and he has no name and no relatives, or so it seems.'

Don Amilcare wiped his nose, unrolling a handkerchief that looked like a napkin. 'The Eternal Father will restore to him what men did not wish to give.'

'I would like to give him at least a name.'

The old priest raised his eyes, which quite suddenly became alive. 'Your determination is worthy of all praise,' he murmured, standing still with a handkerchief in his hand and an expression of amazement on his face.

'It is certainly a duty,' said Soneri in his turn.

'Divine mercy will recognise everyone, but it would do no harm if human mercy would do the same.'

'I'll stop at duty, but I hope I'm not using it as an excuse for another issue.' Soneri stopped there, perhaps because he could not find the words or because he was afraid of them.

'An issue of conscience?' asked the priest, completing the sentence.

'Perhaps. I'm not quite sure myself,' he said, looking down.

'Go forward, since there is obviously a force pushing you on. Fortunately we don't always have freedom of choice.'

'You think not?' Soneri smiled, rising to his feet to take his leave.

He had taken only a few steps when the priest said, 'Yours is more than a police enquiry.'

14

Maresciallo Motti decided to take the matter in hand, and managed to get someone to accompany them on the search of both riverbanks between Sacca and Polesine. Landini was still not feeling well, so the Viking volunteered his dinghy with its one hundred horsepower outboard motor which could fly over the water.

'The Po from the inside is quite different from the view from the riverbanks,' he said. They went up river, passing by Stagno, Isola Pecarolli, Santa Croce and Polesine and then turned to go downstream with the current via Torricella to Sacca, Mezzani and the mouth of the Enza. As a man of the mountains, Soneri was simultaneously fascinated and terrified. He had the sensation of being driven by an immense, unnerving force. Floating on the waters was a risky rodeo ride and on landing he would feel somewhat more alive. The Viking pointed out the places, the sites, the possible disembarkation points, and sounded off with hypotheses on arrival points and escape routes. Soneri did not listen to him. He was thinking of the monster Casimiro had spoken of, of the weird rites in the flood plains, of presences among the poplar trees and of that deeply pagan river peopled by saints, dotted with chapels and majesty. Savage and civilised, duplicitous, gentle and ferocious.

The maresciallo, noting that Soneri was distracted, brought him back to himself. 'Who could ever catch you with all this going on?' he said.

'Especially if you don't have a boat.'

'With something like this,' the Viking explained, pointing proudly to his outboard motor. 'If you know how to use it, all you need is ten minutes' start and you can disappear.' He kept his eyes on the dials.

At certain points, the river widened out and the distance from land made Soneri anxious.

'All Italy is buried here,' the Viking said.

'It's all in the museum at San Damiano,' Motti confirmed.

'There's even the skull of a Nandertal,' added the Viking.

'Neanderthal,' Motti corrected him.

'He didn't come to claim it either,' the Viking added with a grin. 'When all's said and done, none of us will ever really be reclaimed. We'll be forgotten and that's the end of it.'

'Do you remember Carmela?' asked Soneri as the boatman approached a mooring point.

'I met her a couple of times at Trecasali, but she didn't go out a lot.'

'Did she work for the Galleranis?'

The Viking stared at him with both amazement and suspicion. 'Yes, at least at the beginning.'

'And then she stopped?'

'Why are you asking me about that woman?'

Soneri ignored the question. 'Was she a servant?'

'In the early days she worked in the house, but then it changed. She used to take the bus every day to Parma, but I don't know what she was doing. If you didn't see her around much early on, later you didn't see her at all.'

'She was called Caputo like that Gianni. Was he her son?'

'Or her brother,' said the Viking tentatively.

'The age difference was too great.'

The Viking threw out his arms. 'I don't know any more.'

The moment they disembarked, Angela called him. 'That boy's disappeared.'

'Since when?'

'I rang him this morning, but was told there was no such number.'

'More and more people are disappearing nowadays,' Soneri said.

'And lots more split up. A colleague of mine has gone off with a client's money, leaving his wife and children in the lurch.'

'Have you tried finding out about him from his crowd?'

'I've tried, even if I have no right or even interest. He's used to living a solitary life.'

'He'll have fixed himself up in one of those social care centres where you can come and go.'

'I've checked up on his inheritance. There's a fair bit.'

'Wait and see. He'll turn out to be wealthy.'

'No, no, about twenty thousand euros in total.'

'That's a fortune for him.'

'But one he's prepared to turn his back on.'

'If nothing else, he's consistent. No money from the one who's rejected him.'

'When are you coming back?'

'I too am on the trail of someone who's disappeared, and again like you, I've no rights and no interest.'

They said goodbye, leaving that doubt hanging. Soneri made for his car intending to pay a visit to Don Fernando in his Trecasali parish, but he bumped into Casimiro in front of the oil press. He wound down his window to say hello, but Casimiro signalled him to stop.

'Are you going into town?'

Soneri nodded.

'Could you give me a lift? I'm not feeling well and I want to visit my sister.'

Soneri told him to get in. 'You told me you never travel on four wheels.'

The Madman shrugged his shoulders. 'When I can't manage on my own...' There was a strong stench of damp coming off him, so to dispel it, Soneri lit a cigar.

'What's the matter with you?'

'I've got a bit of a temperature.'

'Don Amilcare isn't too well either.'

'No surprise. When the Po rises, it brings all sorts of things with it.'

'Is it the Po or the season?'

'It's got nothing to do with the season. It's the water. You know that all the toilet waste in the plain ends up in the river? And where do you find viruses if not in the toilets where people shit and piss?'

Casimiro seemed tense and agitated, and kept a tight grip on the handle above the door.

'With the life you lead,' said Soneri, 'anybody could get a temperature.'

'Not me,' Casimiro replied. 'I'm too old.'

'You're not old. You could still get married,' Soneri said to cheer him up.

'Oh yes I am. I have reached that age.'

'Age doesn't affect everybody in the same way.'

'You're right there. Do you know when a man is old?'

Soneri waited in silence for the other to go on.

'A man is old when the hairs on his prick turn white.'

Soneri burst out laughing, but the Madman remained serious. Shortly afterwards, when they reached the town, he raised his hand and said: 'Stop. I've arrived.'

He got out without saying a word and turned off into a close.

As he continued in the direction of Trecasali, Soneri remembered having noticed some white hairs, and took that as a worrying sign. He decided to think no more about it. He pulled the hood over his head and got out in front of the church under a baptism of ceaseless rain.

The door opened onto the nave where in the centre, his back towards him, Don Fernando walked by himself, rehearsing hymns, reading the text from a little book. He was tall and looked severe. As soon as he saw Soneri, he snapped the book shut and fell silent, as though he had been caught in the act of doing something reprehensible. When he realised he was dealing with a police officer, he drew himself up even more erect and signed to him to follow him into the sacristy.

'Did you know Carmela Caputo?'

'Yes. I'd just been appointed parish priest. It was many years ago.'

'I'm told she attended this parish.'

'She preferred to come to mass here, even if she lived near Sissa.'

'That's odd. Was there any reason?'

'I wouldn't know. I never asked her.'

'When you knew her, was she still working for the Galleranis?'

'For a time. Then she changed job and I know she found work in Parma.'

'Whereabouts?'

'I believe she had a shop.'

'And she had a son here in the North.'

'Yes, but she never spoke about him. She avoided the subject. I never knew who the father was. The boy was educated by the Salesians in Parma, and she worked her fingers to the bone for his upkeep, because she was a widow.'

'What do you know about the husband?'

'Perhaps he died when they still lived down South. She was Neapolitan.'

'Do you know what she died of?'

'A tumour, I believe. Don Amilcare and I officiated at the funeral.'

'What sort of person was Carmela?'

'Quiet, taciturn. She lived a solitary life, or at least she did here. On the other hand, I heard stories which described her life in the city as being quite different. A joyful woman, sunlit, as they say in Naples.'

'Three years ago, there was a man who was known in these parts, and his name was Gianni or Giovanni Caputo. Could he have been her son?'

The priest looked doubtful. 'It seems strange to me. I don't know anything about him. What I do know is that she got married very young after some mishap. You know what they say down there, a *fuitina*, in other words, she got pregnant and had to go through with it.'

'And then she was widowed.'

'Yes. From what they told me he was a brute of a man, a travelling salesman linked to certain circles. I gather that he didn't die of natural causes, if you follow me. That was one of the reasons why Carmela fled from Naples. She was a good person who wanted nothing to do with that world.'

'What became of that first son?'

'Unfortunately, for young people evil is more attractive than good. I believe he was dragged into his father's orbit and into his gang.'

'The camorra?'

The priest made the same doubtful face. 'Could be. She didn't want to talk about it. She would only say that it was wicked company and she suffered for it. Her aim was to break with that world and those youthful errors.'

'Certainly, here in the Valley...'

'There is some isolation, but don't believe for one minute that being here leaves you in the clear,' Don Fernando warned, ambiguously.

'What do you mean?'

'You'll have heard yourself about what goes on. You're a police officer, aren't you? Everything has altered, apart from the Po and the Eternal Father,' he concluded, as though he was giving absolution.

Soneri went out onto the church steps and tried in vain to light his cigar. The rain was as immutable as the Po and the Eternal Father. Sheltering under a church arch, he phoned his colleagues in the police station in Naples. The telephonist's voice was enough to make him imagine the dazzling light of the Gulf, Vesuvius and the famous pine tree depicted in so many postcards. The officer put him through to the Flying Squad.

Inspector D'Onofrio burst out laughing. 'Dear colleague, with all the camorra alive we have, you're enquiring about a deceased moll! And here was I thinking that you wanted information about the Casalese gang who're doing great business up there among you.'

Once again Soneri felt like a fish out of water, pursuing a whim he could not even define. 'It's a probable murder,' he said, but without much conviction.

'Alright, give me a couple of days.' He put the phone down with a snort.

As he was getting into his car, Motti turned up. 'I've got one or two questions for Don Fernando,' he said.

'He'll sing . Maybe he's actually singing at this very moment.'

Motti was taken aback. 'In what sense?'

Soneri burst out laughing. 'Not in that sense. He's rehearsing sacred chants.'

To see better, Motti adjusted the brim of his cap which was dripping with rain and looked at him distrustfully.

'Any news on the robbery and assault front?' Soneri asked.

'That's exactly the point. The story is getting more complicated.'

'Never thought it was straightforward.'

'We've spoken to the woman going out with the boy who was beaten up, and she's told us about threats.'

'That was predictable. A settling of scores between gangs.'

'Yes, but she told us that the threats didn't come from his countrymen, but from Italians.'

Soneri became more attentive. 'Are you sure she's not lying?'

'Why should she? What reason would she have?'

'I don't know. Covering up for someone else? Didn't you say she was separated? Maybe her ex is tied up in all this.'

'You think it's down to jealousy? In that case, she would've spoken out. It might even have been to her advantage if we had investigated her ex, because he'd been got out of the way. Neither of them wants us getting involved.'

'Local criminal fraternity or something worse?'

'There's no local criminal fraternity worth the name. Is there another possibility?'

'Unfortunately only the one we both imagine.'

'What could be their objective in this place? That lot deal with big business.'

'And there is such here. The Po is a mine – sand, gravel and so on. Isn't the criminal world well placed for sub-contracts with the construction industry?'

'But why bother about the foreigners?' asked Motti?

Soneri made a gesture to signify he had no idea. 'Perhaps those who were doing the illegal excavations didn't want anyone getting in their way, and these people are always pissing you off. Do we have any proof of this sort of traffic?'

Motti made no reply, but after a while he looked down and said, 'Nothing more than suspicions.'

15

Although the Po had finally burst its banks onto the flood plain, it was still possible to walk over it in gumboots, just as the Madman had predicted. Gradually the water flowed into the club courtyard, but a pile of sandbags kept it out of the building itself.

'It's not in a temper,' said Marisa, referring to the river. 'When it's like this, it's just coming up to give you a hug.'

'Just what you're after,' said Cefalú, who narrowly avoided a slap to his face.

After a while, Soneri got tired of hanging about and set off to Sacca to take a look at the houseboats. He was aware of about half a dozen moored there, even though there were more between Felonica and Revere. On the way, he phoned Angela.

'What would you say to a couple of days afloat?'

'And who would be the pilot?'

'We wouldn't move. You and me by ourselves in the mist with the river flowing by and rocking us.'

'I'd rather have a weekend in a spa hotel with baths and massages.'

'You'd run into colleagues with their bejewelled wives.'

'With their lovers, more like. I'd embarrass them.'

'I'll make enquiries,' Soneri said, ringing off.

The man who rented out houseboats was called Battioni, and he seemed to be doing good business. His best customers were men whose hobby was fishing, people who enjoyed casting a line and struggling with a catfish, imagining they had caught a swordfish like the fisherman in Hemingway's novel.

'But there are also couples who don't want to have too much going on around them,' explained the man, with a wink.

'Lovers?'

'Mostly, sometimes men with men or women with women. See what I mean?'

Soneri nodded. 'Apart from yours, are there other, privately owned houseboats?'

'Certainly there are, all sizes. Some look like real apartments.'

'Where are they moored?'

'In the various ports. Some even have engines so people move about as though on a cruise, but the majority have to be towed.'

'Did you say some of them are really large?'

'It depends. Most of them have a lounge and bedroom, nothing much, but the really big ones have a suite of rooms where they can hold meetings. One of the really grand ones belongs to the Galleranis.'

'The Galleranis? And where do they keep it?'

'They've got a range of mooring points where they prefer to stop off. Just now I think they're at Stagno.'

'If you can make a business out of this, it must mean that living on the water has its attractions.'

'In certain seasons it has. In the hunting season, for example. Or at weekends. There're some VIPs who come looking for a place when they have to meet someone for, you know, business.'

Soneri stayed silent; suddenly he felt tired out.

Battioni went on: 'You know what it's like: if someone likes privacy and wants to get away from it all, a floating home is ideal,' he said, with complicit air. 'There're some companies who have their board meetings there. They talk business on the river and then go off to a restaurant for a spot of *stracotto di asina*.'

'Better than in a workshop canteen,' commented Soneri thoughtfully, his eyes still fixed on the current which seemed motionless but was actually rocking the boats a little, making them bump gently against the pier. The rain was not so heavy now, and resembled a heavy mist hanging like a veil over the riverbanks. From the river there emanated something as clandestine and unsettling as a menacing but beautiful snake.

Battioni invited him to go on board one of the houseboats. Soneri found himself in a lounge with matchboard walls, a large table, a cupboard and a mobile bar. Two doors led off to a well- equipped kitchen and a bathroom, while in the centre of the room was a stove placed on a metal strip. Battioni opened the cupboard door to reveal a foldaway double bed.

'After the romance, something concrete,' he said, with a heavy allusion.

To maintain the tone, he picked a bottle of *Bonarda* from the bar and a whole salami which he started slicing. While Battioni was plying the knife with the skill of a pork butcher, Soneri felt his mobile vibrate in his pocket. He went out onto the veranda which was swaying slightly, making him feel tipsy.

'My friend, I told you that you'd run into some fine lad who's doing business in the north,' said Inspector D'Onofrio.

'I've always had a good nose for criminals,' Soneri replied.

'You sure do! Carmela Caputo was the wife of Gennaro Bovino.'

'And who would he be?'

'Eh, who would he be? A member of the Portici gang. Powerful, dangerous people.'

'I was told he was dead.'

'He is, in an ambush years ago, but his son, Carmine, is still around.'

'Is he in prison?'

'He's got a season ticket, but he's been lying low for a while. He came up through the ranks, that one.'

'Any idea if he's hanging about in these parts?'

'Who can say? He's certainly up there in the north, but he's not been fully involved in operations for some time, if you get my meaning?' he ended up, tantalisingly.

'You mean he's not on the front line any longer?'

'Exactly! He's done his time with the guns, so now they'll have packed him off to do a Masters in Economics and Business Studies.'

'Any idea of where he might be?'

'Our cousins in the carabinieri will know more about that. It's been hinted that he might be in the provinces of Lower Lombardy, Mantua or Cremona. There're other gang members there, but nobody could say for sure.'

'And what can you tell me about Carmela Caputo?'

'She got out. As long as Gennaro Bovino was alive, she had to stay with the family, but a couple of years after her husband's death, she set off for the north. It seems the gang didn't take it too well, especially her son.'

'Why was that?'

'Listen, my friend, camorra families are like balls of wool. They won't let one strand slip away, especially not a woman who wants to remake her life far from the gang.'

'So it's likely that this son was here so as, among other things, to keep an eye on his mother?'

'How could I say? Might be. But it's more likely that he was there to keep an eye on the money and investments.'

'If I find anything out, I'll let you know,' Soneri said, winding up the conversation.

'I'll send you the files we have on the woman,' promised D'Onofrio. 'Do you have WhatsApp?'

'No, I don't want the hassle. Just send me an email.'

'You're a fossil! Oh well, I suppose you're quite right, but it's very handy.'

'Bugger all handy. A useless yap yap of chatter that would drive me to an early grave. I want to be master of my own time and not have a cattle prod at my arse.'

As he rang off, Soneri heard D'Onofrio's raucous laugh at the other end of the line, and wondered whether he was being derisive or amused. Shortly afterwards, the promised data arrived. Considering the speed of the operation, it was clear that the file had been drafted on a previous occasion and was simply being forwarded. Carmela had been born in Naples in 1920, and in 1936 had married Gennaro Bovino, ten years her senior. Carmine was born the following year, and by 1946 the husband was dead. He was a travelling salesman by trade, but in truth he was a member of the camorra, and he died during a shootout between rival gangs. Carmela remained in Naples the following decade but in 1956 she cut her ties with her past by fleeing to the north of Italy when her son was nineteen years old and already occupied a position of some respect in the camorra hierarchy. The file contained no information about the woman's life in the north, but it did speak of her son, Carmine. On three occasions, he had been imprisoned in Poggio Reale, and once in Opera for a longer spell. He had a criminal record with more entries than a dictionary, but his criminal CV was interrupted in 2004 on his release from Opera. From then on, there was no further trace of Carmine Bovino.

When he had finished reading, Soneri went back into the houseboat, his mind in a turmoil. Seeing him so preoccupied, Battioni was almost afraid to offer him the salami and wine.

'Have you ever heard any talk of various mafias on the river? I mean, people taking an interest in sand excavations or that sort of thing?' Soneri asked.

'Every so often there is some talk. Anytime around here when tenders are invited for big contracts, the subject comes up but then, as far as I know, it all dies down again.'

'And recently?'

The man shook his head. 'With the current crisis in the building industry, nobody is building as much as a hen run.'

The salami was excellent and the *Bonarda* an ideal accompaniment. When there were breaks in the conversation, a silence so deep fell over them to make it possible to hear the gentle drops of the rain on the edging of the tiny roof. Everything seemed still, but from time to time the current shook the floating house, or a metallic vibration came from the jetty. Some form of tension emanated from that calm, and the combination of movement and sound induced a kind of unrest.

'So, will you want it for a couple of days?' asked Battioni, with a circling gesture taking in the walls, interrupting the embarrassing silence.

'I'd be happy to try out living here. I'm getting my bearings.'

'If you like, I'll shift it and moor it anywhere you prefer,' Battioni went on, taking from the drawer a little map with the riverside ports.

Soneri took a look at it.

'If you want absolute peace, I could see to anchoring it in some inlet away from the current but near to a nice spot.'

'I'll think it over,' Soneri replied, imagining Angela's horror at solitude.

Battioni handed him a visiting card. 'Any time you like. All it takes is one phone call. There isn't much movement on the river at the moment.'

'Or maybe there's too much.'

The man looked at him, giving the impression of having understood. 'Of a certain kind, you mean?'

Soneri nodded. 'Perhaps so.'

16

The rain had almost stopped, but the sky remained grey and menacing, as though on the point of self-lacerating. Soneri found the cruise ship still anchored at the port. He waved to Landini, who opened the railing on the gangplank to allow him aboard.

'I think I've found what they were after,' he announced before saying hello. 'They've taken some pages from the logbook.'

'From what period?'

'Between July and September.'

'Any idea why those months?'

'None at all. It's the busiest time of the year if the water is high enough, and this year it was.'

'With so many sailings, it's going to be difficult for you to remember anything in particular,' said Soneri, with evident disappointment.

'I'll give it some thought,' the captain promised, but then he held his head in his hands and added: 'I still don't feel well.'

'They've given you a right dose.'

The man enquired quietly. 'And how is the investigation going?'

'I might rent a houseboat,' Soneri replied vaguely.

'You should take a trip to San Daniele. Anyone who wants to get to know the river must go there.'

'I want to know about a man who was fished out of the river.'

'There's no shortage of things fished out of the river up there: men, animals, trees, objects. If you do go, ask for Professor Toschi.'

Soneri changed tack. 'Think about it. This robbery stinks.'

'I'm well aware of it. I've taken everything from on board, and now I go home in the evening to sleep. It's not safe here any more.'

'You've done the right thing, at least for now.'

'Until these foreigners clear off,' murmured Landini darkly.

'They don't steal logbooks.'

Landini gave a grimace which suggested he was unconvinced. 'If it wasn't them, so much the worse.'

Soneri was making his way along the gangplank when his phone rang. It was Signora Falchieri, the magistrate. 'How're you getting on?'

'We're a couple of steps forward,' Soneri answered optimistically.

'We're under pressure from the mortuary to free up the space. They're breathing down my neck every day.'

'I've reconstructed something. I should be able to pull out a result.'

'In other words, nothing of any relevance as yet,' said the magistrate, who was familiar with Soneri's strategies for concealing dead ends.

'No, there are clues... I get the feeling that one could...'

'Drop it!' she cut him off. 'I've no desire to start blaming you but there's no point in inventing a justification. There's no need for any deception between us,' she added in a more confidential tone.'

'We can beat each other up with smiles on our faces.'

Soneri heard a snigger from the other end of the line.

'I'll do my best to hold out a bit longer, but I have to advise you that at a certain point even the Maginot line gave way. Your real problem will be with the Police Chief. Just today I heard him say that keeping you on is a waste of public money.'

'It's not true. Anyway, I've decided to take a few days off, since admin is forcing me to use them up.'

Shortly afterwards, he communicated everything to Juvara.

'Oh God, boss, you've no idea what a mess you've landed me in! Who's going to rein in Capuozzo? Now he's even in a bad temper with the cactus plant in the corridor.'

'It'll pass.'

'Excuse me for asking, but where are you off to this time?'

'To the Po, but don't breathe a word to a soul.'

'Don't tell me it's because of that...'

'Exactly that.'

The third phone call was for Angela.

'Pack your bags, because we're going aboard.'

'Do you want me to grow mouldy?'

'It's going to be really chic. Just you and me all alone on the Po. When were we ever so close?'

'In this season?'

'It's ideal. It's not too hot, there're no mosquitoes and there's no shortage of water.'

'I don't know if I could stand it for more than three days before my joints seize up.'

'There's a stove, and in the evening we'll dine in front of the fire. You'll be warmer than in the city.'

Angela said nothing, which was her way of saying yes.

'When?'

'I've taken a week off. You can come when you want.'

Soneri went into the club feeling pleased with himself. If it all went badly, he would at least have had a short holiday in a place well off the beaten track.

'Ah, there you are!' Marisa exclaimed as soon as she saw him. 'Don Amilcare was looking for you two hours ago. He left word that it was urgent. He didn't have your number, so he phoned here.' She handed over a note with the priest's contact details.

'Don Amilcare is leaving in a couple of months,' Ceriani informed him.

'Where are they sending him?' asked the Viking.

'He's retiring to the clergy care home in San Prospero. He just can't take any more.'

'There're two young nuns there who'll see him alright,' Cefalú added maliciously.

'Go to hell,' said Marisa, annoyed. 'It's all he can do to keep on his feet.'

A discussion got underway, but Soneri paid no heed. He went out to the courtyard and dialled Don Amilcare's number, but after a few rings the answering service clicked on. He left a message but without much hope. He was unsure whether to go back to Sissa and get the priest out his bed, or whether to return the following morning. He decided to act immediately, spurred by one of those ideas which occurred to him as suddenly as fear.

'Battioni, you've convinced me,' he barked down the phone. 'I'll take it for a week. I want the one you showed me.'

'Give me time to clean it up. Will it be alright if I hand it over tomorrow around midday?'

'I would like to move in this evening.'

'This evening!' exclaimed Battioni, taken aback.

'Don't you have one all ready, moored at Stagno?'

'I've got a couple you could choose from, but they too have been shut up for a couple of weeks.'

'It doesn't matter. All that counts is that they stay afloat.'

'That I can guarantee.'

'Is the Gallerani one nearby?'

'You can't miss it. It's the biggest one you can see.'

Half an hour later, Soneri had the keys in his hand. Battioni gave him detailed instructions on how to position the gangway; how to light the stove; how to use the gas canister for cooking and how to switch on the electricity at the mains.

Soneri consigned this information to memory but his mind was elsewhere. He was so absorbed in his own thoughts that he was unaware that Battioni was looking at him intently, expecting a reaction which never came. Soneri was about to leave when the carabinieri car pulled up.

'I asked the backroom staff for some information, and they've come up with something,' the maresciallo said.

'Something big?'

'Hints, suspicious companies, some kidnappings. My colleagues are preparing a raid.'

'Is this the 'ndrangheta, camorra or some other body?'

'Camorra around here.'

'What are they dealing in? Sand? Drugs?'

'Drugs, but slot-machines above all. They place them in the bars they take over, using front men.'

'What gangs are we talking about?'

'Ones from Portici, but it seems there's some movement inside them.'

'The usual civil war between bosses?'

'Things have shifted down there, but around here the old balance still holds. However, everything suggests that the new order will move north.'

'There's no doubt about that, and that means that things will be shaken up.'

'It's already underway,' the maresciallo confirmed. 'Just today they've fished out someone else.'

'Where?' asked Soneri in astonishment.

'In the lock at Isola Pescaroli, in Piacenza province.'

'And who is he? Do we know?'

'A foreigner. As if the camorra wasn't enough! This time we have a name because he wasn't newly arrived, and since the corpse was still fresh we were able to take fingerprints.'

'So?'

'A Ukrainian. Dimitri Sekolov, thirty-six, previous convictions for theft, drunk driving and resisting arrest.'

'Was it the water that killed him, or was someone not too fond of him?'

'A blow on the head smashed his skull. What do you think?'

Soneri stretched out his arms. 'In these cases, I am always pessimistic.'

'Neither do I believe it was suicide, any more than I do with the unnamed corpse. Did you note the similarity between the two cases?'

'Do you think there is some connection?'

'It looks self-evident to me. It's the same act. In the last four years, the bodies of five immigrants have been taken from the river between Mantua and Piacenza. It must be another of those feuds between gangs of foreign poachers, or else between them and Italian criminals. Wait and see that the unnamed corpse will be one of them.'

'Have all the others been identified?'

'All bar one, as far as I know. From the reports, it seems that he was found naked and decapitated. There is no way of knowing if his head was cut off by his murderers or by a propeller.'

'Who did the identification of the others?'

'Their friends. A woman in one case.'

'All murdered?'

'Certainly so in two cases. One had a calibre 7.65 hole in his forehead, the other a dozen stab wounds to the body. Two had their heads battered in. That seems to be a trademark. The fifth, as I've just said, was headless.'

Soneri nodded in resignation.

'I imagine that everything's now a bit clearer for you,' said Motti.

Soneri was unmoved. 'It's the name! There's no certainty over identity.'

The maresciallo said nothing. He looked around in evident unease, not really understanding the commissario's obstinacy. 'I've told you everything,' he said after a pause. 'In a short while, my colleagues in Piacenza will deliver their report to their superiors, who will pass it on to the magistrates,' he said, making for his car.

Left on his own, Soneri felt he was losing his grip even on the one handle keeping him linked to the enquiry. All of a sudden, everything seemed clear and his task merely whimsical. He lit a cigar and got into his car. All that remained was to establish what Don Amilcare, the only one who shared his desire to get to the bottom of the story, wanted.

He had to ring three times before the priest came to the window of the parish house. Shortly afterwards, he opened the door and let the commissario into the room he recognised, where the stench of cooking and dirty clothes hung in the air.

'I have some news,' announced Don Amilcare. 'I phoned the bishop's secretary, Monsignor Gorini I spoke to you about, remember?'

Soneri nodded in agreement.

'He finally came up with a baptism dated 15th January 1958, and the child was called Giovanni Caputo, son of Carmela, father unknown. He was her second son, the one she had here.'

'Father unknown,' Soneri repeated. 'That's what they wrote?'

Don Amilcare frowned by way of confirmation.

'The baptism was in the Church of Santa Cristina, the celebrant was Don Guiduzzi, a well-meaning worker priest, who wasn't popular with the Curia. In those days...'

'This Don Guiduzzi, where is he now?'

The priest turned his face to the ceiling and pointed upwards with his index finger. 'I think that at the very least he'll have to spend some time in purgatory, certainly if they sought information from the bishop's office before passing judgement on him.'

'Is there any record of the name of the godfather or godmother? Is there nothing else in the documents?'

Don Amilcare put on his glasses and read out: 'Yes, the godmother's name is Maria Levoni. I don't know any more. She must have been a friend.'

Soneri leant forward, his elbows on his knees and his chin cupped in his hands but he remained silent.

'Do you believe that man might be Carmela's son?' asked the priest, alluding to the unnamed corpse.

'No, there's no guarantee,' Soneri answered, rising to his feet and shaking the priest's hand.

As he accompanied him to the door, Don Amilcare said: 'I don't know if you will find me here the next time you call, but don't give up. I mean it.'

His expression was so insistent that he seemed to be sending Soneri on a mission.

17

On the road to Stagno, it started raining again. It was already dark and everything was so leaden the darkness itself seemed to dissolve into liquid and fall to the earth in drops. When his mobile began to ring, he felt he was under siege.

'One moment. I've got Signor Capuozzo for you,' the secretary trilled, preparing the usual routine.

'You see I was right all along?' began the Police Chief.

'What about?' Soneri replied coldly

'What do you mean – what about? Your man, of course! He's an immigrant, just like I always said. I asked the carabinieri to look up similar cases in the past and up jumped several precedents. I've had a word with the magistrate and she's of the same opinion.'

'So?' asked Soneri in the same glacial tone.

'So close the case down once and for all, get back here and don't let us waste any more time,' Capuozzo ordered peremptorily.

'I've found the identity of a man who was from these parts but all trace of him was lost,' Soneri informed him.

The Chief snorted. 'And what's that got to do with these immigrants?'

'Maybe nothing, it could well be an entirely different story, but we don't know if it's suicide or something else. Even with these immigrants, there are only two cases where we can say with certainty that we're dealing with murder.'

'Be that as it may, the enquiries are going nowhere,' Capuozzo replied, but speaking now in a more measured tone. 'Certain territories are simply impenetrable. My fear is that the whole thing is going to end up in the unsolved file. I'm just off the phone to the carabinieri who assure me they'll carry on with the investigation, but we cannot permit the head of the Flying Squad to be tied up as well. Leave it to the carabinieri.'

'Couldn't agree more. In fact I'm taking next week off.'

'You can't decide that by yourself.'

'The admin people are forcing my hand: sixty-two days in arrears and a non-negotiable deal with the trade unions.'

Soneri heard a kind of grunt, perhaps an oath or a word in some incomprehensible dialect as the receiver was slammed down. That dry sound reminded him of the crack of clapperboards announcing a new scene, and that was indeed the feeling he had. He felt himself free from any need to provide a professional justification for his actions. Happy to be in control of his own time and to decide which way to turn according to his own instincts and wishes, like birds in flight. His instinct took him in the direction of Stagno, which consisted of four houses and two lampposts. He parked alongside the embankment and turned onto the raised roadway, lighting a cigar as he went. The floating apartments came into view a little way beyond the jetty, seemingly its farthest point. The one he had taken was the first and it looked onto the river. He followed the procedures Battioni had showed him, opened the low gate and stepped onto the little veranda. As soon as he pulled up the gangway, he experienced a pleasing feeling of isolation, like a child.

He had stopped on the way to pick up the necessary provisions: pasta, sauces and above all salami, grated parmesan and two bottles of *Fortana*. The light from the little LED bulbs brought out the warm colours of the matchboarding as he sat down to eat. The silence was so deep that he could hear the lapping of the water under the flooring. From time to time, a light, dull thud, accompanied by a slight sway, came from down below. Blackness pressed in from the windows. There was no way of distinguishing the darkness of the river from that of the night and a slow rain, as gentle as a subdued weeping, continued to fall. Every sound in that place so far from anywhere – the leap of a grey mullet on the river, the cry of an animal on the flood plain or the occasional burst of wind – acquired an enormous importance. The small invisible things he discovered as though he was peering through a microscope at a petri dish surprised, even shook him.

Suddenly he felt cold and went out onto the veranda where there was some firewood. It was then that he saw the Gallerani houseboat, its huge outline could be made out some thirty metres ahead. It had private access from a pathway through the poplar wood. Considering its dimensions, it must have a suite of rooms, but it also had a small mooring point for boats allowing direct access from the river. He went back in and lit the stove. There was nothing better than enjoying a glass of *Fortana* while watching the fire chase off the cold and damp. He felt snug inside that warm bubble.

That relaxing thought was interrupted by the phone. 'Are you already afloat?' asked Angela.

'Like *anolini* in broth.'

'A bear going into hibernation would be more sociable than you.'

'Every so often I feel the need to self-isolate because the world is not a pretty place for someone in my line of work.'

'What about mine? You see open violence, I see cunning violence, verbal or actual.'

'Well then, get a move on and come up here for a bit of detox. You could even kid yourself you're by the sea.'

'Yes, with all that mist and pleurisy hanging about!'

'I'm in front of a roaring fire.'

'I'll try, but only for two nights.'

'You'll fall in love.'

'If I do come, don't you think it's because I am already?'

They sent kisses and hung up. Soneri went back out onto the veranda to have a look at the Gallerani houseboat which was so imposing, it was almost menacing. When he went back inside, he noted a reflected light on the water, initially faint but growing stronger. A large boat was approaching, perhaps a barge with powerful search lights. It made its way slowly and cautiously on the current, like an enormous, satiated animal. There were warning lights on both sides, while the pilot in his small, brightly lit cabin could be seen at the prow. The waves made by the boat shook the houseboat, making the crockery on the shelf shake. The noise from the undertow beating against the riverbanks could be clearly heard, like the crashing of the sea against cliffs.

Around eleven o'clock, Soneri went out to get more firewood. A light breeze scattered the raindrops about. He leaned for a while against the railing over the river, which he could sense below him, as terrible and indifferent. He tried to look along the opposite shoreline but could only make out a deep darkness in which to imagine either emptiness or fullness. Suddenly he heard a noise coming from the direction of the Gallerani houseboat, like the sound made by a large fish moving on the surface of the water. He stared hard in an attempt to fathom what was going on, but all seemed still until he glimpsed a light, perhaps from a mobile phone. For a second, the tiny mooring point and a small motorboat, appeared. He saw a man on the steps, framed by the flash of light, running across the veranda and scurrying towards the entrance.

He had not heard the sound of an engine, so the craft must have been electric. At that hour, everything seemed to him suspicious, particularly from that spot hidden from police blocks or CCTV cameras. Soneri stood there, keeping everything under observation until the rain and the cold forced him back indoors. He switched off the lights and continued his observations through the window. Around one o'clock, the man got back into the boat and set off upstream.

Lying in bed later, Soneri thought over what he had seen and tried to work out who it could have been. Perhaps one of the Gallerani family? But what reason could there be for risking the Po at that hour? If it had not been one of the family, he must have been someone trusted, considering the care with which he had moored and entered. He certainly did not look like a burglar.

The following morning, he awoke with the same thought in his mind. The weather was unchanged but the water was a bit higher and the river seemed more threatening. Standing above it, he could appreciate its changeability even from one hour to the next. When he went out, he wanted to have a look along the bank on the village side. In the opening outside the Gallerani houseboat, he noted tyre marks. The rain had partially wiped them away but one seemed fresh. Could it have been someone who had stopped there the night before, gone along the towpath for an appointment at the houseboat on the river? From where he was, Soneri would not have been able to see him.

He had the feeling that the novelty of life on a houseboat had brought him into contact with something unknown, an intuition leading him to imagine its outlines without being able to determine its features. He decided to follow his curiosity. He picked up the phone and called Angela.

'I'm coming to pick you up,' he announced.

'What a cheek!' she replied ironically. 'This is hardly a spring awakening,' she added, referring to the rain and greyness.

'I'm heading for the city because there're some suspicions I need to resolve.'

'Ah, I see! I wondered if it was more than a romantic escapade.'

'It's that as well. Would you prefer to make the journey in the rain and mist?'

'I'm not quite ready. I've got some work to finish off.'

'I have work to do as well. We'll meet in the Milord. Bring your suitcase with you.'

'What suitcase? Two nights at the most.'

Soneri closed his mobile and set off by car for Parma. He took a long way round via some back streets to take in Barriera Saffi, where the San Benedetto Salesian Institute was. The building stood at an angle with the avenues, and retained the structure of the old monastery with a long surrounding wall and wide cloister. The director, a somewhat stocky, sturdily built man, with large, rectangular metallic glasses, was called Benassi. He had that distrustful air of the civil servant which Soneri knew well, always anxious to watch their backs and above all never to expose themselves.

'Has something happened affecting us?' he asked, instantly alarmed at finding himself facing a police officer.

'No, I'm simply looking for some information on a former pupil of yours,' Soneri reassured him.

Benassi put his hand on his desk and seemed to calm down. 'I understand. Which year?'

'The sixties.'

Benassi frowned. 'What's the name of this pupil?'

'Giovanni Caputo. His mother was called Carmela.'

'Carmela what?'

'Caputo. The boy had his mother's name.'

The man frowned again. 'Single-parent family,' he intoned, raising his voice slightly. 'Very fashionable nowadays, but in the sixties...'

Soneri gestured to convey that he considered all this too obvious.

Benassi pulled over the computer keyboard. 'Let's see what I can do. We're in the course of digitalising the entire archive and I hope that the years which interest you... As you can guess, I wasn't here at the time. The director then was Gabriele Cremonini.'

During the minutes it took the man to operate the keys Soneri observed the walls which were covered with diplomas, certificates and photos of monks. There were some silver trophies on a shelf in one corner.

'You did say Caputo, is that right?'

Soneri agreed.

'Yes, here we are. What do you want to know?'

'When did he start with you?'

'In the first year of primary school, 1964-65.'

'And he attended until the final year?'

'Yes, as a boarder. He followed the full school life, eating and sleeping here.'

'Until when?'

Benassi consulted the screen. 'Until the final exams. He got a diploma in accountancy.'

'Who paid the fees?'

'That's not written here. I imagine it was his mother. Didn't you say she was a single parent?'

'Is it possible to say if he received visits, and how frequently?'

'No, I'm sorry. We don't keep a note of such things. You would need to find out from people there at the time, but here everything has changed. We're talking about fifty years ago.'

These last words provoked a surge of dismay in Soneri. They sounded like a bell announcing the end or the beginning of something, and at exactly that moment a bell rang outside the classrooms on the far side of the cloister.

'Forgive me, but what has this Caputo done?'

'He's disappeared.'

The man appeared taken aback by this news.

'He was never seen here after he gained his diploma. Many ex-students come back to visit us even years later, but I don't think I ever heard his name at the annual reunions we organise. Caputo isn't a common name in Parma, so I would remember it.'

'You've no other information you can give me?'

'There's his school record,' said the director, turning back to the keyboard. 'Good marks, no fails. The report cards are always signed only by the mother. There's also a note on his conduct,' Benassi went on, reading out: 'Diligent, shy and taciturn, subject to frequent depressive moods which are holding back his education.'

'Nothing else?'

'Not that I can see,' replied the director, running his eye down the screen. 'Once he was taken into hospital. *Probable psycho-physical breakdown*. That's what it says here. Not long, about ten days.'

'You told me that you knew nothing more about him. Not even an address to send him communications about the Institute?'

'He did leave an address, but for a woman unknown to us. Perhaps a relative.'

'What was her name?'

Once again Benassi turned to the computer. 'Maria Levoni.'

Soneri immediately remembered the name of the godmother Don Amilcare had cited at the christening.

'What's the address?'

'15 Borgo Giacomo Tomassini.'

18

He set off on foot along Via Saffi, but halfway down the street he realised he would come out in front of the police station, and so he deviated into Borgo del Correggio which would bring him out to San Giovanni and Piazza del Duomo. He preferred not to meet his colleagues and to avoid explanations and banalities. To make matters worse, his heavy boatman's waxed jacket was bound to seem at the very least extravagant. As people rushed, frozen stiff, to take refuge in some central-heated bar, they all stared at him from under their throwaway umbrellas as if he were an alien. He walked down Via Cavour as far as Piazza Garibaldi, where the rain added a shine on the hero's granite and bronze. He continued part of the way along Via Repubblica before turning into Borgo Giacomo Tommassini. At number 15, he saw the intercom; the second button on the right was Maria Levoni's. He rang and waited. After a while he rang again, and this time the door sprang open allowing him to go up the stairs. He was halfway up the second flight when he saw a middle-aged woman on the landing, staring at him intently.

'Who are you?' she asked.

Soneri introduced himself and she showed him in.

'Are you looking for Maria?'

'Are you her daughter?'

The woman shook her head. 'I'm her carer. Francesca's my name.'

'One of the few carers who's Italian.'

'We've all got to get by,' she replied resignedly.

'Can I speak to Signora Levoni?'

Francesca looked at him gravely. 'I doubt if you'll get much out of her.'

'Is she not...' Soneri tapped his forehead.

'Dementia or Alzheimer's. The result's the same.'

'I'm interested in a man, Giovanni Caputo, who has vanished

without trace. Maria was his godmother. I was wondering if they'd stayed in touch.'

'I seem to remember hearing some talk about this person before she lost her faculties.'

'Do you remember anything?'

'A depressed sort of boy who caused her some upset. She had no children of her own and I believe she was like a mother to him.'

'To the best of your knowledge, did they see much of each other?'

'I presume so but although I lived nearby, I didn't know him.'

Maria Levoni was seated in a wheelchair with her mouth hanging open and an empty expression on her face.

'The gentleman,' Francesca said in a loud voice, 'is here to ask you about Giovanni.'

The old lady turned vacant eyes towards the commissario.

'I have no children,' she muttered after a pause, shaking her head. 'I never had any. They didn't come to me. I would have liked children,' she continued, in a sequence of short sentences producing an unintentionally comic effect.

'Do you remember Giovanni?' Francesca shouted.

This time Maria made no answer and showed no reaction but then suddenly continued talking. 'It wasn't my fault. It was my husband who wasn't capable. He didn't have the right *substance*.'

The niches her sunken eyes filled with tears which flowed down her cheeks. He thought again about the bell ringing shortly before, as well as the distressing spectre of age.

'Let her be,' he said, giving up further questioning.

Francesca stretched out her arms, defeated.

'Can I have a look around?' Soneri asked.

'It's not my house. It's hers,' she replied, indicating Maria. 'I don't believe it will matter much to her. She only has one brother, but he hardly ever comes to see her. He lives in Verona.'

Soneri understood this as agreement and began a summary search.

'What are you looking for?' Francesca asked.

'I don't know myself. Something that might be a link with the man who's disappeared.'

'In the bedroom a dressing table drawer there're documents and correspondence. Her whole life is there. You might find something useful.'

'I could hardly go rummaging about in her drawers, but I trust your discretion,' Soneri murmured.

The woman made a gesture, implying it did not matter.

Soneri entered the bedroom half taken up by a giant bed with an inlaid headboard. The furniture was in different styles, as though assembled from a variety of inheritances. Against the facing wall there was a piece with a glass back of coloured segments, more a sideboard than a bedroom furnishing. There were several postcards stuck to the glass, as in country houses, depicting holiday destinations. Soneri looked at them one by one: images of beaches, dance halls, bays and mountains. Soneri pulled out one with a city scene, which he turned over and read: Toulouse, Musée des Augustins. Alongside were three words, printed by a shaky hand, as though the writer had been leaning against a wall: Best wishes, Giovanni.

Soneri went back to the kitchen, where Francesca was seated beside the old lady. 'I didn't need to open the drawer,' he said.

'Even if you had... this woman,' mumbled Francesca. She was about to add something, but she hesitated a little, as though searching for the right word. 'She's dead, don't you see? When you no longer have any consciousness, you're dead. I knew her as she used to be, but that person is no longer there, so even if her heart is still beating, she's dead. All that's left is her name.'

'Her name matters. Not having a name is like having never existed, but having one, even if you're no longer the person you were, even if you've vanished, means that you were once there. That's true even for those who believe death is the end of everything. Our little comedy in this world must have a title, don't you think?'

The woman gazed at him without understanding a word, and nodded mechanically.

'Do you know if Maria knew anyone else called Giovanni, apart from Caputo?'

'It's possible,' said Francesca, now somewhat confused, perhaps still thinking of what Soneri had been saying. 'It's a common enough name, and she was well known in this district.'

Soneri turned the postcard over and looked at the badly faded date on the postmark. He managed to decipher the first three numbers, 198... They could have referred to 1988 or 1989, but that hardly mattered.

'I'm going to take this with me for now, but I'll bring it back,' said Soneri, putting the card in his pocket.

'You could just keep it. I doubt she'll be looking for it again.'

'All the more reason for giving it back,' said Soneri, but once again he noticed that the woman did not follow him.

When he was down on the pavement, the church bells of San Giovanni and the Duomo struck midday. As he walked off, he took out his mobile and dialled Juvara's number. 'Forgive me, but I have a favour, in fact two favours, to ask you.'

'But, sir, I thought you were on holiday.'

'A personal foible. I need the numbers of the *gendarmerie* in Toulouse, and then I want you to do a bit of research.'

'Tell me.'

'I'd like to know if in the eighties among the immigrants from Parma to France there was a certain Giovanni Caputo. Perhaps you could find out from changes of residence in the registry.'

'I hope so.'

'You know no limits when you have a keyboard at your fingertips,' said Soneri, who could already hear a clicking at the other end of the line. He took that as an answer.

'While you're waiting, I can give you the number of the gendarmes in Toulouse. Have you a pen?'

Soneri pulled out a bar bill and prepared to take down the number.

'Here it is – 0033 6794. Don't forget the international code. For the other thing, I'll let you know as soon as I get a reply from the office.'

'You're like a flash of lightning,' Soneri said by way of thanks. He sent a text to Angela and made his way to the Milord. She arrived immediately, dragging a suitcase on wheels behind her.

'I'm not sure if I've made a good choice, but whichever way it goes, I'm certain to catch something,' she said.

'It all depends on whether you believe it worthwhile,' replied Soneri, in a seductive tone.

'At our age, if I had to choose between healthy abstinence and unhealthy sex, I' d go for the former.'

'What cynicism!'

'Foresight, I'd say. Is one hour of pleasure worth a week of ill health?'

'You won't take sick,' Soneri assured her as Alceste escorted them to their table.

'What are you having?' he asked.

'Nothing liquid. We'll see enough of that,' Angela giggled.

'This is the season for *anolini in brodo*,' Soneri stated firmly.

'For two?' asked Alceste.

They both agreed.

'And tripe to follow,' said Soneri.

Angela ordered *melanzane alla parmigiana*. A bottle of still *Gutturnio* completed the order.

'Has the young man shown up again?' asked Soneri.

'All I've had is an email from an address I don't recognise. He told me the cash will come in handy, but that for now he's lying low and can't come himself to a lawyer's office.'

'What about his court problems?'

'Since he has no previous convictions, he's got off with a sentence of a couple of months.'

The *anolini* were floating in a broth in which oily transparent circles joined together or drifted apart when moving the spoon.

'The eyes of the broth,' Soneri said, pointing to them.

'One of the few things that hasn't changed,' Angela confirmed.

They both contemplated that observation, exchanging a look which was at once loving and sad and which counted for dozens of words. Before they could sink into nostalgia the *Gutturnio* once more raised their spirits to a joyfyul mood.

'*Gutturnio* is better than any psychic drug,' Soneri said.

They were in a euphoric state when they returned to the car. 'I am keen to see this new den of yours,' Angela said.

'Floating is a bit like flying.'

'Is all this jollity the *Gutturnio's* affect?' Angela sounded incredulous. 'Normally a whole demijohn isn't enough for you.'

'I think I know who the unnamed man in the river was. I need one more piece of proof, but then I'm in the endgame.'

'And who would he be?'

'You speak French, so you can help me,' said Soneri.

'Can you tell me who he is?'

'His name is Giovanni Caputo. He's the son of a Neapolitan woman who ran away to the Po Valley to escape a camorra gang her husband was a member of. He was killed in a shootout. The first son was the product of a youthful affair, and in his turn he became a camorra boss.'

'And she had another son here?'

'Exactly. Father unknown.'

'In a village, nothing is unknown,' said Angela.

'I haven't got to the bottom of it. She was a woman who always tried to hide.'

'Not completely, I would say,' said Angela, ironically.

'We'll soon find out. Meantime, I'll have to make a final verification and then I'll pass it all over to the Prosecutor's Office. That's where you can help me.'

'Explain yourself. You know I can't be too involved in your investigations. There's incompatibility issue.'

'I'm on holiday and can do what I want.'

'What should I do?'

'Phone the *gendarmerie* in Toulouse and tell them you're calling on behalf of the police HQ in Parma, and would like to know if one Giovanni Caputo is resident there or if he appears to have disappeared.'

'Do you think they'll reply without an official request in writing?'

'We can try. At the end of the day, it's only a piece of information. And then with your seductive voice...'

She made as if to slap his cheek, but her attention was distracted by the side street Soneri had driven into, bumping over the holes in the road.

'Are we going to end up in the water?' she asked, mildly alarmed.

He made no reply and parked alongside the embankment. He helped her out and led her along the pathway by the river. He fixed the gangway in front of the houseboat and escorted her over it before pulling it up and closing the little gate. At that point, she announced: 'Farewell, world. We're now *boat people*, and I'm adrift.'

The rain had made the river level rise and the current seemed faster and more agitated. Soneri lit the stove, and the flames seemed to reassure Angela who had been observing the flow of the current through the window.

'Do you like it?' he asked.

'I feared worse,' she said, in her usual indirect style. Changing subject, she went on, 'Weren't you supposed to phone your colleagues in Toulouse?'

He had been about to embrace her, but felt a sense of duty. He fumbled in his pocket and brought out the bill with the number. She took it from him and began dialling.

Soneri stood listening while she spoke in fluent French. From what he understood, the officer on the other end was saying he was of Italian origin.

'*Mais oui! Votre grand-père vient de Padoue? Je connais Padoue, très jolie ville...*' Angela skilfully steered personal questions towards matters concerning Caputo. With typically feminine tact, she succeeded in charming the man into him giving her his mobile number.

'You've obviously got a way with police officers,' said Soneri.

'French policemen are much nicer than Italian ones.'

'Not body to body,' said Soneri, trying to pull her to him.

'Not now.' She pushed him away. 'After dinner. I want to be a bit tipsy and this swaying is perfect for making me believe I am.'

'You've fallen in love with that guy, and now you're rejecting me,' said Soneri, in a mock rage. 'At least tell me what he said to you.'

'He said he would call me back in half an hour. That's another reason why I don't want you to come on to me now. Some things must not be interrupted.'

They kissed and stood embracing for a little. A boat passed by and made their houseboat rock. It was then they realised that darkness had fallen and it was raining more heavily, creating a din like a flock of birds on the roof. Angela looked out, a little concerned and a little excited at a darkness so deep making it impossible to distinguish the outlines of the poplar trees. The telephone brought her back to herself.

'Allo Cédric, bonsoir,' she said, making a sign to Soneri.

'Comment? Onze Rue Maupassant? Il vit avec une femme? Comment elle s'appelle? Lorette Martignon? Vous pouvez la contacter, s'il vous plaît? Génial!'

'I presume you're keen to meet this Cédric now,' Soneri suggested when she hung up.

'And I presume you're keen to meet this Lorette,' Angela shot back. 'Your man has been living in 11 Rue Maupassant since 1986, but they don't know the date he arrived in France. Perhaps he'd lived in other places, but they would need to research further. He's in a relationship with this Lorette, or at least that's what they think in that she lives in the same house.'

'Did he say he would talk to her?'

'He promised me. But is this important? Isn't it enough to know that Giovanni Caputo is resident in Toulouse and that the body found in the river had a photo of that city in his pocket as well as a metro ticket? And then there's the fact that he's probably disappeared from home...'

'Yes, yes,' said Soneri, still beset by doubts.

'The case is settled, commissario,' said Angela, in a voice imitating judges in an American TV series. 'Tomorrow you can phone your magistrate and tell her to proceed with the judicial identification by the usual fingerprinting system, then she can bury the man with his full name, leaving us to enjoy this short break without more arse ache.'

Soneri smiled and agreed without saying anything. She was unconvinced and decided to let it drop. The boat continued to rock gently in the current. Every so often a lament could be heard from the willows around the inlet. The occasional craft sailed slowly by in the darkness at a distance, marked by a row of lights. After a few minutes' silence during which Angela attempted to comprehend Soneri's perplexity, his good humour returned. They prepared dinner listening to the murmuring water against the houseboat.

'I have to admit it does have a certain charm,' Angela conceded as they ate. 'You're on the brink, anchored at the very edge of things, brushing against an immense force which could seize you and carry you off. It's like standing outside the cage of a starving lion.'

'Facing death sharpens life,' pronounced Soneri.

'That's what the Po does: establish limits.'

At intervals, in time with the gusts coming down the chimney, the stove gave a kind of rumble. The bottle of *Fortana* was now empty and the two of them stood, arms around each other in the half darkness of the floating lounge. The total solitude added to their state of excitement, but just as they were undressing Soneri's mobile began to vibrate.

Angela reacted with annoyance. 'I told you I didn't want to be disturbed.'

Soneri had already grabbed his phone and was speaking to Juvara. 'Number 84, did you say? In Montpellier? Good. Thanks.'

'It's him. From Parma to France only to end up in the Po.'

'What a dreadful end!' said Angela.

'And an obscure one,' added Soneri, once more plunged into doubt.

'You don't want to start again now, do you?'

'Not right now,' said Soneri, taking her in his arms.

19

'Good! Good!' The examining magistrate, Signora Falchieri, was delighted when Soneri communicated the news to her by phone. 'You've no idea what a weight you've lifted from my shoulders. I couldn't stand it any longer. Day after day, one call after another from the mortuary and always more demanding. They were just about begging me.'

'Where will you bury him?' Soneri asked.

'If no-one comes to claim him even after the identification, the law says he must be interred in the cemetery near where he was found.'

'He had a partner in Toulouse.'

'If she's failed to come forward in all this time, not even to the French authorities, perhaps they were no longer together.'

'They lived in the same house, 11 Rue Maupassant.'

'I could send a request to our French friends for information.'

'I've opened a direct channel with the *gendarmes* in Toulouse. No harm in that,' he said, looking at Angela while driving.

'You should be pleased. The case is solved and you're on holiday,' said the magistrate.

'I'm happily afloat,' Soneri confirmed, once again throwing an understanding glance at Angela.

'I too was keen to give that corpse a name. There are too many bodies with no dignity these days.'

'It wasn't just an investigation. It was more than that,' Soneri agreed.

'Some times our professions compel us to confront doubts that aren't only judicial, and that has to be good.'

'That's the way it should always be.'

'Nevertheless, the majority of cases deal with merely technical and procedural issues. Enquiries are like knives. It all depends on who's holding them.'

Angela's mobile rang and Signora Falchieri heard it. 'I'll leave you alone. I can hear you're in company.' Before ending the conversation, she added: 'By the way, did he really commit suicide?'

This question resonated with Soneri for a while until he was distracted by Angela who was speaking in French.

'*Merci beaucoup, Cédric.*' She put her phone away. 'While you were chatting with the prosecutor, I was at work for you.'

'It sounds like a hot line when you talk to that officer.'

She gave him a pat on the back. 'This Lorette says they had separated but he had never officially changed residence and they remained on good terms. She thinks he stayed a bit with a friend and a bit with another woman. They continued to bump into each other from time to time in Rue Maupassant and they phoned each other on practical matters, picking up correspondence, that sort of thing. The house is in her name.'

'Did she say anything else about him?'

'She reported to Cédric that she just couldn't put up with Caputo. He was too unstable, with frequent bouts of bad temper or depression.'

It all began to fall into place. An illegitimate child kept hidden away out of shame or to escape a criminal gang, a boy who grew up in boarding school and who after his studies decided to go his own way, marked by an unhappy childhood and with a difficult and fragile character leaving him isolated. Then the return to where he was born, probably a visit to his mother and placing that enormous vase on the tomb, perhaps a symbol of gratitude. Finally, given the impossibility of carrying on with a life that continued into emptiness, the end. One last attempt in Righetti's clinic where, between the embankments and the flood plains, he perhaps felt drawn to his roots. Could it all have gone like that? Angela was certain. 'He had no-one, as is clear from the fact that they've never come searching for him. When that's the way it is, for someone who's already unstable, it can lead to a no-exit.'

'Off a bridge,' concluded Soneri.

'You couldn't do anything more. You've found a name for a man who until a few hours ago was only a corpse. What else could you hope for?'

'Perhaps nothing,' he said, fixing his eyes on the glistening roadway.

'Exactly. Let's not think about it any more. Do you know, I like your little floating abode.'

'I'd never have bet on it.'

'I won't be able to stay long. I've a case coming to court in a couple of days.'

'Then let's not waste time.'

'Where are you taking me?'

'To the museum, and then out to dinner.'

'No, I'd rather have dinner on the river.' A few seconds later, Angela reflected on their first destination. 'But which museum? Are you having me on? Here?' She looked out at the grey rain and at the mist making the countryside fade away.

'In San Daniele there's the Po museum with all that the river has given up over the years teaching us that it's eternal and we have only walk on parts.'

'The meandering thoughts of the commissario,' Angela teased him.

He turned into the car park and switched off the engine. Toschi, the director, was waiting for them in a small office which Angela welcomed for its warmth. There was, on the other hand, no central heating in the rooms, and in them hung the cold, damp air of the granary which was perhaps what it had previously been. The bare walls still gave off the smell of grain.

Toschi led them along corridors where rows of display cases were lined up and stopped in front of a jaw bone equipped with a full set of teeth, with one enormous, protruding canine.

'Here we have one of the most recent and interesting finds,' he announced. Noting Angela's aghast expression, he explained, 'It belonged to a lion.'

'Here?'

'Not to mention mammoths, elks, bisons, fossils of the megacero deer as well as predators like hyenas and leopards. We've also been able to document the presence of the predator *par excellence*,' the director concluded, plainly pleased with himself.

'When do these date from?' Angela asked, still bemused.

'To the Pleistocene, or at least, that's the best estimate.'

'Didn't I tell you the Po is eternal and wants us to know that?' said Soneri.

'Can you see the colouration of the teeth, and the light beige of the bones?' asked Toschi. These are the fossils from the Quaternary flooding of the Po. It's presumed that this breed of lion originated in Asia, moved through India, Russia and finally got to Europe in the first Pleistocene.'

'The lions arrived then and the catfish today,' commented Soneri.

'The lions arrived by themselves,' Toschi said, to clarify. 'The teeth are intact and they allow us not only to obtain DNA and establish the sex of the animal but also where it lived, what it ate, its habits and, exactly your point, its place of origin.'

'Isn't that exciting?' Angela said to Soneri, who had been distracted by a display cabinet which contained a skull with a large hole on the left side.

The director noticed his interest. 'That's another of our jewels, at least it is for palaeontologists like me.'

'Whose was it?' Soneri queried, totally ignoring the lion's jaw.

'Neanderthal man. We gave him the name Paulus.'

'Why?'

'Well, everyone must have a name.'

'There I do agree.'

'Our dead must have one so they're at peace and we with them. As well as that, we have to be able to summon them up in our memories.'

'There are some who will never have a name. Think of those people lost at sea in our own times.'

The man bowed in agreement. 'Without an identity, we regress to the banality of our chemical components, an organism with no history. And what are we without history? Nothing, a piece of waste. When all's said and done, it's an ethical problem.'

'So what do you know about this one?'

'Exactly. We have chemical information about him thanks to DNA, the same as with the lion's jawbone. We even know when he was alive, that he was male and his likely age. We also know what he ate, so I can tell you he was a carnivore, certainly a hunter and perhaps a warrior.'

'And he has a name,' said Angela.

'At least the one we gave him. In this way, I can refer to him in our research papers, and delude ourselves that he is what he would have liked to be.'

'And how did he die?'

'That's a real policeman's question,' Angela observed.

Toschi smiled. 'Our hypothesis is that he was killed. You see the fracture in the cranium? He was a young man as you can tell from the teeth, and in good health. The most probable hypothesis is that he was involved in warfare with another tribe and was the victim of a skirmish. The splintering fracture leads us to conclude that it was a blow compatible with the weapons of the time, principally clubs.'

'Could it have been an accident, like a fall?' asked Soneri, whose curiosity was aroused.

'It could have been, certainly. His skull was broken by a blow from above, but perhaps it was caused by tumbling down from some height.'

'What do you think happened?'

'Are you trying to reopen the inquest?' joked Angela.

'The guilty party can't be located now,' Toschi replied jovially. 'The case has been studied by anatomical pathologists.'

'And what did they conclude?'

'That the man was killed. That's my own opinion, considering the times and the level of the Neanderthal civilisation.'

'Can we rule out suicide?'

The director burst out laughing once more. 'At that time, survival was already so difficult that no-one thought of that. Nature did a good job in seeing you off.'

Soneri too smiled but with a dreamy look as if he was elsewhere.

'The Po is a formidable container,' Toschi continued. 'The summer dry spells and the big stretches of beaches they reveal are archaeological sites which are as important as Pompeii. There's everything there . All human life, starting with a multitude of ancestors.'

'A crowd with no name,' said Soneri.

'The wreckage of time. That's what we'll all become. In thousands of years' time, people might well struggle to remember Dante, Michelangelo or Leonardo da Vinci, and we will exist only because some chemical components of our bodies survive, perhaps scattered by these waters and their currents,' suggested Toschi with a trace of sadness.

'Or as a plate of *tortelli* and a bottle of *Bonarda*, as far as he is concerned,' broke in Angela, referring to Soneri.

Soneri had gone back to staring at the skull, with its receding, strongly curved forehead.

'He must have been none too bright,' the director informed him, noting the commissario's curiosity.

'Another reason for ruling out the suicide hypothesis,' murmured Soneri.

The director did not seem to understand and remained silent. Angela, however, began to feel cold. Toschi started talking again in an attempt to attract the attention of the couple to a section of the museum which was full of fragments of amphorae and vases, but Soneri's mind was now definitely focused on Toschi's tale.

'I hope I've not been boring you,' said the director when he noticed that neither of them was following him.

'Not at all, this visit has been a revelation,' was Angela's comment, although she was now shivering.

'Apart from anything else, there's the unsolved crime,' said Soneri.

'If we look back to those times, this was the case for the majority.'

'Don't imagine that it's much better nowadays,' concluded Soneri.

'If we'd stayed any longer in that frigde, I'd have become as rigid as one of those fossils,' Angela protested as she climbed into the car and turned the heating up to the maximum.

'In no time at all, we'll be back in our little den, we'll turn on the stove and keep each other warm,' promised Soneri.

The arrived at the embankment and parked the car. The silence was profound, broken only by the river's delicate gurgle and the light beat of rain against the steel of the nearby houseboat. Everything seemed to have a fixed place, the silence, the darkness, the flowing river and time itself which seemed to keep abreast of it.

Soneri cooked some *gnocchi al pomodoro* topped with a generous layer of parmesan. They moved in total silence. Their deep understanding had no need for words. It was cosy inside the houseboat as it swayed gently, growing so warm that the colour returned to Angela's cheeks. A couple of boats passed on the river. The barge which Soneri had seen earlier looked like an ocean liner with all its lights shining brightly fore and aft, and as they stood admiring it with eyes wide-open they became aware of being slightly tipsy. Pervaded by a glorious sense of changing mood, they made love, each conscious of living a moment of perfection. They had no awareness of time until they heard a church bell ring out languidly in the mist and rain. Soneri got out of bed and a few seconds later realised that the happy mood had passed, replaced by a vague sense of satisfaction far removed from their previous consummated passion. Angela dozed, curled up under the sheets. Soneri gazed at her in that state of abandonment making her seem like the young woman she must have been. He was not sleepy, so he sat down at the table quietly, so as not to disturb her. After a little, he got to his feet and went over to the window. There was nothing to be seen other than a darkness so dense that it might be possible to dig a tunnel through it, but after a while it was suddenly pulled apart. Someone opened a door in the Galleranis' floating home and the interior light pierced the night. Two men came out onto the veranda and stood for a while in front of the door before closing it, allowing Soneri a glimpse of the two moving figures. They went down towards the little jetty and got into a boat which set off soundlessly upstream.

Soneri looked at his watch. It was half past one. He took out a chair and sat astride it keeping his eyes fixed on the houseboat. Just as he was beginning to drop off, he saw the door open again, a light shine over the veranda, a figure stand on the threshold before darkness closed in again. The figure seemed to be that of a tall, corpulent man, and as he walked around, the creak of the planks on the veranda could be clearly heard. Unlike the other two, he did not make for the river. He climbed off on the land side, and walked along the embankment. Soneri wondered about the meaning of all that silent, nocturnal movement, but could not find an explanation. None of his various conjectures stood up, leaving him with only one deep suspicion.

20

They were woken at eleven o'clock by the church bells ringing along the riverside. The stove had gone out some time before and the room was chilly. Angela shivered as she looked out at the incessant falling rain, at the grey mist and at the river which seemed on the point of carrying them away and she concluded that it was better in the dark. Soneri lit the stove and prepared some breakfast, but his eyes were continually drawn to the Gallerani houseboat. Angela could not help noticing his obsessiveness.

'You're like a dog on a chain. What's attracting you so strongly?'

'Strange things. You know how sensitive I am to anything unusual. It's a professional peculiarity.'

'What unusual thing are you talking about?'

'A certain coming-and-going by night.'

'Lovers in search of excitement? Like us, after all.'

Soneri shook his head. 'I've only seen men.'

'All the more reason for them wanting to hide.'

'I don't think it's got anything to do with sex. I've never heard of anyone going off for a screw in a boat with an electric engine.'

Soneri's phone began to ring.

'I've learned about the official identification from Signora Falchieri. The Prosecutor's office got hold of a dental X-ray done in France,' Motti blustered. 'Congratulations. The provincial command is a bit disgruntled, but the Police Chief has said it's the fruit of joint work between the police and the carabinieri.'

'Winning praise was the least of my intentions,' said Soneri.

'Since we've collaborated, I wanted to inform you of a new development,' the maresciallo went on.

'Go on?'

'We've been checking some mobile phones in connection with the robberies, and there's something that might interest you. You remember that row boat found smashed against the breakwater at Stagno? Somebody saw it being stolen.'

'And who is this witness?'

'He's not exactly a witness. The question came up during a conversation between the wife of a Moldovan who's in prison for attempted murder and a fellow national, one of those catfish poachers. The guy in prison, according to his wife, seems to have seen two men put the boat into the water. One was big and sturdy, the other smaller.'

'Was the Moldovan there?'

'Yes, he worked in the houseboat at the jetty. Maintenance was his job. It's not clear why he was there that night, but perhaps he had some business of his own.'

'The boat belonged to a certain Andalò, ex-husband of one of the Gallerani family.'

'I know,' replied Motti. 'And it seems his firm is in deep trouble.'

'Not as deep as his boat,' was Soneri's snide response. 'Did the wife have anything else to say?'

'According to her husband, those two weren't involved in any robbery.'

'So what were they up to?'

'They were quite simply taking the boat. They were working away quietly, and from what he remembers almost all the boats on dry land were chained together for security, and he didn't seem to see anyone prowling about for any length of time.'

'But why did he put it into the water at nighttime?'

'Well, it was summertime, the Po was in spate, but it was bizarre,' Motti agreed, while Soneri struggled to arrange these new pieces of information into some plausible sequence.

The maresciallo changed tack. 'In a short time, we'll go and interrogate that guy who was beaten up. Maybe he knows something about this story as well.'

'Do you think he'll talk? They nearly killed him, so I wonder if he'll take any more risks.'

'He said it was an Italian who threatened him,' Motti reminded Soneri.

'That's even worse.'

Before they hung up, they agreed to meet.

'Your mind is already elsewhere,' said Angela over breakfast. 'We were supposed to be having a couple of uninterrupted days,' she added, fully aware that the previous night's excitement was already a distant memory.

The beginnings of disappointment hung over them. Everything suddenly seemed too narrow, too precarious, too grey, like the implacable rain that never ceased.

Soneri made a sudden decision. 'Let's go to Torricella.'

Angela, overcome by an untypical feebleness, raised no objection. She got ready and followed him.

They travelled between puddles, flooded fields and water-filled ditches. Every so often, they came across houses of the same colour as the mist, their backyards piled high with assorted objects as though in preparation for a removal.

'Could you bear living here?' asked Angela, for whom the very idea caused a surge of anxiety.

'Only peasants and the poor live here. These are the new slums. Houses here are cheaper, as used to be the case in districts furthest from the city centre. Now even they've become luxury quarters and the poor have ended up in the mists. Unseen in every sense of the word.'

'I wonder if the next step will take them to some damp houseboat?' asked Angela, who was recovering her good humour.

'Perhaps they'll form communities, like the one the lad you're dealing with is going to.'

'Or perhaps they'll just sink into solitude, left to themselves like Caputo.'

The mention of that name had an immediate impact on Soneri. 'I dreamt about that broken head.'

'Caputo's?'

'No, the one in the display cabinet. The Neanderthal, remember?'

'It made an impression on me as well. Could it be because we've foreseen our own destiny?'

'It did look as though it had been left there deliberately.'

'Do you think so?'

'I had that impression,' concluded Soneri, turning into the yard outside the nautical club. On Sunday morning it was full. The *aperitivo* the main drink of choice.

'There are always more folk here than in the pews of the Assunta Church,' moaned Marisa.

Captain Landini was on his own, with only a glass of *Ortrugo* for company. They sat down beside him.

'I'm getting better,' the captain said. 'I must have digested the poison.'

Ceriani and the Viking came over. Soneri introduced Angela and took a cigar from his pocket.

'Who'd ever have imagined that man was Carmela's son?' said the Viking. 'Not that we'd have ever recognised him. He left when he was a boy.'

'There's always a lot of movement around here,' said Soneri.

'Have you heard the latest?' asked Ceriani.

Soneri shook his head.

'People with more money than sense have bought the poplar grove beside the oil press and want to build a village.'

'The law won't allow them to build on a flood plain.'

'They don't want to build anything traditional. They want wooden houses standing on great stilts, towering over the embankment. They've taken on the Madman as consultant.'

'Do you know who they are?'

'Rich folk who can indulge their fancies. They love nature so much they want to live among the trees, but they turn up here in cars that look like space ships,' said Ceriani.

'Some folk from Cremona and Mantua used motor boats. It's quicker by water, and there's no traffic on the Po.'

'Business will flourish,' said Angela.

Marisa shrugged her shoulders. 'There's plenty as it is.'

When they were left alone, Landini said: 'I think I know why they stole those pages from my logbook.'

Soneri was all ears. Landini got up and invited them to follow him. When they were outside the club, he said: 'Better if nobody hears.'

They went on board his boat. Angela was enchanted. 'This reminds me of Salgari's adventure stories about pirates in Malaysia,' she said, as she examined the walls of the downstairs, matchboard decorated room.

Landini said, 'I remembered that something odd happened last summer. I think I mentioned it to you.'

'You chanced on suspicious movements between two houseboats,' Soneri reminded him.

'Exactly. People reported hearing some shots, but the carabinieri couldn't find any proof. There was some suggestion of settling of accounts between the poachers.'

'But since you'd seen...'

'All I saw was some coming and going near Polesine. I was going back after dropping off some people who'd been on a cruise.'

'But they might have been afraid that you'd noticed something.'

'I don't know any of them.'

'Maybe there was one who had reason to fear being recognised.'

'Then it must have been someone from here.'

'Can you be sure?'

Landini fell silent, thinking it over, then he said, 'No.'

Meantime, Angela had gone off on her own to look about. 'A magnificent boat,' she said.

Landini looked at her with a sad smile, disturbed by the thought of the attack.

'Would you let us hire it for one night?' she asked, paying no heed to the captain's tormented state.

'I'd be happy to let you have it. I sleep on land.'

When they got off, Soneri said he was surprised by her idea. 'What made you think of sleeping on that motor boat?'

'It'll be my last time on the Po, and I want it to be like last night. It won't be possible to repeat it there. You need a change of scene and this one excites me.'

Soneri was relieved. Wakening up in Stagno had also brought him back to day-to-day tedium. He aspired to live moments of intense joy and then put up with an apnoea of routine in wait for the next burst of passion, but it was precisely that incessant need for happiness which made the gaps unbearable and made him long for time to fly past and with it the life frittered away in that longing.

'I can't wait to get back on board,' said Angela, turning back to look at the boat.

'Do you wish to skip the afternoon?' replied Soneri. 'Saying I *can't wait* sounds as though you were considering suicide.'

'Look, you'll spend the time asking questions and thinking of broken heads. I told you it would end up this way if you didn't switch off your mobile.'

On cue the phone rang, but Soneri did not reply. They were now back in the club.

'It won't be dangerous?' she asked, gripped by a sudden fear, pointing down to the boat almost obstructing their view of the river.

'They knew what they were after and they found it, so they won't be back.'

'I don't understand about those pages on board. It seems so out of proportion.'

'That's exactly why I think there's something much bigger at stake.'

'But what?'

'I don't know. Without the log and GPS confirmation any evidence that Landini could give would be of little value because he couldn't show that he had been in a certain place at a certain time on a certain day.'

'He says he didn't recognise anyone,' Angela objected.

'But someone might have recognised him, and might have suspected that it worked both ways.'

'You think it was someone from here?'

'If it had been an outsider, he would've had nothing to fear. They know Landini but he doesn't know them.'

Angela stood in silence and then asked: 'What does all this have to do with Caputo?'

'Apparently nothing.'

'Then forget it. Leave the whole business to the carabinieri.'

With the ghost of a smile, Soneri agreed, but he was still riven by doubt. Just then, Marisa came over.

'If you want to eat, you'll have to tell me. We're only serving those who order in advance.'

They looked at each other, and Angela decided for both. 'I don't fancy getting caught in the rain again.'

'Have you seen the river?' asked Marisa. 'It has risen a full metre and this time it's really serious.'

'When is the evacuation?

'Between tonight and tomorrow morning it will rise even higher. It will reach the embankment so I think we'll have to move some things around by the afternoon.'

'Will we be safe on the motor launch?' Angela sounded doubtful.

Marisa shrugged her shoulders. 'It wasn't even moved by the flood in 2000.'

'Are you all getting out?'

'If the water comes over the embankment onto the flood plain, we'll have no choice. The Madman says it will reach one and half metres here.'

'So we would be cut off,' said Angela.

'There are plenty of boats and dinghies. A flood can do some good. It cleanses everything,' said Marisa with another shrug, which quickly changed into a groan as she looked out at the riverside where some fishermen had set up their camp.

'Are they getting out?' asked Soneri.

'I hope so. What are they here for? With the Po so high and full of rubbish, they can't do any fishing.'

Over at the jetty, there was a great bustle of tractors and boats being dragged onto dry land. They passed by the window one after the other in procession. From the oil press too there emanated a grim, non-stop crunching noise.

'They're filling sandbags to raise the embankment, if needed,' said the Viking.

'For the river, this area is like Russia for Napoleon,' explained Pezzani, seated at the next table. 'The main embankments are more than a kilometre away and when it reaches here, the water spreads out over a wide front, loses power and drains away. Thanks to us, Mantua and further down remains safe.'

'How much time have we got?' asked Marisa.

'Ask him,' suggested the Viking, pointing to Casimiro who was just making his entrance.

'Feeling better?' said Marisa, changing subject while serving a tray of *culatello* at the table.

'That's the best medicine,' replied Casimiro, looking at the slices of meat spread out like tiles.

'Well then, when do we have to evacuate?' the Viking asked him.

'It will really start gushing down around midnight, and from then on it will build up, because the water pressure in the mountains is high.'

'What have your snails got to say?'

'At the top end of the poplar grove, they're up to one eighty, in the shelter of the main embankment they're at one fifty.'

'So here it will rise to one and a half metres,' Marisa deduced.

Soneri's mobile began ringing, but once again he ignored it.

'We might as well finish the lot,' said Marisa, opening the cupboards and pulling out a large chunk of parmesan, a whole salami and a few bottles of wine. She emptied the contents of the pantry onto the table and distributed paper plates and napkins. 'Less stuff to carry away,' she said. The mood was jolly in spite of the impending threat from the river.

Soneri looked down at the banks, and it seemed that the launch was much higher in the water.

'How long is it since we last saw floods like this?' asked Ceriani. He was seated behind them, his back against the wall, one arm on the table and the other slung over the back of the chair.

'Three years,' said the Viking.

Marisa corrected him. 'No, it was four, the year Gualtiero died.'

'Old Gallerani?' Soneri ventured.

'Yes,' Marisa confirmed.

The mobile rang for the third time. Irritated, Soneri got up and went out onto the club's front porch.

'My dear colleague, I was afraid I wouldn't get a connection through all that mist you have up there,' D'Onofrio said, jocularly.

'I had to use a metal detector to make a call to a Neapolitan.'

'You up in the north have got it easy. Here if we don't reply at once, we get a right bollocking.'

'As it happens, I'm on holiday.'

'Now? At least tell me you're in Sicily.'

'No, I'm here on the banks of the Po, and there is a flood on the way.'

'Great! Everyone has the right to muck up his own life. Anyway, I've called you because you asked me about Gennaro Bovino, but if you're on holiday, I'll leave you in peace'

'No, I'm interested. I'll be back in a couple of days.'

'It turns out that his son, Carmine, is up there. He's seen so much mist that he's vanished into it.'

'Are you sure?'

'Ninety-nine per cent. He's done well for himself. The camorra dispatched him to the north to attend to their business. He's in charge of Emilia, but things are getting tough. It's war inside the Portici gang.'

'What sort of business?'

'All sorts. Usury, drugs, but above all investments using front men in companies, bars and shops.'

'How long has he been here?'

'He's always kept in touch with his mother. When he wasn't in Naples, he was with her.'

'Was his mother involved in the business?'

'I don't think so. For the camorra, she was a disgrace. They couldn't accept that she had gone off and made a new life for herself. The wife of a boss can't abandon the family.'

'But her son rejected her.'

'Ah well, you know what it's like. The mamma is always in the heart.'

Soneri groaned something implying that he understood.

'I imagine the local Anti-Mafia Department has got everything.'

D'Onofrio raised his voice. 'If only that lot would deign to pass information onto us! They're scared we'll take all the credit.'

'Who cares about the credit?' burst out Soneri, ending the call.

When he went back, he found that the maresciallo had joined the company round the table. He must have come in through the door on the jetty side. They greeted each other with a nod.

'Civil Protection has ordered an evacuation by 11pm,' Motti was explaining.

'The water will arrive at midnight,' the Madman said.

'We know what to do,' the Viking added.

The maresciallo shook his head in as a conciliatory gesture. 'I know, I know. But don't get me into trouble. If the people at the Prefecture find you here, they'll take it out on me.'

'The people in the Prefecture all live inland. What do they know about it?' sniggered Cefalú.

Motti had to restrain a smile. 'Do we understand each other?'

On his way out, he gestured with his head to invite Soneri to follow him. Once outside, he drew close as though he wanted to speak in confidence. 'The immigrant who was beaten up was responsible for the robbery at Sissa.'

Yet again, Soneri struggled to put this news into some logical framework, but failed.

'That's not the only news. Come along to the police station tomorrow, and I'll brief you.'

Without leaving Soneri time to reply, the maresciallo disappeared into the rain still falling in the gathering darkness.

21

By mid-afternoon, the port resembled the rearguard of a war front. Waves were arriving in slow, inexorable formations, and watched with apprehension from the trenches on the embankment. The activity on the flood plain was frenetic. Everything possible was being transported beyond the towpath which for more than an hour had been packed with sentinels on the lookout over the main embankment. A disarmed army in retreat was carrying away anything they could from the invader, leaving only the trees and the fishermen's cottages on stilts behind. And the nautical club would soon be receiving a new baptism.

Marisa, climbing up and down a ladder, continued to move objects from the shelves, while outside a crane raised and lowered its hook onto boats. Sandbags were piled up along the perimeter of the club, leaving only a space leading up to the door. A man showed up and shouted to Marisa: 'All done?'

She waved over to Soneri and Angela, who stood up and went out to the courtyard. A few seconds later, Landini appeared. 'Are you still sure?' he asked.

'It depends,' said Soneri doubtfully. 'Can you guarantee we won't be devoured by the catfish?'

'The cruise ship is the most secure place of all. Wasn't it an ark that saved humankind from the flood?'

'Of course we're sure,' Angela said, to Soneri's surprise. He remained silent to conceal his own fears.

'In that case, let's get a move on before Civil Protection turns up and forces us all to evacuate. If they find you here, they'll make you go.'

'Which means there is some risk,' Soneri deduced.

Landini shrugged his shoulders. 'They know nothing about the river but they're covering their arses.'

On board the captain showed them all the rooms and gave them the basic information.

'We could kid ourselves we're in Venice,' enthused Angela. 'Isn't this exciting?' she continued when they were on their own. 'The risk is the unknown, a better high than cocaine.'

'I thought you were afraid.'

'Of course I am, but that's precisely we'll live this night so intensely. Just imagine. You've never before been in a situation like this.'

At seven o'clock, Battioni phoned to tell them the houseboats had been moved because of the high water, and were now unfit for purpose. From the cruise ship windows they could see the club courtyard was once again calm and completely evacuated. Some people had remained inside to await the water and they would leave only when it was up to their boots. Soneri imagined they would include the Madman, the Viking, Ceriani, and perhaps Pezzani and Cefalú. All that could be seen now and then were shadows passing backwards and forwards behind steamed-up windows.

While they were at dinner, the pitching of the boat became more furious and on the the river they noticed the dark outlines of objects being dragged downstream, for the most part trees whose protruding branches looked like the arms of people lost at sea.

'Was it a night like this when Caputo was drowned?' asked Angela.

'Who could say?'

'Spring and summer are the fiercest seasons, when you feel time rushing and fleeing by. It's the sunlight itself showing you the end.'

'Every time I think of Caputo, I see that split head,' murmured Soneri.

Their thoughts were interrupted by the flickering orange light of a car, which must have been Civil Protection asking anyone still in the club to get out. Two of them came out and from their build Soneri recognised the Viking and the Madman. They began arguing, and after a while they started gesticulating wildly before the new arrivals climbed into their car and made off with a screech of wheels. Not long afterwards, another car turned up, this time, the carabinieri. Motti got out and conferred briefly with the two men before setting off again. Soneri imagined they had negotiated an honourable retreat. On the towpath, lights went on, trained on the flood plain to illuminate the rising water. Some were fixed, others in movement, swaying back and forth.

'Like fireflies in summer,' said Angela, pulling Soneri close to her. They tumbled onto the divan and made love to the accompaniment of the slow, gentle sway of the boat. When they were back on their feet, they felt a more violent surge from the water. The prow of the boat rose and fell amid the screeches and laments of the anchorage. At that point they looked over to the club and noticed that it was now besieged by a tide of water pressing against the sand bags. Soneri glanced at his watch and saw that it was now midnight.

Suddenly the floodlights on the embankment came on and the light flooded in through the window panes of the boat, bouncing off the river but growing faint before reaching the opposite bank. A tide of water, awash with an emporium of relics, swept by with the force of a riot. Soneri trembled and felt himself in danger. Angela put her arms around him and dragged him back to the divan.

'I've never felt anything more exciting,' she whispered in his ear. 'Do you think it's like this with those extreme games when people experiment with suffocation?'

'Or with drowning?' said Soneri, and at that moment Caputo came back to mind.

'Tonight you must think only about us, and nothing else but us,' Angela said, intercepting her partner's disquiet.

There was a little Sauvignon left and she poured two glasses. 'Let's get drunk so that at least, if we do drown, the last taste in our mouths won't be the river water.'

'I'm not keen to quench my thirst that way,' said Soneri, gulping down the wine.

'Let yourself go. The morning will dampen our happiness.'

The boat was now being battered by short gusts with ever greater force. Soneri feared that at any second something would give on the moorings, leaving them to an unplanned voyage into the darkness of the river. Once again the floodlights on the banks came on. The water had almost reached the top of the sandbags defending the club. It was up to the branches on the poplars, and the flood plain was totally submerged with the current flowing slowly there too. Soneri kept watching the towpath where the floodlights were placed, thinking that the distant boundary meant safety. They had another drink, embraced and so remained afloat until morning.

When Soneri opened his eyes, it was already daylight and his first thought was wondering when they had fallen asleep. Perhaps it was when the floodlights were switched off and darkness returned to the river, allowing them to drop off.

He looked outside. The water was falling and the flood plain now seemed like a calm, muddy lake sited on a sandbank. Being awake threw him and Angela into a hazy present. Excitement had been transformed into exhaustion, and the dreamy other-worldliness of the night had given way to the dense gloom of the rain and flood. The hours ahead seemed purposeless and aimless.

'Maybe we should have stayed asleep,' said Angela, but then the noise of a boat could be heard. They went out on deck and recognised Landini. He pulled up alongside his cruise ship and climbed aboard.

'I imagine you've had enough of water,' he said, observing their faces. The river level had dropped and everything appeared calmer.

'I have to get back to the city. I have to be in court tomorrow,' said Angela.

'I hope everything was to your satisfaction,' the captain continued, before going out on deck to examine the anchorage. Soneri said nothing. He remembered he was still on leave, but at that moment so too was his will power. He followed Angela and Landini mindlessly, boarding the dinghy which gently drew up in front of the plank leading to the embankment. From there they proceeded on foot to Torricella, where they had left the car.

'I'll give you a lift,' said Soneri.

'Let's have breakfast and then I'll get a bus,' said Angela.

They had a cappuccino at the bar and saw the bus pull up in the piazza. Angela gave him a kiss on the cheek, took her trolley case and walked off. He watched her disappear inside the bus, and he suddenly felt alone, as though saying a final goodbye.

He forced himself to shake off his moodiness. He remembered his appointment with Motti and decided to head for the police station. The maresciallo arrived shortly afterwards.

'Odd, is it not? Or perhaps totally clear. What do you make of it?' He was referring to Iosif Milick, the immigrant who had been assaulted and who had confessed being guilty of the robbery.

'Both. It is odd that he's confessed but if it's true everything becomes clear.'

'It was the first question I asked myself. Why did he confess? We had no proof against him.'

'He did say he had been threatened by an Italian?'

'That's what he said.'

'Anything else useful?'

'The threat was made over the phone. He gave us the day and hour. We've checked and we've verified that in fact he did receive a call, but whoever made it was no fool. He used a phone box.'

'This doesn't look to me like a straightforward quarrel.'

The maresciallo agreed. 'I doubt if he's telling the truth.'

'You think he's scared?'

'His fellow nationals are leaving. He'll be on his own and the only person he can count on is that woman.'

'An easy target,' said the maresciallo.

'So he might prefer prison and taking the blame for somebody else rather than risk another beating up.'

'That might be it.'

Motti seemed uncomfortable. 'As if the flood wasn't enough, now there's this problem,' he grumbled. 'My wife never sees me now.'

'Where does this woman live?' asked Soneri.

'What are you planning to do?' asked the maresciallo, taken aback.

'Give you a hand. I'm on compulsory leave.'

'Do you have any suspects?'

'I thought I had it all tied up, but now...' Soneri's voice trailed off.

'What's puzzling you?'

'Several things. First of all the fact that Carmine Bovino's active in this district.'

'That does worry me too,' agreed Motti. 'The woman who's with the immigrant is called Adelaide Moretti, and she lives in Coltaro, at 13 Via Roma.'

Soneri made a note of the address, then got up and headed for the door. 'I'll keep you posted.'

'Don't you want to tell me what you have in mind?'

'I don't rightly know myself, so how could I explain it to you?' replied Soneri, on his way out.

Coltaro suddenly came into view beyond a curve on the road, cutting across the plain above canals, ploughed fields and newly harvested maize. The woman lived in one part of a house, embraced over its whole facade by a wisteria tree.

'You'll have heard a lot about me,' joked the woman.

'What should I have heard?'

'Don't play the fool. You're from the police, aren't you? My sin is, at the age of forty-two, to have taken in a young lad. If it had been a grown man, no-one would have said a word.'

Soneri waved his hand to show that the subject was of no interest to him. 'I'm trying to understand who attacked him and why.'

She looked at him gratefully. 'Unfortunately I don't know much about it. A week before it happened he returned home really upset. He'd received a phone call but had no idea how that person could've got his mobile number.'

'What did this person say to him?'

'I don't know the exact words, but it was a death threat.'

'And did he tell you why?'

'Iosif is always very reserved with me. He doesn't tell me what he's up to on the river, but I got the impression that maybe he'd done something that had stirred up trouble.'

'Like robbery. He has confessed that it was him at Sissa,' Soneri said.

Adelaide shook her head. 'I don't believe it.'

'You've just said he didn't tell you everything he did.'

'Because he's a quiet boy, but it's just impossible to imagine him robbing a bank.'

'But he's confessed.'

'I don't know what to say. Female intuition. Can I put it that way?'

'That's not going to be enough to get him out of this hole.'

'What can I do?'

'Tell me all that Iosif told you. Even the things that might seem insignificant.'

Adelaide thought it over for a while. 'He must have told you it was an Italian who threatened him?'

Soneri nodded. 'Did he also tell you about the southern accent?'

'No, he didn't say that. From where in the South? I don't think he'd be able to tell accents apart.'

Soneri got up. 'Do you know what it means to drop him off by a cemetery?'

The woman indicated she had understood. 'Try to get him to talk. He might tell you things he would never say to us.'

Adelaide watched him go out and closed the door behind him without saying any more.

As Soneri was on his way back to Torricella, Battioni came on the line. 'I am sorry about last night, but it would have been too risky to leave the houses exposed to the river at Stagno.'

'No problem. We found another solution.'

'I'm at Torricella now, and if you like... The danger has passed.'

'I've still got the key.'

'To compensate in the name of the Po, I'll let you stay another night free of charge.'

'Some times this river seems none too kind.'

'That's another reason for giving compensation.'

'I'll take advantage of this credit right away. I was thinking I might stay another couple of days. Have you rented out any other houseboats at Stagno?'

At the other end, the man hesitated a little. 'Only one,' he said warily.

'To whom?'

Battioni's tone changed to the laconic. 'To a company.'

'And which one would that be?'

'It's called River Blues,' he answered resignedly.

'What do they do?'

'I've no idea. We fixed everything up by email. The payment was made by bank transfer.'

'But you must have handed the keys over to someone, didn't you?'

'A young man came to pick them up.'

'Did he give you his name?'

'Yes, but I don't remember. A foreign name.'

'So the lad was a foreigner?'

'Yes, from the East, I would say. One of those who work on the river. Perhaps they are the company.'

'Could you give me a description? Physical description, I mean.'

'Medium build, fair hair, thin. He had a scar on his forehead. That's all I can remember.'

22

'I'm becoming obsessed by your stories,' Angela said over the phone. 'It's as if the Po had burst its banks and is flooding the city.'

Soneri had called her, expecting her to be at home, but she was at the court.

'It's because of that lad and his legacy,' she explained. 'The judge has summoned me and wants to close the case.'

'What's that got to do with me and the Po?'

'I've come across some business involving the Gallerani family.'

'What's it about?'

'An inheritance again. It's a case which has that's been dragging on for years as far as I can see.'

'Between whom? The two brothers?'

'Not between the two of them. The other party is Elvira Gallerani.'

'She's a cousin.'

'It seems they've reached an agreement but I don't know much about it.'

'Can you manage to find out?'

'How come it interests you so much? You seem more excited than you were on the boat.'

'I don't know. Maybe it's because whenever there's money, you always find some shady business.'

'The only one who couldn't give a damn about it is this lad who hasn't been seen.'

'I admire him for that, but see if you can find out more about the Gallerani family.'

'I know one of the lawyers quite well. He's a friend, but I'll have to tread carefully because he might get ideas. I suspect he knows about the two of us.'

After he switched off his phone, Soneri's mind filled with apparently unrelated images and scenarios, like brief, incongruous dreams. He got into his car and drove to Torricella. When he reached the embankment, the first thing he saw from the towpath was the Madman sitting at the stern of his boat with his trousers down. From time to time, he pulled slightly on one oar, causing it to turn in the flood plain in a kind of slalom among the poplars. Soneri discreetly hid, not wishing to interrupt that intimate, physical daily rite, an act to bring together matter and spirit at the same time. After about ten minutes, Casimiro tied his boat to his tree trunk construction and tested its solidity. When he caught sight of Soneri, he rowed over to the bank and got out.

'It has withstood the test without even leaning over,' he declared proudly.

'All you have to do is tidy up,' was Soneri's considered reply as he took a look at the rubbish carried down by the current. It was everywhere. The lower branches of the poplars were loaded with debris and loud autumnal colours.

'These are our sins,' said Casimiro, dreamily. 'Every item of rubbish is a sin, as is simply dumping something.'

'Caputo threw himself away,' Soneri recalled.

'The Madman shook his head. 'If anyone goes that far, it's because he already thought he was a piece of rubbish. And that's even more true when you're dead.'

'After death, we're worth only what we leave behind. Did you know anything about old Gallerani?'

'Gualtiero? What am I supposed to know?'

'About his legacy. There's a dispute.'

'Between Fabio and Rinaldo? Fabio always was a bit of a bully.'

'No, with their cousin, Elvira.'

The Madman seemed taken aback, but a malicious look passed over his face. 'That one...' he muttered, but caught himself at once.

'That one what?'

'I've never had any time for people who don't have to work.'

'Elvira's never worked?'

'Not for a single hour. She married a man from Cremona and she stayed with him as long as he had money, but when everything began to fall apart for him, she dropped him and took every penny he had.'

'As far as I'm aware, her ex-husband still has his own business,' said Soneri.

'Yes, I know, but with whose money, I wonder? Nobody here knows the answer to that.'

'Gualtiero left a lot of money, and that's why they're at odds.'

'I don't know what Elvira has got to do with it. She's the daughter of Giacomo, Gualtiero's brother, but the two of them divided things up earlier. They'd reached an agreement.'

'There must have been something in the will,' Soneri suggested.

'I don't think Gualtiero made a will. People like him think they'll live forever, but then some years ago, his number was called. He was over ninety,' explained the Madman with an eloquent gesture. 'He died a horrible death, poor man,' he added.

'How did he die?'

'He had a stroke while walking in a field of maize two-metres high. He frequently went off on his own, and his family had no idea where he was. Righetti did his best to revive him but there was nothing doing. His brain was shot to pieces.'

'He died in the fields where he came from,' murmured Soneri.

'They found him with his dogs four days later.'

'Was it on his own farm?'

'More or less. Not far from Via Bassa dei Folli.'

'The right place.'

'It seems he always went in that direction, the one that goes to the Po.'

'It's always the river you're searching for.'

'We have it here,' said Casimiro, placing his index finger on his forehead. 'I've asked them to throw me in when I'm dead. It'll be up to him to carry me to heaven or to hell.'

Casimiro tossed back the hood of his jacket leaving his head uncovered and it was only then that Soneri realised it had stopped raining. The water was draining away from among the poplars.

'The water is higher on the flood plain and empties quickly, like a colander,' the Madman informed him.

'So they'll be able to start work,' said Soneri, indicating the red tape marking off the area among the trees where the village was to rise.

Casimiro shrugged his shoulders. 'What a bunch! They think they can come here and live as though in the city. They slap cream all over themselves, they bring along their air conditioners, the women wear high heels or little mountain slippers, they're so skinny and full of allergies. They can't even have children, so they bring along loads of little dogs.'

'But they pay you, don't they?'

'I've told them to where to go. They introduced me to an architect from Milan, and he wanted to show me how to work with wood. I took one look at his hands with fingers like the worms in cheeses, and I told him to go shit himself.'

Soneri felt in sympathy with the Madman and his savage simplicity. He guessed that old Gallerani was like him, and brought the conversation back round to him.

'Did Gualterio get on well with his brother?'

Casimiro furrowed his brow. 'In families there is always one who forges ahead and one who follows along. He was the one who forged ahead.'

'The dominant partner?'

'The one who did the business. It's the same thing but it sounds better. It's always that way with brothers, one's a leader and the other does what he's told. If they're on the same level, sooner or later they'll come to blows. Gualtiero's sons were well matched. Fabio commands, and Rinaldo obeys. That's why they get on so well.'

'So Giacomo also went along with what Gualtiero decided?'

'Giacomo worked away and was hardly ever seen. In the market, in the bank or where there were decisions to be made, it was always Gualtiero.'

Vans and lorries with lights flashing appeared along the towpath.

The Madman looked at them with contempt. 'They come out when it stops raining, like snails,' he commented.

The carabinieri car brought up the tail of the procession. When he was alongside the commissario, Motti wound down his window. 'How did you get on with Signora Moretti?'

'She didn't have much to add to what we already knew. She doesn't believe it was him who robbed the bank in Sissa.'

Motti gave a shrug.

'The only new detail is that whoever threatened Milick had a southern accent.'

The two men exchanged knowing looks. 'You get it?' asked Soneri.

The maresciallo nodded. 'I think we're going to have to disturb the peace of the Anti-Mafia Directorate,' he said.

'Do you know what he looks like, this Milick? Does he have a scar on his forehead?' asked Soneri.

'If you could see him now, you wouldn't be talking about *one* scar. He would have been better off fighting a duel with Zorro.'

'But is he of medium build, fair skinned?'

'I've only seen him on a stretcher after they'd beaten him up.'

The car departed and Soneri took out his mobile. 'Ciao, Juvara, everything OK?'

'Well, that depends,' came Juvara's ambiguous reply.

'Listen, two things,' Soneri went on, scarcely noting the embarrassed silence at the other end of the line. 'Can you handle social media?'

'Nearly everybody has a profile,' said Juvara with a little laugh.

'Could you look and see if there exists a certain Iosif Milick, and if there're any photos of him?'

'I'll look him up right now. Just stay on the line.'

Soneri heard a rapid click-click on the other end. 'Ah, here we are, Milick!' exclaimed the inspector. 'Should I send you some images?'

'Yes, but tell me first if you see a scar on his forehead.'

Juvara took a few seconds to look. 'In the most recent photos, yes he has – a fine disfigurement.'

'And he's light skinned, quite fair?'

'Affirmative, sir. I'll send you the best photos.'

'How?'

'Via email.'

Soneri heard another quick-fire clicking of keys, and a few seconds later felt the mobile at his ear vibrate.

'One other thing. Could you do a quick check on a company called River Blues?'

'I'll need to call you back on that one. But aren't you supposed to be on holiday?'

'Yes, I am, but there are always things that turn up to make me curious.'

'You really pulled it off when you found out the name of that guy who was drowned. Signora Falchieri is delighted and said she'd felt it was a duty.'

'That's at least one job done.'

'Why? Is there something else?'

'I don't know. We've given that poor soul a name, but the whole affair still looks a bit fishy to me.'

'What makes you unsure?'

'A broken skull.'

The inspector's silence made it clear he had not understood, and there the conversation ended. Juvara knew perfectly well that when the commissario entertained that kind of doubt, there was no point in pursuing the matter, since he was incapable of explaining the reasoning even to himself.

'I'll let you know about that company,' he said, ending the call.

Soneri opened the email which the inspector had just sent through. There came up the face of a young man with tousled hair, a bold expression and a large V on the right side of his forehead. He was unsure whether to be more surprised by the speed with which he had received the photo or by the confirmation of his suspicions. But why had Milick gone to pick up the keys of a houseboat? The deeper he burrowed into the case, the more questions emerged, as happened again shortly afterwards when Juvara called back.

'Sir, this company has only one director, Rinaldo Gallerani.'

Soneri was taken aback. 'What's the business?'

'The corporate description is a bit ambiguous. It speaks vaguely about services to businesses, logistical support, consultancy on warehouses. Everything and nothing. It has registered capital of around two thousand euros. It sounds to me more like a shell company, to be used like a taxi.'

'What I don't get is why the Galleranis rented a houseboat when they already had one of their own, and a big one at that.' Soneri was thinking aloud.

'They might have had guests,' suggested the inspector.

'Maybe you're right about the guests. Important people. We need to find out who they were.'

'I don't believe they could have been that important, otherwise they would hardly have put them up in a place like that.'

'It has its admirers.'

'I could be wrong, but it seems to me more like a den for lying low,' Juvara said. 'By the way, if I were you, I'd keep a low profile and switch off my mobile.'

'Why? Has the hunting season opened, and there's a risk they might mistake me for a pheasant?

'I bumped into Capuozzo who was moaning to personnel about your obligatory holidays. He was trying to get them to revoke them.'

'So much the worse for him. I've decided not to reply to calls from the station. If you or Musumeci need me, send me a text and I'll call you back.'

Soon afterwards, Soneri made his way along the embankment until he came in sight of the nautical club. The Viking, Ceriani and Cefalú were at work up to their knees in water, removing rubbish from the sandbags defending the walls. The three signalled to him to come over, but he pointed to his shoes. The Madman had told him that after getting a waterproof jacket, he should equip himself with a pair of boots. 'You don't go up and down the Po in sandals.'

He got into his car and set off for Colorno. On the way, he thought about Milick going to pick up keys on behalf of a company owned by the Gallerani family, and then being beaten up by some Italians in a typical mafia-style warning. In the fluid magma of all that information, something was beginning to take shape. At the same time, on either side of the road he was travelling on, everything seemed to be falling apart: fields flooded, the ploughed land soaked and the walls of houses dark with damp, so when he turned into the piazza on the far side of the hump-backed bridge, the straw-like colours of the Palace of Colorno seemed like a beacon of light. He stopped to admire its smiling magnificence and never before had he been so convinced of the importance of a few glimpses of beauty in the midst of workaday routine.

He had arranged to meet Bosi in the café beneath the portico to learn more about what he had spotted through the window. Bosi arrived punctually, slightly bent as he walked. His rounded shoulders resembled an old log of wood. He signed for him to take a seat. The Chinese barman came over and they ordered two glasses of Prosecco.

'It's the only wine they have,' Bosi said by way of apology.

'We're reduced to barbarism,' Soneri replied, shaking his head.

They spent a short time in silent recrimination before Bosi said, 'I've been thinking it over.'

Soneri knew what he was referring to and kept his eyes on him as if inviting him to continue.

'Sometimes I did go and pick up Gianni at Pizzo,' he explained.

'Where the Galleranis live,' Soneri reminded him.

'Not exactly there, a few kilometres further on, in Via Bassa dei Folli.'

'Did he wait for you out in the fields?'

'There was an old, long-abandoned house. He would sit quietly there if it was raining or if he was tired.'

'Did you ever ask him why he went there?'

'I did try once, but he didn't reply. I would pick him up from other spots as well.'

'How did he get in touch? Did he have a mobile?'

'Yes, he would call me direct. I should still have his number somewhere among my contacts. I remember it was very long because it was a French number.'

Bosi put on his glasses and took some time to bring up the number. Finally he dictated it to Soneri who took it down on a bar bill. 'It's odd that he went there,' he said after a brief silence.

'It seemed odd to me too. There's nothing to see in that place; a house now in ruins and some fields. It's different with the Po which you never get tired of watching.'

'Do you know whose house it was?'

'I think it's Gallerani property. Around there, everything belongs to them and not only there. About three hundred metres away is where they found the old man dead. Did you know that?'

'Yes, among the maize.'

'They didn't make much effort to search for him. He had gone mad and had no control.'

'I know, dementia.'

'I was told by one of the tenant-farmers who worked the fields.'

'How did he know?'

'He was ploughing a field nearby. He related that he used to take his trousers down and play about with his whatsit. On another occasion, he had seen him battering his fists against the door, bawling and shouting.'

'What was he saying?'

'I don't know. Maybe he hadn't understood what was going on, or maybe he just didn't want to tell me.'

'Did you get the impression he was trying to hide something?'

Bosi heaved a sigh. 'Well, I just wouldn't know. He was still his boss.'

They sipped the Prosecco, which was very poor quality and warm into the bargain. 'They should be paying us to be here,' Soneri complained. 'I can't stand these fashionable wines, nor people who don't know how to treat them.'

They gazed at the Palace, which seemed to be fading as the sun set. 'And that woman,' Soneri went on, 'the one who came to get Caputo at the clinic. Do you remember her?'

'Vaguely. She was quite young.'

'Did she seem on good terms with Caputo?'

Bosi reflected for a while. 'No. Gianni appeared a bit intimidated by her.'

23

'You know, I'm very envious,' said Signora Falchieri, the magistrate, when she picked up the phone.

'You're the first one,' replied Soneri with some surprise. 'When I say I'm on the banks of the Po in this season, everyone else commiserates.'

'I speak as an orphan of the sea, where I was born. The river helps make up for that loss.'

'In the days when the river is in full spate, it'd be easy to kid yourself you really were at sea.'

Soneri heard a sigh. 'You're lucky to be on holiday.'

'On holiday...' he repeated vaguely. 'I thought I'd finished but...'

There was a silence which neither felt like interrupting until the magistrate, again sighing, picked up the thread. 'I didn't want to say anything, because initially it all seemed nonsense, but when I examine the whole story, I do get suspicious.'

'There are too many things that just don't add up,' agreed Soneri.

'From what I've read in your report, at least some short additional investigation... there's this matter of the son in the camorra.'

'Exactly,' Soneri interrupted brusquely. 'I would need access to Caputo's mobile records.'

'There's never been any mention of a mobile.' The prosecutor seemed surprised.

'I guess it's down there keeping the fish company. It's a French sim card.'

'That's going to take some time.'

'It'll be worth it.'

'Let's hope they kept the records. It was four years ago.'

Soneri looked at the current, once again calm, as the high waters receded. He was at the houseboat window, now anchored at the nautical port in Torricella.

'Admire the water for me too,' said the magistrate.

'I'm doing that.'

Yet another sigh before he heard the phone being put down.

Soneri got up to poke the fire. He enjoyed the slow rhythm of the river, the boats passing every so often and making little waves, the noise of someone working on the vessels as well as the sounds coming intermittently from the oil press nearby. The thought of Caputo disturbed his leisurely reflections. He took out his phone and called Angela.

'How would you like testing your French again?'

'Don't you think we have tried the gendarmes' patience more than enough?'

'That Cédric will be more than happy to hear your voice again. I'm surprised he hasn't invited you to Toulouse already.'

'Maybe he's found a photo of me and decided I'm not his type.'

'If I were him, I wouldn't hesitate.'

'Should I take that as a compliment, or are you trying to dump me?'

'For now, you're too useful.'

'Don't push your luck. You're toying with fire,' she said, playing along with him.

Soneri turned serious. 'I want you to ask this Cédric for another favour.'

'I can have a go. What's it all about?'

'The records for a French mobile.'

'Are you aware that you need authorisation from a magistrate for that?'

'That's already seen to, but it'll take days. If in the meantime you could tell Cédric that he's covered, that the procedure is underway.'

Angela snorted. 'And then your Police Chief is going to give me a medal?'

'Don't count on it. I'll make it up to you.'

'You're too mean, unlike me who's getting you out of trouble.'

'Just because you know French.'

'Is that the only reason?'

'You were about to tell me if there was any news.'

'I'm in charge of this investigation.'

'I'll leave it to you as my legacy.'

'That's the very word – legacy. The cousin has the little brothers over a barrel. That woman is capable of anything, and she's very bright.'

'A great talent,' Soneri confirmed.

'She's managed to bring up a question regarding DNA.'

'What's that got to do with it?'

'She's so cynical and unscrupulous that you've got to admire her.'

Soneri was distracted by the sight of a large barge passing by the window. By association of ideas he thought everything was floating gently towards some port.

'Elvira Gallerani believes that she's Gualtiero's daughter,' said Angela.

'Is that why she's asked for a DNA test?'

'Her story is that her family and Gualtiero's lived in the same house and that there was a dependent relationship between the two brothers as well as between their wives. Gualtiero was in command and Giacomo did as he was told, but it was the other way round with the women. Elvira's mother was brash, while her sister-in-law was more reserved. Now do you understand what happened?'

'Giacomo's wife went to bed with Gualtiero.'

'A highly ambitious woman who couldn't put up with a submissive man. Gualtiero was the opposite of his brother: a man of action, with no principles when it came to business matters, decisive in behaviour, untroubled by doubt. Giacomo shy, sensitive, other-worldly, with a passion for music just couldn't compare.'

'So Elvira is now demanding her share, and it will be much more substantial than what she got from Giacomo, whose name is on her birth certificate. Do you think she's telling the truth?'

'Who knows?' replied Angela. 'She's a woman who knows how to play poker. She might be bluffing or she might be sure of having the right cards in her hand. What can you say about a woman who won't hesitate to make her dead mother a whore for the sake of money? She's ruined her reputation.'

'How are the brothers going about their defence?'

'They've engaged a top lawyer, an expert in civil law, whom I know well. I invited him to lunch yesterday, and I gave him a real going-over.'

'Going-over in what sense?' asked Soneri, deliberately ambiguous.

'He's seventy, he's fat, balding and he's not my type. Remember that I'm making enquiries on your behalf, and faced with your jealousy, I could throw it all up so as not to upset you any further.'

'I'll keep my feelings under control,' chuckled Soneri.

'Anyway, the two brothers are unsure, so much so that they seem to be reaching an agreement with Elvira to convince her to abandon the DNA test. My colleague thinks that would be the best solution, especially taking account of the fuss there would be over this kind of controversy. There's too much already for a family always trying to stay out of the limelight.'

'At least they're concerned about their father's reputation.'

'As if! They know that he had no scruples about women even before he was widowed. They can't exclude that he had it off with his sister-in-law, and not being sure they've chosen the lesser evil. If it all goes badly for them with the DNA test, they'd have to fork up more money than with some agreement.'

'Have they made up their minds?'

'The lawyers are trying to sort something out. As usual it's a question of figures. There's also the matter of the property which might come into the equation.'

'Houses, land... do you understand what that's all about?' Soneri asked, thinking of the spot where old Gallerani was found.

'Not really. My colleague spoke about property, but I didn't ask him what kind of property.'

'I'd like to know.'

'Are you asking me to delve further into the enquiry?'

'I think it's necessary at this point.'

They said goodbye. She was at the entrance to the court and he afloat on the Po.

Soneri went out, crossed the courtyard to the nautical club, nodded to Marisa, whom he saw through the window. He was curious about something, and as he was getting into his car he heard someone call his name. He turned round and saw Battioni.

'I came to check everything was working,' he said.

'Everything's fine.'

'You're safer and better served here. There's always the club.'

'The Galleranis have moved here too,' said Soneri, pointing to their giant houseboat.

'They follow the movements of my houseboats, but it's not them that make the decisions. They've got a guard who attends to everything.'

'And who is he?'

'Boschi, but maybe that name doesn't mean anything to you. Around here he's known as the Viking.'

Soneri was surprised by this information and duly registered it. As regards the Gallerani family, there was a level of confidentiality close to *omertà* which hid any actual plots.

'Have you ever come across the people who use the houseboats you rent out to River Blues?'

'I never met any of them whenever I went to check up.'

'Did you know it's a company managed by Rinaldo Gallerani?'

Battioni hesitated a little before stretching out his hands and raising his eyes in a way resembling that of statues of saints in churches.

'The one person I met was that foreign lad who I handed the keys to,' was all he would say.

Soneri realised that his questioning was going nowhere, like flat stones tossed over water, so he bade Battioni a brusque 'goodbye' and got into his car.

He travelled along roads which as usual felt like being in mid-air, or of flying low alongside the fields. He came to Pizzo, passed in front of the Gallerani courtyard and carried on for another kilometre until he saw the abandoned house. He concealed the car in a little clearing behind a ridge and got out to have a look about. The door was closed and the lock seemed to have been changed recently. The chrome was shiny, not yet having been dulled by the damp. He wandered about. The downstairs fittings were, on the contrary, in a poor state. At the back, the bricks not covered over by plaster were sodden with the rain. At the side facing the fields, brambles had grown over the low windows. Peering through them, Soneri noted a way down to the cellars, blocked by a wooden door which had been worn away by the water. He moved closer and saw that it would not take much to force it open. In a kind of conditioned reflex action, he took out his Swiss Army knife and began to twist it in a crack in the wood. With some patience, he managed to overcome the lock's resistance and pushed into the dark cellar, where he was assailed by the stench of mildew, stale wine and rat shit. He switched on the torch on his mobile and made out broken shelves, spiders' webs, flasks, wooden boxes and layers of dust. A woman's bicycle with flat tyres was leaning against the wall. On the far side, he made out an old grape press.

He located the staircase leading to the upper floor, and on the second landing he found the door into the flat. A faint light filtered through the cracks in the wood. Soneri fumbled about in the grey light with everything suggesting a state of widowhood. It was an abandoned house, not a house awaiting someone's return. He could not have explained why, but he felt that sensation so strongly as to leave no doubt. Perhaps it was because of the dated furniture, the moth holes in the curtains, or the dead flies on the lamp hanging from the ceiling, but then as he looked around more carefully, he noticed signs of a more recent presence, even if somewhat rushed. The dust on the kitchen table had been casually wiped aside in some places and all around there were traces of rapid movements, like those of a burglar.

Soneri stood quite still for a while in an attempt to relate to that abandoned room. The effect of the ancient furniture projected him back many years to some imprecise time in his youth, but before nostalgia totally overcame him, he set out to explore the house. In the sideboard he came across a complete set of plates, pots, pans, dish cloths and napkins which still retained the odour of stale bread.

Then he spotted some letters sewn onto the corner of one of the napkins. He pointed his torch at it and read: 'C. C.'

He wondered whose initials they could be while examining the drawers, in one of which he found a notebook. It was filled with annotations, each line corresponding to a date, and against each date there was a figure. Since there was no entry for Sundays, they must have been the daily takings from some commercial activity. The mystery was suddenly solved when among the pages he found an invoice in the name of Carmela Caputo referring to the purchase for 140,000 lire of male knee-length stockings. So it was here that the woman had lived. The initials were hers, as was that rudimentary cash register.

He had no time for further reflection because he heard a car pull up in front of the house. Soneri pushed the drawer shut, moved to the door and went back down to the cellar. He was afraid that the new arrival would prowl about in the courtyard, so he preferred to hide in the cellar. From there he heard the lock click followed by heavy steps on the tiled crossbeams of the flooring. Who had come in? One of the Galleranis, if the house was theirs. He heard three, four thuds at intervals, a period of silence, then the same sequence repeated, like a series of quick moves made by a cook in a kitchen. After a while, the steps again but this time going across the room in the direction of the cellar door, which was then flung open, causing Soneri to tremble all over. He crouched down behind a row of demijohns and waited. A beam of light from a torch appeared, first aimed downwards then shone in all directions before being withdrawn. At the same time, the exit was pulled shut and the footsteps resounded once again on the ceiling. These lasted a few minutes until the outside door was slammed and a key was heard turning in the lock. Soneri ran out just in time to see a man climb into a large, brightly coloured Range Rover. Peering round a corner, he managed to make out and memorise the number plate. Ten minutes later, he called Juvara.

'Can you check a car number for me?'

'Still on holiday, eh?' the inspector said ironically as he worked the keyboard. 'Sir, it's registered in the name of Gigabyte Store, 15 Via Torriani, Cremona.'

'And whose company is that?'

'Hold on and I'll look it up.'

While waiting, Soneri looked over the house. He noticed a niche above the entrance with a shattered statue of a saint. Someone had been throwing stones at it and had broken it in half.

Juvara distracted him 'Here we are. The owner is called Sandro Andalò, Cremona, Via...'

Soneri did not let him finish. He hurriedly thanked Juvara and switched off, overcome by a sudden euphoria.

24

The Viking was sitting next to Ceriani and Cefalú at a table in the nautical club, when he noticed the commissario he looked over at him but immediately turned his eyes away, seemingly afraid.

'You've got a taste for life afloat,' said Marisa from behind the bar.

'You see the most interesting things,' Soneri replied.

'The mist is settling in, so very soon you won't see very far.'

'This is its time,' Ceriani commented without turning round.

Soneri walked over to pick a chair and moved to the table. The Viking looked at him sideways and filled his glass from the bottle of white wine.

'Marisa, another glass,' he shouted.

'We're neighbours,' said Soneri, pointing to the floating lodgings at the mooring.

'I don't live there,' said the Viking, without taking his eyes off the river.

'How did you manage to get it up against the current?'

'I called a company in Viadana that does river transport. They have a three-hundred horsepower boat.'

'There's a fair bit going on in that houseboat.'

'The owners are there a lot,' the Viking confirmed.

'The Galleranis?'

The Viking nodded.

Soneri turned round in surprise. 'At night time?'

'Yes, quite late on.'

Silence fell.

'It's gone down about a metre and a half,' said Ceriani, pointing to the river in an effort to change the subject.

'I doubt if they're here to check the river level,' said Soneri, keeping his eyes on the Viking.

'Ask them,' said the Viking, sounding annoyed. 'I'm guarding the boat, but I'm not their guardian angel.'

'It'd be better if you were,' sniggered Cefalú, with his usual malice. In return he received a threatening, sideways look.

'You're all afraid,' Soneri insinuated.

The Viking and the other two made no reply. Ceriani shrugged his shoulders.

'I wonder why,' Soneri went on, breaking the silence in a patient tone of voice.

The three men continued staring outside. Their tense expressions seemed to quiver, their eyes fixed on some imprecise point among the poles at the mooring. It remained like that until the Viking could stand it no longer. 'I don't trust those people,' he said with annoyance.

'Did they tell you to say nothing?'

His eyes rolled. 'That's what I was made to understand.'

'You know who they are, don't you?'

By way of reply, the Viking shook his head. 'They're from the south. That's all I know.'

'Are you afraid they might be dangerous?'

'Could be.'

'The people who beat up Milick are southerners as well. Do you think they're the same ones?'

'Wasn't it a settling of accounts between immigrants?' Ceriani enquired.

Soneri shook his head.

'Why are you asking me all these questions?' It was again the Viking who spoke up.

'I'm curious about all that coming and going at night time.'

The three seemed reassured. 'Have a drink with us,' said Cefalú.

Before Soneri could reply, his phone rang. Angela sounded weary. She was walking somewhere and the traffic could be heard in the background.

'They fished up Ragu. I'm rushing to the police station.'

'When you said 'fished up,' you made me think of someone else.'

'The umpteenth bit of nonsense. He's getting me down, that boy.'

'What's he done now?'

'He's been scrawling graffiti on the walls of the Teatro Regio.'

'The Teatro Regio no less.'

'Caught red-handed by a patrol. It's not the first time.'

'Always public buildings?'

'He goes for big targets. In Bologna, he was doing the same thing under the Pavaglione portico in Piazza Maggiore, but they stopped him before he could do anything.'

'He's a crazy exhibitionist.'

'He declares it's a kind of protest. He says writing on walls is the equivalent of rebelling in the face of a world that's ignored him. Defacing a public building is a way of demonstrating his existence. The building is a bit like a stage, it's the public facade of respectability, it's history as it's narrated to us. Ragu and these other youths charge in with rage and irreverence. They're taking revenge with these symbols.'

'Maybe Ragu has that awareness, but for so many of these vandals it's like a dog peeing to mark out his territory,' Soneri commented sceptically.

'It's the same with all other actions like this. There are those who believe in it and those who go along with it because it's the fashion.'

'Nothing new about the legacy?' asked Soneri, changing the subject.

'My colleague must have smelt a rat. Now when I question him, he replies with a little smile and tells me to be good girl. No beef, I'm afraid.'

'A big blow to your reputation as a temptress.'

'Don't underestimate me. In the end, I accidentally trumped him.'

'What do you mean?'

'This information is going to cost you.'

'Money's no object.'

'He let it slip there's a third party in this story, as well as the two brothers and Elvira.'

'And who would that be?'

'Do you seriously believe he'd tell me? He realised he'd gone too far, and even tried to take it all back, but by then I'd got it.'

'Male or female?'

'How can I make you see there's no beef?'

The idea of beef reminded Soneri of the hunger he had momentarily suppressed when talking to the Viking. 'All right, send me the bill,' he said.

'Payment in kind, obviously. I am keen to be afloat once again.'

He was so deep in thought when he switched off his phone he did not notice Marisa standing beside him. She put her hands on the table and leaned over to ask, 'Are you eating here?'

Soneri nodded and continued to stare into the middle distance until Marisa said: 'I've made a risotto with strolghino.'

The word strolghino aroused Soneri and his stomach proved stronger than his brain. The thought of delicate salami sliced into little cubes, mixed with rice provoked a surge of delight and a flow of the gastric juices.

'For the main course, I have boiled beef with tomato salsa,' Marisa added.

'Just the thing! With a half litre of Bonarda, I'll be in heaven.'

The rice was of the finest, cordon bleu quality he could remember, and the beef topped with a thick concentrate of tomatoes was a most effective antidote against the bitter cold mist advancing along the embankment. Soneri finished his lunch but stayed seated for a few minutes, thinking over the various new facts which had emerged. His mind was now more relaxed, as though the food and wine had lubricated its workings. The first thing he thought of was the abandoned house and the mysterious visit by the man with the Range Rover. It was the same place which had frequently drawn both old Gualtiero, now suffering from dementia, and Gianni Caputo on his solitary walks. Then his mind turned to the presence of the camorra and the assault on Milick, for which there was some element of unfinished business. Soneri told himself that he would have to go back and see the woman who lived with the young man. He got up, paid his bill and set off for Adelaide's house in Coltaro.

He drove for a quarter of an hour in a mist as thick as a curtain.

He rang the bell and was invited in. Judging by the mess, the woman would appear to have only just returned home.

'Have you been to the hospital?'

'Among other places,' she replied gravely.

'How was he?'

'His condition has suddenly deteriorated. He's in intensive care. There's internal bleeding.'

'Can he talk?'

'No. They're keeping him sedated and semi-conscious because of his head injuries. Those thugs have destroyed him.'

'So you know them?'

'Do I really have to teach you that there are mafia gangs around here?'

'I meant the persons.'

'What do you mean? Do you think they leave visiting cards?' she reacted angrily.

'Try to help: details, descriptions, tall, short, fat, thin, fair or dark... anything that distinguishes them. I don't know, maybe their car.'

'OK, the car,' Adelaide remembered. 'A big car, a jeep.'

'Colour?'

'Bright. Maybe white or cream.'

Another piece slotted into place in the assorted jumble of the story. Could the jeep the woman spoke about possibly be the Range Rover he had seen drive away from the abandoned house?

'I'd really like to give you a hand.' Adelaide's change of mood surprised him. 'Seeing Iosif in that state provoked a sense of rebellion in me. I'd like to make them pay, the pigs.' She seemed sincere.

'Get him to talk as soon as he's able. He'll talk to his partner without fear.'

The woman made a sign of assent.

Soneri got up to go and was about to say goodbye when she gestured for him to stop. She disappeared into another room and came back almost immediately with a mobile phone.

'This belonged to Iosif. He forgot it the evening he was assaulted. If they'd found it on him, no doubt they'd have destroyed it.'

'Sometimes it's pure chance that saves us. Other times it condemns us,' commented Soneri, putting the phone in his pocket.

At the wheel of his car on the way back to Torricella, he pondered the number of expectations he entertained for that device. What he had said about chance was still echoing in his mind, and he suddenly started feeling confident.

He went into the houseboat and was immediately overcome by a vague sense something was amiss. Like an animal sniffing an unusual smell in its den. He had no idea why but he had the feeling that the houseboat had received a visit from someone. He observed assorted odds and ends and they were all in their proper place. He guessed that the impression he could not shake off was the result of a changed perspective on the jetty as he glimpsed it through the port hole. The water had gone down and on that side everything seemed gigantic. He made an effort to turn his attention to Milick's mobile, which he set down on the table. He opened the top drawer in the sideboard to take out his notebook but could not find it. He remembered with absolute certainty definitely having put it there after his call to Angela. He opened another two drawers and finally found it in the bottom one. It seemed to have been tossed in there hurriedly, as though in an emergency. He became certain that someone had been there, and he found himself suddenly vulnerable. He picked up his mobile and dialled Battioni.

'Apart from you, who else has the key to my lodgings?' His tone was threatening.

Battioni reacted with an embarrassed grunt. 'I've got one, but you would expect that, wouldn't you?'

'So you've been in my place?'

'Absolutely not.'

'Someone's been here, and the door wasn't broken down, so whoever it was had a key.'

Battioni remained silent for a few seconds, perhaps attempting to work out a plausible reply, or perhaps simply because he was taken aback.

'Sorry, I forgot. Today's the day the cleaning woman goes there. I give her the key. She's totally trustworthy.'

'Would she go raking about in the drawers?'

'I've never had a complaint, but I'm not there while she does the cleaning. Anyway, if she did do it, I'm sure there was nothing to it. She's nearly seventy years old and gets by with her old-age pension and little jobs like this.'

This time it was Soneri's turn not to know what to say. This sounded like a plausible explanation.

'I'll ask her if it was her, but you'll see it was the way I said.'

When he finished the call, Soneri was gripped by a sense of unease. His anxiety made him forget Milick's mobile, but he remembered about when he saw it on the table where he had absentmindedly laid it down. He checked the contacts, and found about a dozen foreign names, presumably of co-nationals who were fishing on the Po. He found Battioni's number as well as those of an ironmonger in Sissa, a takeaway pizzeria in Coltaro, Adelaide and another woman with an international number, possibly his mother or a sister back home. There was nothing else. He turned to the log of calls made and received, almost all from Adelaide, as were the texts. He made a note of the unknown numbers, tore out the page and put it in his pocket. He would have to call Signora Falchieri for further authorisation to check the phone records, but his impatience made him take a shortcut.

'Juvara, are you still in good standing with the telephone companies?'

'Well, yes. The same as before,' replied the inspector nervously, fearful of some new request from Soneri.

'If I sent you a number, could you let me have a list of the calls made?'

'I could try,' he replied wearily. 'Will you be getting the magistrate's authorisation soon?'

'I'll request it immediately. By the way, have you had any word from France? The magistrate should have forwarded the request by now.'

'Not yet. I'm afraid it might take some time.'

'I hope you'll be quicker.'

'Here in the station, they believe you're on some undercover mission. In other words, that you're making out you're on holiday but in reality you're engaged on something really big,' Juvara whispered, speaking with his mouth against the receiver.

Soneri gave a little laugh in denial, but then burst out with a guffaw. 'Might be. They'll find out in a day or two.'

There was no reaction on the other end, so Soneri ended the call, and phoned Signora Falchieri.

'Still on the river?' she said before he had time even to say hello.

'Still there, but you'd never be satisfied with this miserable strip of water now that the river is back inside its banks.'

'I know that when the level drops beaches emerge, so I could deceive myself.'

'I'm calling to seek authorisation to consult another telephone log,' said Soneri, steering the conversation to what he wanted to discuss.

'Who are we talking about now? Another Frenchman?'

'No, a Hungarian, name of Iosif Milick.'

He heard the magistrate making a note. 'Get them to send me the request and the data from your office. This time the telephone doesn't belong to the missing person, so it would be better to explain the reasons for the request.'

'He's the young man who was assaulted by Italian criminals.'

'Ah yes, I remember the case but, commissario, you'll have to tell me what you're up to. You've found the name of the unknown man in the river and that was a great relief to everybody, but now I just can't follow your trajectory.'

'Nor can I. Let's just say I'm firing in all directions.'

'I have no intention of doing your job for you, but I suspect that this might be my job as well,' the prosecutor suggested.

Soneri did not reply right away and did not really know what to say. He was aware of having bundled together a series of things which were beginning to give off a bad smell.

'Is there something rotten in all this?' asked Signora Falchieri, almost as though she had really caught a whiff of the stink.

'There might be,' Soneri replied, lighting a cigar as though to dispel the stench. 'I'm not completely convinced that Caputo did actually commit suicide.

'Just what I suspected,' the magistrate muttered. 'I thought it was strange that you were prolonging your holiday.'

'Checks on the log should clear up a lot of things.'

'You'll receive them as soon as possible,' said the prosecutor as she hung up.

Juvara's reply arrived a few minutes later, which seemed miraculous to Soneri. 'This lad didn't have much of a social life, sir. Of the roughly ten calls he made and received, I doubt there is even one of interest. Two calls to discos, one to a doctor, one to a bar in Sissa, three to a fishing and hunting store, one to a delivery service, and then two to the Gigabyte company in Cremona. If I'm not mistaken, that's the company who owned the car you got me to check out.'

Soneri gave a grunt but sounded satisfied.

'What was that?' asked Juvara.

'Nothing at all,' he rushed to reply. 'You've been very helpful.'

25

Angela got off the bus at the piazza in Sissa feeling exhausted. 'Once it was men who travelled for miles, defying the raging elements to reach their beloved,' she snarled.

'The world is upside down: the Communists are in favour of the free market and the Liberals impose tariffs on trade,' replied Soneri.

She tried to put on an irritated expression, but instead burst out laughing. 'I could eat you whole. I'm as hungry as a lorry driver.'

'That might be quite enjoyable. Certain practices conceal unexpected pleasures.'

They had a look in the window of an *osteria* under the portico, about a hundred metres along from the bank that had been robbed a few days before. A little table with a napkin around a bottle of wine had been placed at the entrance to the establishment.

Angela looked around the place and shook her head. 'It's a bit rough and ready, but promising,' she pronounced as they went in.

There were only two tables taken. One was occupied by a couple devoutly focused on their mobiles, while four young people at a nearby table were talking loudly, exploding from time to time into a raucous guffaw, like a bomb going off. Angela continued to inspect the place before turning to Soneri with a somewhat uneasy look.

'Vulgarity does have its attractions,' said Soneri.

They sat down and gave their order to the stocky restaurateur, who wrote it down. He had a protruding paunch so his apron was hanging half a metre above his feet, like a tent flap. Soneri chose the *tortelli di zucca*, and Angela, tempted by its vaguely vegetarian promise, did likewise and shortly afterwards two plates appeared before them.

'Now that the flood has passed, we can't expect the same adrenaline surge,' she said, 'unless you can arrange your own,' she added teasingly.

'There will be some kind of adrenaline charge. Just today someone broke into my place to have a look around.'

'Do you mean to say that while we're in bed we might be caught *in flagrante*? Maybe by some jealous woman? That would be one for the books.'

'I think it's a bit more serious than that,' said Soneri, frowning.

'So it's no longer safe for us to stay there? Would you prefer to move to the first rundown boarding house we come across? That way we could extend our adventure in bad taste.'

'I've purchased a chain like they use on motor bikes. If they come, we'll know all about it, but I think they prefer to drop by when there's no-one there.'

'You don't even have a pistol. Are there any suspects?'

'Nothing more than a confused idea.'

'And that is?'

'There're all sorts of criminals hanging about around here, and they live partly in the light of day and partly just out of sight.'

'Have you worked out what they were after?'

'They consulted a notebook, and the person who examined it didn't bother putting it back where he found it. That's why I became aware of the break-in. The owner of the boats told me he gave the keys to the cleaning lady, but I doubt it was her.'

'You think they'll be back?'

'Who's to say? I've no idea of what they're interested in. Anyway, I don't think so, unless...'

'Unless what?'

'Unless it was a warning.'

'What's it got to do with you?'

'I have my doubts about how Caputo met his end. Maybe it wasn't suicide. I must have stirred the waters a bit too much.'

'I think that's the right line to take, considering the nature of the case.' Angela gave laugh. 'Anyway, you're right that even a person who meets his end in the water must have a killer. At least indirectly,' she added, pointing to the newspaper lying open on the table with a story about the latest migrant deaths at sea.

'The killers are the ones who put them to sea, both those who force them out and those who don't save them,' was Soneri's comment.

'And in this case, who was it who failed to save Caputo, or who made him jump into the river?'

'I don't know yet,' said Soneri, shaking his head. 'But I've got an idea of him as a lost soul, one of those who live on the edge of things, just like the lad who paints graffiti on walls.'

'I get the impression you've really landed me in it.'

'You can always refuse the assignment.'

'You'd never do that. Anyway, when he phones me it's because he needs something or other. He seems so naive and defenceless. I mean, he's located some maternal instinct in me now that it's too late.'

They were interrupted by the waiter bringing the main course, a steak *alla Robespierre* for the commissario and a salad for Angela.

'I'd never have guessed you could pronounce *alla Robespierre* so perfectly,' she laughed.

'The usual prejudice. They'd have immediately chopped off the head of an aristocrat like you.'

A yell from the young party drowned out their words. The couple were still staring at their mobiles, perhaps texting each other.

'Let's turn our minds to the bourgeoisie. The most mean-minded of them survive here, clinging on to their possessions, but taking that into account, I prefer them to the other lot with their passion for algorithms,' said Angela.

'Are you referring to the Gallerani family?'

'Who else? Their lawyer told me that the two brothers carry on living as they did thirty years ago, but their sons splash out on cars and nightclubs. Fabio develops liver problems every time he sees something new delivered to their home.'

'He must have money coming out his ears,' said Soneri.

'There's news about the squabble over the inheritance.'

'Have you resumed your seductive ways?'

'No, but I did get access to some reserved information,' she said with a wink. 'After twenty years, you get to know everyone in court.'

'Who have you corrupted now?'

'Professional secret,' she said, sitting up straight. In order to move the conversation away from her source of information, she chose to arouse his curiosity on another front. 'There's a shop in the centre of Parma which is part of the inheritance, a haberdashers in Via D'Azeglio.'

Soneri raised his eyes from his plate and looked straight at her. He made a sign to Angela to invite her to go on, and she intercepted his thoughts. 'Exactly, the shop where Carmela used to work.'

By now, various loose ends were knitting together to form a pattern which Soneri was struggling to decipher, a decidedly troubling pattern.

'You see? It's me who's leading this enquiry,' Angela said in a sing-song voice as she leaned flirtatiously forward over the table.

'I have to admit that the best information has come from you.'

'This is perhaps the most useful of all, not least because I detect something else.'

'What would that be?'

'Why would old Gallerani, notoriously mean as he was, invest money in a clothes shop?'

'Maybe it was a good deal. Bricks and mortar are the safest investment for someone who makes a cult of possessions.'

'These people are more likely to think of land, salami, jam factories, slaughterhouses, things useful for their trade. They've got their feet on the ground and intend to remain there.'

'So you think that...'

'You obviously don't have a woman's brain, nor do you understand women,' sighed Angela. 'We are more intuitive and refined, I mean. But you got there in the end.'

Soneri ignored the irony. His mind was on other matters. The idea of some link between Carmela and old Gallerani seemed plausible: she a widow fleeing from an oppressive, suffocating world , and he a widower still nurturing fantasies of conquest; she poor with a son in the camorra, he wealthy and a lady's man. Here was a situation which could easily evolve, as had probably happened.

They polished off the bottle of *Gutturnio*. Nothing induces light-headedness like wine. Feeling weightless, they wanted to remain in that near Dionysian state, with reality reshaped. It felt like a flight with no wish to return to earth. The mist outside besieged the houses and rested on the window sills. Afraid of breaking the enchantment and of returning to the world, they remained as long as possible inside the calming, dark womb of that autumn evening until they realised they were the only people left. They heard the dishes being cleared away, and when they saw the waitress appear with a brush in her hand, they rushed off in search of some new enchantment which they hoped to find on board their floating home. For a moment, Soneri's worries and suspicions came to the fore, but then adrenaline began to flow and desire flamed up.

For a time, the gentle flow of the river kept time to their feelings. When they got up, Angela looked out the window.

'Everything seems so gigantic now,' she said in surprise.

The river had gone down and the riverbank looked like a city wall. The bollards on the mooring even looked a bit like battlements on a castle.

'We've fallen down a rabbit hole,' said Soneri.

'Exactly,' replied Angela, returning to the ongoing enquiry. 'You thought you'd cleared everything up but here you are back at square one.'

'It all started with the discovery of Caputo's identity, an ending now transformed into a beginning.'

'Eternal snakes and ladders.'

'Life is a game of snakes and ladders.'

They both found themselves plunged into a serene melancholy, perhaps after a satisfactory lovemaking or perhaps a weariness, and all the while the dark river flowed around them, causing slight bumps and jolts and reminding them of rhythms long buried in time: of cradles and nursery rhymes, of summer travel by coach or car, afraid of vomiting. The night was still, apart from the rushing water, but then a light pierced the darkness and for a second shone through the window. It came from the land, almost certainly from a car's headlights. It was unclear whether it had gone to the nautical club, or had made some manoeuvre on the towpath. It might even have gone down towards the oil press. The gleam had rebounded in their direction, like light reflected from a knife blade. Soneri instinctively looked at his watch. It was a quarter past two in the morning.

'We didn't even notice it was so late,' he said to Angela, somewhat surprised.

'That's a good sign,' she replied, still peering into the night.

'Yes, but that car is not,' Soneri said.

'Could they be the same people who broke in here?'

'They could be, but whoever they are, there's something rotten about the whole thing.'

There was now tension in the air. The darkness seemed to vibrate with menace, and danger seemed to be hanging over them from high on the towpath, as though the water from the far side were on the point of sweeping them away.

'Have you put on the chain?' Angela asked.

Soneri nodded and lay down on the bed. She lay beside him, almost on top of him. Only the surrounding silence seemed to offer them protection. They surprised themselves by whispering to each other in fear before falling asleep at almost the same time. They slept deeply, as though knocked unconscious, but it was not long-lasting for they were awakened by a sharp, sinister noise which seemed to Soneri, still only half-awake, like the sound of a bone being broken. He sat up in bed, gripped by foreboding. The stove had gone out and the cold in the room heightened his unease. He took a few steps towards the door in the dark. Angela sat up against the headboard, following his movements. When he reached the door, he found it still tightly shut. There had been no attempt to force it. There was nothing much to be seen from the window. The clock struck quarter to five. They had been asleep only two and a half hours.

'What was it?' asked Angela in alarm.

'I've no idea,' he replied.

The ensuing silence deepened the tension, even if seemingly nothing had changed, not the slight rocking of the houseboat, not the darkness and not even the overhanging riverbank with the same grim look.

'But something's been going on. Did you hear that crack as well?'

He did not reply immediately, but continued staring out the window into the dark. Gradually his eyes adjusted and his sight became sharper, allowing him to focus on the mist as it moved in time with the rhythm of the river. Something was certainly badly amiss. The Gallerani houseboat was tilting towards the water like a tree perilously perched on the edge of a ditch. The crack they had heard must have been caused by the snapping of the wooden walkway to the jetty, caused by the weight of the residence now no longer afloat.

'It's completely twisted,' announced Soneri to Angela who had come to his side, staring like him at those blurry outlines now at an angle to the vertical lines of the poplars.

'What's going on?' asked Angela.

'The houseboat is sinking into the river.'

'It looks as though it's hit a mine.'

'It must be leaking, but what was the mine?'

The water was now up to the window, perhaps gushing in. Another crash jolted the houseboat, making it tilt further over into the river reclaiming it. It was now only linked to the jetty by one thin but strong strip of wood, looking like an arm stretched out in a desperate attempt to reach safety. After a few minutes with the houseboat dangling, as if suspended in a vacuum, the river succeeded in snapping the wood, and the houseboat, jutting out of the water, was dragged away like a man overboard.

26

A faint light, little more than a glimmer, woke them both at the same time. Without speaking a word, both made for the window. The damage was now clear. The stump of the connecting walkway was still attached to the jetty, and where it had been fractured, the frayed ends of the wooden planks hung over the water like the outstretched hands of beggars.

'Where's all this going to end?' asked Angela.

Soneri shook his head. 'The river will choose where to deposit what it has taken.'

'I think it wasn't so much taken by the river as delivered by someone or other.'

'You're right, but that doesn't change anything.'

'Who did you think did it?'

'You remember the car headlights? I think it was them. Maybe other people came to the river as well. I did see them arrive once before.'

'But why?' Angela wondered.

'An ongoing war. If nothing else, at least everything's a bit clearer now,' replied Soneri, but his words were enigmatic.

'What's clear is the Galleranis are under fire, even if nothing else is,' she went on.

'When I understand the motive, I'll be on the right road.'

'You think it's to do with the inheritance?'

'There could be more to it but everything seems to point that way.'

A confused murmur could be heard coming from the direction of the nautical club. Soneri noted some people congregating at the jetty and looking out at the empty space where the houseboat had been, which now seemed laden with devastating symbolism for the village. The Gallerani family, so wealthy and powerful, now seemed to be threatened by someone who had dared to take something from them. They all knew how attached they were to that floating home. They were river folk, as amphibious as frogs, incapable of living their lives on dry land.

Soneri and Angela slipped out without letting themselves be seen and got into the car.

'Are you leaving as well?' asked Angela in some surprise.

'I'm following the lead you gave me. I'm curious about that shop.'

'Now you'll never let go of this case. You've sniffed something.'

As they left the village, they passed the carabinieri car going in the opposite direction, with the maresciallo and an officer on board.

'I prefer to stay out of sight for now and leave Motti to get to work on the Gallerani houseboat.'

'You're behaving like an ordinary private investigator ensnared by some nosey female lawyer.'

'I'll put my uniform back on when the time is right,' promised Soneri as he drove down the Po Valley.

They said goodbye in the car park alongside the Pilotta. Every time he saw that imposing, austere palace, Soneri was struck by its authority and power which clashed with his own anarchic spirit. In particular, those walls battered by bombs in 1944, tilted over Piazza della Pace like broken, bleeding limbs suggesting an image of a veteran who had survived a war wound. The history of the city was engraved there.

He walked along Via Garibaldi, turned under the portico in Via Mazzini and crossed the Ponte di Mezzo. The mist on the river was not as thick as on the Po, but was enough to mask the soul of the city which was half mountain and half plain. Only on a few, rare windy days in spring, from the top of the hump-backed bridge, looking towards Filippo Corridoni, struck by a bullet and immobile in bronze, could the white hills on the left and the wisps of smoke over the industrial plain on the right be clearly seen.

Soneri headed for the *Oltretorrente* district. Carmela's former haberdashery was halfway along Via D'Azeglio, a little before the Paolotti Towers. The shop had two front round windows and looked fairly large, but it must have been lying empty for some time because the windows were covered with newspaper pages and the iron grate was rusty. The small space between it and the door was strewn with rubbish and little bottles. Soneri stood for a few seconds examining what remained of the shop without really knowing what to do. On one side, there was a kebab outlet giving off a pungent odour of meat, and on the other a Pakistani fruit shop, with a large doorway between the two from which an elderly lady was emerging. He turned to her with a warm smile but she, perhaps precisely because of it, looked at him distrustfully.

'How can I be sure you're from the police?' she said doubtfully. 'Nowadays there're people who pass themselves off as officers or local authority employees to get into your home and rob you of all you have.'

Soneri invited her to the café to convince here that he was not interested in getting into her home, but simply wanted to have a chat with her.

'You just can't trust anybody anymore, can you?' she apologised once she was seated at a table and was reassured by the bustle of the customers.

'You're quite right,' he said, to offer further reassurance. 'At the police station we advise people not to let strangers in.'

'You see! But there are still people who fall for it.'

'What'll you have?' he asked when the barman came over.

'A Fernet,' came the surprising answer. She relaxed and stretched out a hand over the table. 'I'm Angiolina,' she said, with almost girlishness.

Soneri took advantage of the unexpected confidentiality. 'Did you know Carmela Caputo?'

The elderly lady looked at him, once again frowning.

'I've been living in the place you saw me coming out of ever since I was born.'

'I've got the right person then.'

Angiolina made no reply but kept her eyes on him. Soneri began to feel uncomfortable with such intense attention.

'It's high time,' she murmured.

'What is?'

'That someone came to enquire about her.'

'About Carmela?'

'Who else? When she became unwell, they took her away and I never saw her again. I went to the hospital to visit her, but she wasn't there anymore. I didn't even manage to say goodbye.'

'Did she die in her shop?'

'She fainted there. It was wintertime.'

'Was the shop closed or had it been sold?'

'It was closed. After a few days they cleared everything into a van. Months went by before someone re-opened it. An ice-cream shop, a café and then a perfumery. There were other things as well, but I lost count.'

'Did you ever see the owners?'

Angiolina threw a malicious glance at him. 'Of course. He came regularly, usually on Wednesdays.'

'A Gallerani?'

'Gualtiero.' She gave his name as though in confidence.

'Did you know him well?'

'No, he kept himself to himself, but Carmela spoke to me about him. We were good friends.'

'What sort of relationship did they have?'

Angiolina once more stared at him intensely, uncertain whether he was being naive or just prying. She decided on the second option.

'You're not really pretending you don't know that...'

'What?'

'That they were lovers!' The old lady burst out, raising her voice a little too much and attracting the attention of the barman.

'Of course I knew,' he replied quickly. 'I meant to say, was Carmela happy? Did the affair make her content?'

'What do you think?' She leaned her head to one side, with an expression of wistful coquetry. 'He was older but she had to make do. Down south they weren't pleased she had her own life here, nor that she had completely cut off from her relatives.'

'From the camorra, you mean?'

'Ah no, I don't know...' Angiolina pretended to be in the dark, and retreated into an attitude of discretion. 'She did tell me her son came looking for her here in the north, and that they often quarrelled, but it all seemed quite normal to me.'

'Did he want to stop her seeing Gualtiero?'

'There are certain traditions... you know what I mean... stick to your own kind. They wanted her to stay in Naples, maybe even to marry a relative of her late husband. It's a funny family,' she ended, shaking her head.

'A camorra gang,' Soneri said.

The old woman made no reply.

'Did you ever see the son?'

'The elder one, no, never. However, Giannino was a boarder with the Salesians. The poor boy,' she murmured.

'He didn't have an easy life,' Soneri confirmed.

'It seemed Carmela wanted to keep him out of sight. She used to go and see him during the afternoon break, and he came to the shop in the evening after he'd done his homework, but then he went back to sleep there.'

'Was she ashamed?'

'I don't think so. I think she wanted to protect him.'

'From whom?'

'From his half-brother, perhaps. Or from gossip.'

'Were there problems with the Gallerani family?'

'I don't know. We were good friends but not close enough to speak of that sort of thing.'

'But do you think he was the son of a Gallerani?'

'Listen,' she said, sitting upright. 'Carmela was already the object of much gossip, and I wouldn't like to add any more.'

'Do you think that she and Gualtiero were in love with each other?'

'I really do think so. Female intuition. It might look like self-interest, but that's not the way it was. These were two broken lives and they tried to put the pieces together again. I'd be the first to admit it was hardly an ideal situation, especially for Carmela, but when certain misfortunes occur, you've got to make the best of it.'

'Have you any idea what became of Carmela's second son?'

'Ah, so it was him!' Angiolina's mouth fell open. 'I read in the papers that the body in the Po was called Giovanni Caputo, but here everyone called him Giannino and he hadn't been seen for years.' The old woman looked disconcerted. She stared at the floor for a few seconds before raising her head and muttering, 'Poor boy! Tragic!'

'When did you last hear of him?'

'I don't remember, but it was some time ago. I thought he was in France.'

'When did he leave?'

'You're asking too much of my memory. As soon as he could. He was very young. He couldn't stand the situation here any longer,' Angiolina explained, wringing her hands to make up for the words which just would not come.

'Do you mean, life at boarding school?'

'That, and everything else... An absent father, a mother under surveillance, a hostile half-brother... and that loathsome label of illegitimacy which must have weighed on him. Who wouldn't want to get away?'

Soneri agreed. 'Did the elder son threaten his mother?'

'Carmela told me that he treated her badly, and that if she hadn't been his mother...' Angiolina said, expressing the unspoken words by an eloquent gesture. 'Rejecting your own family is considered treachery by people down there. She once told me that she didn't care if they killed her since life in the mafia world had become more unbearable than death itself.'

'Can you remember how old Giovanni was when he went to boarding school?'

'As soon as he reached school age. He left at eighteen.'

'Before that he lived with his mother?'

'When he was a child there was no alternative.'

'And the whole town knew whose son he was?'

'I didn't live in that town. Carmela told me there was plenty of gossip and that tongues were wagging. In the early days, she told them her husband lived in Naples, but everybody knew he was long dead and that the child wasn't his.'

'Did they also know about her relationship with Gualtiero?'

'Do you really imagine that in a place like this they wouldn't know? They were cautious and met up in Parma, but they didn't live all that far from here in the Po valley. You see what I mean?'

Once again, Soneri nodded. 'Giovanni, Giannino or whatever he was called, was he a difficult character, prone to bouts of bad temper, depression?'

'He was a very unstable, fragile boy, but how couldn't he be? Wouldn't you suffer from depression?' said Angiolina, summing up, draining the last drop of the Fernet.

'He sought treatment from time to time,' said Soneri. 'Before ending up in the Po, he was in a clinic in Sissa.'

'Nobody wanted him. The only people who went looking for him were you police, and that was hardly out of affection.'

'Affection, no, not that,' admitted Soneri. He would have preferred to go on. He felt he should explain his persistence, but the words stuck in his throat.

The old lady held up her glass to the barman, who immediately filled it up. 'When will I next get the chance to have a drink with a police officer?' she said with artificial jollity.

Soneri noticed that her eyes were laughing and becoming watery. 'Don't blame me if you end up drunk,' he warned her.

'We're all to blame for something, including other people's unhappiness,' Angiolina replied, her mood darkening. 'Old folk like us feel like Giannino, but perhaps it was more serious for him. When you're old, feeling shut out is more bearable.'

She took another sip of Fernet, and once again her face was shining.

'It's not good for you,' Soneri warned her.

Angiolina looked at him gratefully and Soneri imagined her forty years younger, putting on the same intimate expression for some man.

She raised her glass. 'It's cheaper than pills and more effective.' She burst out laughing and downed the rest in one gulp.

27

The Madman was walking along the empty mooring of the Gallerani's houseboat, turning an expert eye on specific details from different angles.

'You see, it's come back?' he said under his breath, without looking at Soneri but continuing his inspection of the fractured wooden beams.

'Who?'

'The beast of the Po. I've located new footprints on the sandbanks.'

'I'd like to see them.'

'You'll need to get up early. He wipes away most of them with his tail, but he misses some.'

'Were they fresh?'

Casimiro nodded. 'Did I tell you about the pair of wolves under the bridge at Ragazzola?'

'No, or else I've forgotten.'

'Doesn't matter. For some days now only the male has been seen, and he seems to be injured. There were three cubs as well.'

'Do you think it was the beast?'

'Who else could get the better of a family of wolves? The wild boars have vanished as well.'

'The same story?'

'The beast is always famished. The only ones to escape him are the mountain goats, but he's wily. He uses a courgette as bait and traps them after scaring them. That's why he's planted it everywhere.'

'Surely the carcasses must be left.'

'He drags his prey down to the river and eats the lot. He even devours the bones.'

'Are you telling me it was the beast who wrecked the Gallerani houseboat?'

The Madman looked at him askance. 'You don't eat a house.'

'Perhaps not, but there might be something good inside, like inside nuts.'

'If there's anything good, it's not edible.'

'Where do you think the houseboat will end up?'

'Wherever the Po wants. The river's always changing and makes up its own mind, but never twice in the same way.'

'Who do you think it was?'

'That's for the police to find out. The maresciallo is on the job.'

'You must have some idea.'

'Who cares? I'm supposed to be mad and my ideas don't matter. What I do know is it was the work of an expert. It's not easy.'

'There are plenty of experts around,' Soneri agreed.

'They might have bored a hole below the waterline, let the water in causing the structure to tilt over and the walkway to the jetty to break apart. Then the river would do the rest.'

'Would they have come by land or by the river?'

'I imagine by the river. It's easier. But they might have forced the door and at that point all they had to do was break though the flooring.'

'Maybe they didn't even need to force the door,' Soneri suggested.

Casimiro stretched out his arms and said nothing. He took one last look at the stumps of wood, then started to move away, making a sign to Soneri to follow him.

'I'm back in my house,' he announced, pointing to the wooden structure. They walked down to the flood plain, along the riverbank and went in. Soneri was surprised to find how comfortable the place was inside. He saw a kind of delightful, rustic simplicity enhanced by the bright poplar wood. The trunks were the colour of chicken bones, but the Madman had arranged everything with unexpected taste.

'From here I can hear every noise made by the current and everything that moves inside the flood plain.'

'And what does move?'

'So many things; animals, monsters, people.'

'I'm interested in the people.'

'In the morning, I find the ashes of fires lit during the night. I've spoken to you about them.'

'Have you seen who lights them?'

'No. I'm afraid of the night because the water has the same colour as the land.'

Without speaking a word, Casimiro took out a package wrapped in a cloth. It was a little cardboard folder with flaps folded over, secured by an elastic band. The water had made the exterior swell, but the inside was not too badly soaked. On the outside, it was still possible to make out: 'Notary's Office', and underneath in handwriting, Gallerani & Co.

'This is what the Po's given back to us, at least so far.'

'Where did you find it?'

'What does it matter?'

'Alright, it's not important.'

'Anyway, I found it next to Curve 39, where the suicides jump from.'

'Did you have a look at them?' Soneri asked, indicating the papers.

The Madman shrugged his shoulders. 'Why should I? I've no wish to nose about in Gallerani family affairs. There might be all kinds of unpleasant things there. A guy in town answered the phone for a colleague, a notorious womaniser, and found his own wife on the other end of the line.'

Soneri took the package, heavy with water. He thanked Casimiro, who brushed it aside with another shrug. He was about to go when he heard Casimiro behind him say, 'The river never returns anything by pure chance. It's his way of speaking.'

Shortly afterwards, Soneri was back in the houseboat. He placed the package on the table and it reminded him that he had done the same with Milick's mobile. He should have phoned Adelaide for news about the young man. He looked around the rooms but this time nothing was out of place. He picked up the folder and opened it. It must have been recycled for documents they wanted to keep. The water had got inside and many of the sheets at the top and bottom were sodden, forming a compact, glutinous, lard-like mass.

The middle sheets were safe, but many of the edges were stuck together. Soneri patiently and delicately picked them apart and laid them out on the table. In total, about twenty were still legible. There were invoices for food purchases, a television guarantee, an orthopaedic report, an old electricity bill, some letters, part of a manual for a boiler, the electric wiring plan for a cabin, a photo, and an estimate for building work. Soneri first turned his attention to the photo which showed a couple, a man in his sixties and a much younger woman. He was staring hard at it, trying to work out who the two people were when he noticed a sign in the background. He put the photo under the light to get a better view, and deciphered the graphic 'Gigabyte.' He guessed that it must be Andalò with his secretary, his new partner. He slipped the photo into a plastic envelope and started looking at the letters. There were five in all, four of correspondence with accountants and lawyers. The fifth was a plain page torn out of a notebook with a hand-written message: 'Maybe it would be better if Giannino stopped coming here: too much chatter and gossip. Carmela.'

It must have been a message for old Gualtiero. In those few lines he detected a mother's embarrassment in a place where everybody knew everything about everybody, but only spoke the truth in whispered exchanges in fear of the Galleranis. At some point even the whispers must have become too loud.

Soneri was still engrossed in making sense of this new information when he heard a dull rumble outside. He went over to the window and saw Landini manoeuvring his motor launch up to the mooring.

He picked up the photo and went out. He had no more than a suspicion, perhaps even a wild surmise, but until he cleared it up he would have no peace. He got into his car, and just as he set off, Signora Falchieri called him.

'I believe I can hear the water flowing,' she began.

'You're the only magistrate who could start a phone call that way.'

'Only with you. I assure you that with Maresciallo Motti, I speak an impeccable, legal jargon.'

'Motti is a well-balanced man.'

'Whereas you're all over the place, like me, and so much the better for it. It's like having several eyes looking in different directions, like a Picasso painting.'

'Do you really think that's an advantage?'

'Undoubtedly. Especially for somebody whose job's to investigate and who has to stick his nose in all over the place.'

'Right now, one of my eyes is curious about a woman.'

'Is it preparing to make advances?'

'Merely to ascertain her identity. I have discovered the joy of enquiring when not driven by pressure or sense of duty.'

'The pleasure of speculative, unbiased enquiry can produce the most surprising and profitable results,' Signora Falchieri confirmed. 'What's it all about?'

'It's about a photograph of a couple. I have reason to believe that the man is Andalò, the businessman from Cremona whose houseboat was stolen, remember?'

Soneri heard a murmur of assent from the other end.

'It's the younger woman at his side I'm curious about,' said Soneri. 'I imagine she's his new girlfriend, according to what his ex-wife had to say.'

'And what's this all got to do with the Caputo story?'

'I don't know,' Soneri had to admit. 'I've got a half-idea but it might be nothing more than a than a wild guess.'

'You know perfectly well that I'm on the side of adventurous investigators. Fantasy and imagination are a policeman's best gifts.'

'I'll let you know if I got dazzled, or if it was all worthwhile.'

'Yes, keep me informed. From what the maresciallo's been telling me, this affair is spinning off in a direction I don't like. There are too many ambiguities and too many murky coincidences.'

'That's the way I see it too,' Soneri said, before ringing off.

He crossed the bridge bringing him out in front of the Palace of Colorno, and parked his car. As soon as he was in the portico, he saw Bosi through the bar window, sitting alone with his newspaper.

'In this mist, I almost wish I was back at work. At least I'd have someone to talk to,' he complained, looking around the establishment where there were only three young people, each occupied with playing the slot machines, as well as the Chinese woman behind the bar, as still as a statue.

'It's dead at this time,' said Soneri.

'I'm afraid it's us who are dead. There's no conversation even in the villages.'

They ordered two glasses of Prosecco.

'Even the wine,' said Bosi with a scowl. 'It tastes as though it came from a box. I don't know why I keep coming here.'

'Do you remember the woman who picked up Gianni in the taxi?'

'You only remember out of the ordinary things,' Bosi said.

'Would you recognise her?'

'I'm getting on a bit, but my memory hasn't gone altogether. Do you want to introduce me to her? She wasn't too bad looking.'

Soneri took out the photo and showed it to him. Bosi focused on it, holding it at the right distance from his eyes. He muttered something and began to agree by moving his chin up and down.

'Yes, that's her. Lovely woman, isn't she?'

'Do you know her name?'

'Ah, after all this time... I don't even know if we were ever introduced. If I remember correctly, you said she was a relative.'

Soneri shook his head. 'She's the lover of the ex-husband of Elvira Gallerani, Fabio and Rinaldo's cousin.'

Bosi indicated he knew nothing about it.

'It's an important detail,' said Soneri, as he put the photo back in his pocket.

'Do you know something?' Bosi exclaimed all of a sudden. 'I don't believe Gianni was really sick at all.'

'What makes you think that?'

'He once confided in me that he was there in the clinic after doing a deal, because it was cheaper than going to a boarding house.'

'You mean he deliberately arranged to stay in hospital?'

'I have no proof, but since he'd had a nervous breakdown, it wasn't difficult.'

'It's surprising that he chose Righetti's clinic of all places.'

'That's the area where he'd lived with his mother before going to boarding school.'

'He could hardly have had a happy memory of it.'

'I agree with you, but you know how the mind works. The things that you grow up with when you're a child... Maybe he was just curious.'

Sonieri made no reply.

'And then he told me he was short of money. I think that might be why he chose a brief spell in hospital instead of renting a room.'

Running away from France, thrown out by his girlfriend, having no relatives, away at boarding school, the object of gossip, Gianni had possibly surrendered to despair.

'Do you think that's why he ended it all?' asked Soneri.

'Could be. He seemed cheerful enough, but the reasons for taking your own life are so deep they're never really clear,' said Bosi.

The midday bell rang out as they went their separate ways.

28

The mist grew thicker, falling against the windscreen, swirling around, unsure where to go. Soneri observed its silent impact, imagining he was walking into a giant's sneeze. The ringing of his mobile shook him back to reality.

'I've had a horrible dream, a sort of premonition,' Angela started.

'Don't believe this crystal-gazing nonsense,' said Soneri, playing down her warnings. Instead of taking the road to Sissa, he instinctively turned off in the opposite direction, onto the Asolana motorway to the city.

'I don't believe it, but it's the same with astrologers. We think they're a bunch of charlatans, and yet we listen to them.'

'I don't believe in warning dreams, but I like hearing about them.'

'Ragu and your corpse in the Po appeared to me together.'

'And what were they doing?'

'They were chatting, then they embraced each other. They were wearing a sort of robe, sitting on a bench, I don't know where. They could have been at a swimming pool or in a sauna.'

'And what do you think all this means?'

'That there are other people like them, suffering the same fate, but Ragu isn't as far down the road. He still has to follow the path taken by Caputo.'

'And that's why you think this dream is a premonition?'

'Yes, and I'm a bit afraid.'

'They're only suggestions,' said Soneri, cutting her off.

'Yes, but those two have a lot in common, and we know where that path leads.'

'You've still got time to make the other lad turn back.'

'It'd be easier to make a pigeon change direction. But where are you going?' she asked when she heard the engine rumbling in the background. Only then did Soneri notice that he heading in the direction of the city.

'In the direction of a meteorite attracted by a planet.'

'And which planet would that be?'

'You.'

'Have you grown tired of growing mouldy on the river?'

'No, it was an unconscious turn, perhaps it's your magnetism.'

'Don't be so ridiculous,' she warned him. 'You know very well what the unconscious is. You must have a whole store of repressed intentions inside you.'

'And couldn't you be one of them?'

Angela emitted a kind of gurgle sounding like a mixture of satisfaction and uncertainty. 'Drop by at my place to say hello, but I won't be able to dedicate much time to you today. Just a few minutes to let you feel my magnetism,' she said seductively.

After the call, Soneri made for the city centre. At the crossing of Viale Solferino and Via Pizzi, he remembered about Elvira and turned alongside the Cittadella. It was obviously a day for instinctive decisions, a freedom suddenly offered to brighten his days, like summer afternoons in his boyhood.

He pulled up at Elvira's house and sat for a few minutes deep in thought before convincing himself that there was nothing to be lost by making the effort. He got out the car and pressed the button on the intercom, to be greeted by the woman's somewhat irritated voice. He said simply, 'Soneri,' and the door clicked open. Elvira looked her customary forbidding self, showing off her suntan.

'Perfect timing,' she said. 'I just got back yesterday.'

'End of the holidays?'

'I'm not going to hang about too long in the city. This mist gets me down. Just long enough to attend to some outstanding business.'

'Like investing the money you're going to get from your cousins?'

Elvira stared at him impassively, giving the impression she wanted time to study him and understand how much he knew.

'There are agents who attend to that,' she replied coldly.

'You're going to rake in a tidy sum,' Soneri said, deliberately provoking her.

'The Tax Office will take some interest in these matters, don't you think?'

'Your cousins, they must be apprehensive, aren't they?'

'If they are, there must be some reason for it.'

'Indeed. Your uncle was a smart man.'

'Men are often like that. Maybe you are too,' Elvira insinuated.

'And women are too often complicit, especially mothers and daughters. They keep secrets. But not you. On the contrary, you've revealed some very intimate facts.'

The woman started to laugh. 'You didn't know my mother. I'm sure she would've approved, anything to squeeze some cash out of that family of misers.'

'Are you bluffing, or are you sure you're Gualtiero's daughter?'

Another burst of laughter. 'The moment of our conception is the most important point in our lives but we have no recollection of it. That's a bit of a bluff, isn't it?'

'Don't take the piss,' replied Soneri, giving no ground.

'Listen,' she replied, in no way intimidated, 'what I do know is my mother went to bed many times with my uncle. I often saw them emerge together from the house in Via Bassa dei Folli. Do you imagine they'd been there for a game of cards? Anyway, that loser of a wife of his was no good for anything.'

'The house in Via Bassa dei Folli,' repeated Soneri thoughtfully.

'They called it the 'slaughterhouse' because that's where my uncle used to take his lovers.'

'Even after Carmela Caputo went to live there?'

'That I don't know. I was off the scene by then, but he kept seeing her even after he was widowed. His ardour diminished as he grew older, and perhaps she was his only *fixture*,' was Elvira's malicious theory.

'And he had a child by her,' Soneri added.

For a fleeting moment, the woman seemed embarrassed. 'Do you really think Gualtiero was so stupid? He would never have got a woman like that pregnant. He liked women but he liked money more. In my mother's case, he was in the clear. Officially, I was his brother's daughter.'

'And why did he get his sister-in-law pregnant?'

'Because my mother wanted children, and it hadn't happened with my father.'

'So you'd rule out the possibility that Carmela had a son by your uncle?'

'I believe there was some sort of feeling between him and that woman,' Elvira replied. 'When you feel old age coming on, you stop fighting the world and try to come to terms with it. Carmela needed support, and he was happy to provide it. Even if they lived in different houses, everybody knew what was going on, but I'd still rule out the possibility the boy was Gualtiero's son. Do you really believe Carmela didn't have other affairs in the city? Do you know what family she came from?'

'Is another family's reputation about to be shredded?' Soneri asked dryly.

Elvira was unmoved. 'I'm only telling the truth. I've done the same with my own mother, so why should I hold back when we're dealing with an outsider?'

'You're completely unscrupulous,' Soneri admitted.

'It might seem an unpleasant quality, but it's a necessary one. I've no time for hypocrisy. I've learned that everything must be out in the open, however obscene it might appear. Just imagining things to be different is a fool's errand.'

'Is there much obscenity in your family?'

'No more than in others. The stakes are higher and that's a risk. But then so is poverty.'

Soneri got to his feet with a vague sense of bitterness. Elvira made to accompany him to the door, with a benevolent, sneering victor's smile.

'Is the business with the inheritance all settled?' Soneri asked at the doorstep.

'I believe so,' Elvira replied complacently.

When he was outside, he called Signora Falchieri. He needed to get himself out of the swamp he had been wading in for some days.

'Any news from France?' he asked.

The magistrate was obviously in a meeting, since voices could be heard in the background. Her reply was brief and to the point. 'No, none. These things take time.'

Soneri was disappointed. When he switched off his phone, he found himself in Via Farini. He walked under the portico and turned into the *Da Bruno* wine bar.

He ordered a plate of *culatello* topped with Parmesan shavings. As an accompaniment, he opted for a *Malvasia amabile* because he felt the need for something sweet. Before setting off again, he was considering a brief encounter with Angela who was expecting him, when his phone rang.

'Where have you been?' It was Motti.

'In the city. I have some business to attend to.'

'You'd better get back here fast, if you're still interested in what's going on down in the Po Valley.'

'What's happened?'

'They've killed Bovino,' came the cold reply.

The slice of *culatello* almost fell from his hand. He did not speak for a couple of seconds until he heard the maresciallo repeat from the other end of the line – 'Hello, hello?'

'When did this happen?'

'Last night. The forensic team are trying to establish the time.'

'Where was it?'

'Casimiro found the body in the flood plain near the poplars, not far from that makeshift construction of his.'

'Did he have his skull broken as well?'

'No. Three shots in the chest should have been enough but they gave him the *coup de grace* in the face. Execution with disfigurement.'

'Have you spoken to anyone yet?'

'Who do you want me to speak to?' replied the maresciallo. 'No-one lives there apart from Casimiro, and that lot will have used a silencer.'

Soneri ended the conversation, paid the bill, alerted Angela and got into his car. On the way, he called D'Onofrio in Naples. All of a sudden, everything was falling into place.

'And what did I tell you?' replied the inspector. 'Bovino is on the losing side, and when it's like that, you either clear off or else they wipe you out. There are no half measures. He attempted to take care of his affairs up your way, and they've made him pay. That's the way it goes.'

'Who's on the winning side?'

'The Cenciarello mob. They've been on a killing spree down here.'

'As far as you know, are there any of Bovino's associates in this area?'

'You should know that. According to your prefects and police chiefs, there is no such thing as a mafia of the north.' D'Onofrio's tone was sarcastic.

'What does the Cenciarello mob deal in?'

'Primarily drugs and property investment. They leave sub-tendering and slot machines to the 'ndrangheta.'

Soneri was about to hang up when the inspector added; 'Keep me posted. You know how tight-lipped our good friends in the carabinieri are!'

Soneri reassured him, and as he drove along he persuaded himself that at long last this unbearable stillness had been jolted. This must be the *coup de scène* in the final act. For some days now, he had felt that some silent, barely contained energy was about to burst the banks of apparent normality. The nighttime movements, the assault on Milick, the bank robbery, the corpse of an outsider, the break-in on the motor launch – all in a tangle of lines – were about to converge.

When he arrived in Torricella, there were groups of people on the river bank as happens when the Po rises and when the locals pray that the river will not come at them. He climbed over the white and red tapes and went down to the flood plain. The carabinieri were already at work and were surprised to see Soneri turn up.

One of them came over to enquire about Nanetti, their colleague from the forensic section. 'What are you doing here anyway?' he asked.

'I'm on leave and the Po is a place I love.'

The other man looked at him strangely. 'Well, you're out of luck. You're dogged by misfortune,' he said, as he turned away.

Soneri went over to Motti, who was gazing intently at his colleagues working on the corpse. 'She's dead, and now her sons are dead,' he murmured, referring to Carmela.

'They slaughtered him like a lone wolf,' the maresciallo said.

'Maybe he was trying to put together a new pack.'

'You can't do that on your rival's territory.'

'Did they shoot him on the spot or was the body dragged here?'

'We've found footprints and traces of something being hauled along the ground.'

'I wonder why they didn't weigh the body down and toss him in the Po?' Soneri said, almost speaking to himself.

'Before being posted here, I did five years in Catania and I learned mafia symbolism. They brought him here so as to warn others of the fate awaiting them.'

'Do you think there are many of them?'

'No, just a handful of poor devils. The small fry already understand whose side they have to be on.'

The forensic medic, impossible to miss with his tie and coat among the array of uniforms and overalls, was on the scene. He had rolled up the bottoms of his trousers to stop them getting wet in the grass. When he saw him prepare to leave, Motti went over to speak to him. He came back to report that the time of the murder was between two and four o'clock in the morning.

'The execution hour,' Soneri noted. He saw Casimiro going towards his house of trees, and went over to him.

'You nearly bumped into the killers,' Soneri informed him.

'Did they do it here?'

'It would appear not, but the time of death might have coincided with the time you leave your place.'

'I didn't see him immediately. It was later when I had a walk around to see if there were any mushrooms. They spring up in this season after the water has drained away from the flood plain. They appear overnight, like so many things in these parts.'

'Such as dead bodies.'

'Do you know what I did? I touched it and it was still warm, not the face or the hands but under the jacket.'

'What time was it?'

'Just before six o'clock, when it was still dark. I noticed something standing out among the poplars, and that seemed strange to me. Here everything is flat.'

'Did you call Motti right away?'

'I don't have a phone. I went over to the club and waited for Marisa to arrive. He wasn't going to come round.'

'Had you ever seen him around?'

'How could I tell? His face looked like a crushed tomato. No, I don't think I've ever seen him, but I've seen his car.'

'How could you be sure it was his car?'

'Well, I don't know if it was really his but I've seen it being driven around, and there's no-one here who has a big car like that. And there was something else I realised this morning.'

Soneri listened carefully, his face inviting Casimiro to continue.

'It's parked in front of the house in Via Bassa dei Folli.'

29

As the rain started again, Soneri made his way back along the tow-path to the house where Carmela had once lived. The Range Rover was still there, open with the keys in the ignition. Perhaps someone had lain in wait for him, or perhaps the driver had tried to escape when he realised he was in a trap. There were no clues in the car, which could have been cleaned up, but its very presence at that spot signified something of great importance to him. He went round to the rear of the house to try to force the door through which he had previously made his entrance. It was not a problem. He climbed up to the apartment and now had more time to inspect it. Nothing much was changed: the same dust, the same abandoned state. The only room showing any sign of recent use was the bedroom where an unmade double bed occupied half the space. A pair of slippers lay on the floor and on the far side there was a dressing table with a mirror. The bathroom was a stinking hole with yellowing tiles. In the dressing table drawer he found a few uninteresting objects – a couple of combs, shaving sticks, razor blades, some holy pictures and some photos, perhaps of deceased relatives.

He switched on the torch on his mobile to check if there was anything else in the drawer and noticed a kind of false bottom where he found a diary with a bank's logo as well as a thick, transparent folder containing passports and identity cards which he started to examine. They belonged to Eastern European women, Romanians, Bulgarians, Poles, eight in all between eighteen and twenty-four years of age. As he replaced the documents in the folder, he saw a name written at the bottom: Seskolov. The same name occurred in the diary presumably to keep track of the gang's accounts. A profitable prostitution ring, judging by the sums involved. On another page the name Milick appeared, and in this case it must have had something to do with drugs because expenses were listed alongside earnings. Other foreign names made up the list, and

Soneri assumed these were fishermen from the East because unaccountable takings had been entered alongside words like 'supplies to client No 6' or 'client No 10.' The numbers undoubtedly corresponded to some clandestine register.

He pocketed the diary and documents and made his exit. On the short journey to Torricella, Soneri attempted to clarify his thoughts. Bovino had obviously set up a drugs and prostitution ring on his own by signing up the fishermen from the East. Perhaps he was also selling catfish and other types of catch to the restaurants along the riverbanks. In other words, he had set up on his own behalf in a territory which was no longer his. Probably the assault on Milick and Seskolov's murder were part of this scenario.

He parked in front of the club. The crowd of onlookers had cleared, and the corpse had been taken away.

Pezzani came up from the jetty. 'Everything seems a lot clearer now, doesn't it?' he said.

Soneri's frown expressed his uncertainty.

'This victim has a name and that explains a lot,' Pezzani insisted.

'What does it explain?'

'The robberies, the thefts, all these strange comings and goings.'

'Are you going to add Gallerani houseboat wreck as well?'

'Are you telling me there's no connection? Maybe that *camorrista* was blackmailing them? Maybe he was demanding protection money.'

'I don't believe he was demanding anything from the Galleranis,' said Soneri, cutting him short and making his way into the club where Ceriani, the Viking and Cefalú were in animated conversation. In a corner, Casimiro was wholly engrossed in spinning a glass filled with white wine, the last of several to judge by his appearance. Soneri took a seat beside him, causing Casimiro to look indifferently in his direction.

'Why did they drag him in front of my house?' he wondered in a whisper, as though just coming round. 'I've always done everything to keep myself to myself.'

'Pure chance,' Soneri reassured him, although he was none too sure himself. 'It was the handiest spot.'

The Madman shook his head. 'Nothing is ever pure chance. They must have seen me talking to you and so they sent me a warning.'

Soneri thought this was a plausible suggestion, but said nothing.

'I've been having bad thoughts,' Casimiro muttered again, taking another sip. 'Do you know how my father died?'

'Yes, I do know.'

'He was burned alive inside a wooden house. I learned from him how to build with branches and tree trunks, and now I fear I will meet the same end. I too will die in a fire. I've built the bonfire myself.'

'They wouldn't dare. They've no interest in doing such a thing, and you know nothing about them.'

Casimiro gazed at him, reassured. He found that argument convincing. 'It's true. I know nothing, but they might suspect I have some arcane knowledge.'

'The mafia is ferocious but they kill as little as possible. They prefer to travel out of sight.'

'That's why they are so feared. They're there but you don't see them.'

'Like the beast of the Po,' Soneri suggested.

'I think he's out to protect me. I'm the only man who believes in him and respects him. If the rest have their way, it'll be the end of the wolves and the wild boar.'

'Who knows?' murmured Soneri, trying to conceal his scepticism.

Casimiro seemed to be carried away by his thoughts or, more probably, by the wine.

'It's the river who'll decide, as usual,' he replied, as if in a dream. 'Doesn't everything spring from water?' he asked, gazing hard at Soneri as he waited for a reply.

Just then, under that intense stare, Soneri had an intuition. 'Did anyone take over from Venanzio, the frogman?'

Casimiro shook his head. 'There's no-one else. They all gave up.'

'No money in it?'

'That's not the reason.'

'So what was it?'

'They're afraid,' said Casimiro moving close to Soneri with a conspiratorial air. 'It's the same fear that Venanzio felt when he saw the beast in the depths at Stagno. It never left him. They're all afraid of raking about in the Po among the things it keeps concealed. There are vile things the river keeps out of pity: curses, threats, old crimes, sacrileges. Everything is there.'

The capacious warehouse Angela had spoken about, came to Soneri's mind subconsciously.

'Sometimes there's no choice but to face things you'd rather not. The police have always had to do that,' he said, rising to his feet.

He had an idea in his mind and went off to find the maresciallo, but first he called Signora Falchieri. 'We're going to have to dive into the river.'

'Which one? The Po or the Ganges?'

'You know I only move within a short range.'

'Not in your mind,' the magistrate said. 'I think I'm in general sympathy with you.'

'I would like to bring in some frogmen.'

'In connection with what?'

'The Gallerani houseboat that sank to the bottom.'

'What do you suspect?'

'I can't be too sure, but I believe it could tell us a lot. In any case, it'd be worthwhile to take a look.'

'You always operate outside every known perimeter, a real stray dog when it comes to enquiries. I end up reining in your intuitions with risky procedures.'

'In this case, criminal damage causing the sinking has been established.'

'And just as well too, otherwise I'd have had to come down hard. Bear in mind that employing divers is a costly business and the Administration is getting more and more tight-fisted. If you don't come up with something interesting, they'll be straight in with their protestations.'

'No operation is ever free of risk. You should know that.'

'All right. I place my trust in you. If anybody else had asked me, I'd have refused,' she said, making herself sound complicit.

Soneri met Motti on the towpath. 'I've asked the magistrate to get the frogmen involved, yours,' he said.

The maresciallo looked at him in surprise. 'So you're no longer on holiday?'

'I'm in the mood for being generous with the Executive, and without the Chief on my back it's easier to get on with work.'

'What are the divers for?'

'The houseboat. I've this idea that it had become a battleground between Bovino and the Cenciariello gang.'

'And you think you'll find proof of that on the inside?'

'I don't know. Maybe, but it might also be no more than a hole in the water,' he laughed.

Motti did not immediately understand, but then he joined in the laughter.

There was nothing to be done but wait, the maresciallo for results from the investigative unit, Soneri for the arrival of the divers, and the townspeople for what was happening to the place where they lived. As he continued along the towpath, Soneri saw the arrival of some reporters surrounding Motti with their cameras. A superintendent from Parma came along and was also encircled. Soneri drew aside and as he continued on his way, Angela called.

'This time you did have good reason for making yourself scarce,' she admitted.

'This phoney normality has finally been shattered. Now I hope we can see through the cracks.'

'Cracks are good for that, provided you know how to look.'

'It's like peering under the surface of the water,' Soneri replied, the submerged houseboat still on his mind.

'Since I fear I won't be seeing you for a while, I'll report by telephone of something told to me in the strictest confidence, but will be of interest to you.'

Soneri grunted.

'It's to do with Caputo's mobile. Do you know who carried out the check on the French contacts list?' Before Soneri could open his mouth, Angela answered her own question. 'The *Gendarmerie* in Toulouse.'

'Your little friend Cédric!'

'Yours too, seeing that he's facilitating the enquiries. He's already informed me there were at least twenty calls from an Italian number with the Parma code, 0521 8713..., to be precise. That's not all. There have also been a dozen conversations with the mobile number 335 6532... I'll leave you to draw your own conclusions.'

'I get it,' he said, copying out the two numbers on the back of a bar bill.

'This isn't the official version yet, but Cédric wanted to pass this on. He said he understands the requirements of someone conducting an enquiry, and in his eyes the real detective is me,' added Angela.

'My debt to you increases, just as your understanding does with that Frenchman.'

'I should inform you that I will apply a loan shark's interest rates and that I have no time for love at a distance. The distance between the Po and Parma is already too far.'

'It won't be long before we can end this separation. I have an idea that the cracks will reveal more than I thought.'

As he switched off, he realised someone had sent him a text. He read, 'Come and see me. I have something to report. Adelaide.'

He got into his car and set off for Coltaro. The mist was as thick as ever, while the mist over the mystery he was investigating was lifting slightly. En route, he called Juvara and asked him to find out who the numbers Caputo had been calling belonged to. The inspector took note without saying a word, and then said: 'A right mess. I see you're keen to get to grips with it.'

'The carabinieri have turned out in force. The place is overflowing with gang leaders.'

Juvara mumbled something expressing incredulity.

'I'll wait for the next surprise,' he said as he signed off, but he did not sound convinced.

Just then Soneri arrived in Coltaro. Adelaide let him in and stood waiting at the door. She seemed even more tired and tormented. Her face was pale. She showed him into a living room with a round table, lacquered chairs and an inlaid cherrywood sideboard.

'Have you found anything? Do you feel free to talk?' Soneri asked.

'Maybe,' muttered the woman, 'or maybe not. What Iosif told me has nothing to do with what's happened.'

'Did you know that from the outset, and just didn't want to tell me?'

She nodded her head. 'It was him who robbed the bank. He needed money to send home for his father who's unwell. He did it without informing Bovino.'

'Was it him who beat him up, or others?'

'The others. Bovino was in a rage but he already had too many problems with his rivals. The assault on Iosif was a warning aimed at him as well.'

'What actually happened that day? Did he tell you?'

'They were lying in wait for him while he was on his way home from Torricella. Between the mist and the darkness that falls mid-afternoon, you're more alone here than anywhere else.'

'Did they ask him anything about Bovino's whereabouts?'

'He didn't tell me, but I imagine they already knew everything because one of the fishermen had changed sides. Iosif didn't, and he paid for it.'

'What kind of job did he do for Bovino?'

'Drug pushing all along the Po. The handover took place on the banks, inside the houseboats.'

'Which ones?'

'I don't know. The pushers pretend to be tourists on the river. They would rent one houseboat and let the rest of them know. No-one can see you on the Po.'

'Iosif picked up the keys of a houseboat on behalf of a company owned by the Gallerani family. Did you know that?'

'No, I didn't, but it's plausible, seeing what he was involved in.'

'Did he have any dealings with that family?'

'How could he? Iosif is young, not well off, and scarcely speaks any Italian. They're powerful and keep themselves to themselves. Only old Gualtiero, when he turned up at markets to do his business, was ever seen out and about in the Po valley.'

'But Iosif did pick up the keys for the River Blues Company which is controlled by Rinaldo Gallerani.'

Adelaide shook her head. 'Believe me, I know nothing about that.'

'Iosif had already been assaulted. Do you know who gave him the beating?'

'With the people he hung out with, stabbing and punches were the least of it. I did my best to get him out of those circles, but I didn't manage in time.'

Adelaide lowered her eyes and stared at the floor. She seemed sincere and may well have been in love with that younger man. Perhaps that relationship was the result of two solitary existences on the margins of everything. Ragu and that army of the unseen which also included Caputo came to his mind.

Adelaide saw him out, and made a promise. 'You'll see that when he comes out of the coma he'll tell me everything, and then we'll cut free from the past. We'll go away from here,' she ended, with a gleam of hope in her eye.

Soneri got back into his car, buoyed up by that brief flash of light. The daylight, on the other hand, was fading in the brief autumn afternoon. As he drove along the road, he picked up his mobile and saw there were a couple of new calls. Just then, Juvara's call came in.

'Sir, I have those numbers you were enquiring about,' he said.

'I hope they're what I figured.'

'The landline is in the name of Gualtiero Gallerani, while the mobile belongs to Fabio Gallerani. Was that what you figured?'

'A perfect match, like water in a glass.'

'There's one thing I should warn you about. I understand that Capuozzo is gunning for you. He got all worked up when he heard about the murder of that *camorrista*.'

'Don't worry. I'll ignore him.'

'Be careful. He's capable of borrowing a telephone from someone in admin and taking you by surprise from a different number.'

'Where can he have learned all these tricks? They don't teach them at the police academy,' said Soneri, with heavy irony. 'Anyway, I never reply to unknown callers.'

In fact when he switched off his mobile, he noticed two unanswered calls from a number not among his contacts, and imagined Capuozzo cursing and swearing while the phone rang out.

He arrived back in Torricella through a sudden, swirling mist. A wind had blown up and seemed unsure which direction to take.

'Perhaps the weather is changing,' said Marisa, and Ceriani confirmed this because of the pain in his arm which he had broken years before.

'Yes,' said Soneri. 'I do indeed believe there is a change.'

30

Soneri too felt the need for a change of scene. He took the *autostrada* towards Cremona, where he would see the famous Torrazza and ask Andalò a few questions. An hour before, Signora Falchieri had given him the findings on Caputo's mobile. Soneri had to fake his ignorance, accompanying her account with a series of little grunts. He was genuinely surprised when the magistrate updated him on another series of calls to a phone with a foreign code.

'In Portugal,' the magistrate went on. 'Do you know of any contacts Caputo had in that country?'

He thought for a while, then remembered Elvira Gallerani's visiting card. He took it out and asked Signora Falchieri to repeat the number. It was the same.

'It's the phone belonging to the cousin of Fabio and Rinaldo. She's in dispute with them over the old man's inheritance. She lives part of the year in Portugal.'

'I'm coming round to the fact this Caputo was very well-acquainted with the Gallerani family.'

'If you ask me, it was if they were his own family.'

'Yes, indeed! Considering he had no family of his own and may have felt the need of one,' she commented, before adding, 'There are other calls from Caputo, three to be precise.'

'Who to?'

'To a certain Professor Righetti, who seems to have died.'

'He was the director at the private neurological clinic in Sissa.'

The magistrate gave a squeal of surprise. She seemed to have understood. Pieces of information and odd details were changing the angle from one moment to the next, but some things were coming into focus.

'I do have to admire your stubbornness in persevering with this enquiry,' she concluded, in a complicit tone.

In Cremona, he was surprised to find himself so much at home. The cities in the Po Valley all resembled one another, so he found something there of his native Parma. The Torrazzo was divided by a sizeable, mid-air cornice, while in that dark atmosphere, the marbles of the Duomo shone as brightly as the Palace in Colorno. He found the Gigabyte Store, a luxury shop with two oval lit-up windows, situated in a pedestrian precinct in the centre. A young, highly attractive woman, wearing high heels and a mini-skirt, stood behind the counter. It did not take him long to recognise her. She was the woman in the photograph who had picked up Caputo in a taxi from Righetti's clinic.

Soneri introduced himself. She said her name was Erika 'with a K,' she declared, as though it was a university degree. She called over a colleague and told her to take over at the counter while she escorted him into the back shop. She sat down behind a glass and ironwork desk, cupped her face in her hand and looked at him with an air of annoyance.

Soneri asked: 'Did you know Giovanni Caputo?'

'No, I've no idea who he is.'

'He's the man you met in a taxi three and half years ago at the clinic in Sissa.'

She gave a start, looked confused and then pretended to remember suddenly. 'Ah yes, him!'

Soneri nodded gravely.

'I'd forgotten his name. It was a long time ago,' said Erika in self-justification.

'Had you ever seen him before?'

'No.'

'So how come you went there to meet him?'

She blushed slightly and moved a little on her seat. All of a sudden, she seemed troubled and defenceless. It took a few seconds for her reply. 'Sandro asked me.'

'You mean, Andalò? Your man, ex-husband of Elvira Gallerani?'

She nodded, as though swallowing an enormous mouthful.

'Why did he send you?'

'I don't know. If I remember, he asked it as a favour.'

'Did you talk on the journey? Did Caputo tell you anything?'

'Only that he was waiting for someone. He didn't know where. He was astonished when he saw me. He thought some man was supposed to come for him.'

'Did he tell you who the appointment was with?'

'No.'

'When you got out the taxi, did you accompany him somewhere?'

'Not at all! We said goodbye on the pavement. I got back into the taxi and he went into a café.'

'Did you wonder why Caputo didn't call the taxi himself?'

'I've no idea. Obviously they'd told him someone would come for him.'

'Or perhaps there was some other reason?'

'Sandro told me it was all paid in advance.'

'Why was Andalò mixed up in this business? And what reason was there for sending you? A favour? Doesn't it all seem a bit odd to you?'

Erika was growing more uneasy. Her eyes met Soneri's resolute expression, and gave in. 'I was to pretend I was someone else,' she confessed, to ward off his gaze.

'Who?'

'Elvira Gallerani's daughter.'

'So it was Elvira who'd made the appointment with Caputo?'

'How do I know?' she burst out, turning hysterical. 'Maybe! Could be!' She raised her voice. 'All I did was take him to Viale Duca d'Alessandro. If you want to know anything else, ask Sandro.'

'That's why I'm here. Where is he?'

'Having breakfast in the Bar Duomo, or maybe in his office in Via Milazzo.'

As he went out, Soneri ran through the conversation with the woman. He thought of Elvira making an appointment with Caputo shortly before he disappeared. Or perhaps it was Andalò who had arranged things, sending his girlfriend along and telling her to make out she was his daughter. The problem was he had no proof that Andalò had been in contact with Caputo. He went into Bar Duomo and enquired about Andalò, but they told him he had left about a quarter of an hour earlier. He made his way to Via Milazzo.

He found him in his office, which looked like a cross between a surgery and a studio. Andalò showed no surprise when Soneri made his way in and first adopted the phoney cordiality of a salesman. His smile faded when the commissario asked about Bovino.

He feigned ignorance. 'I don't know him.'

'And yet he was driving about in a Range Rover which belonged to your company.'

The man was taken aback, and immediately tried to recover lost ground. 'I sold it through an agency, but obviously the change of ownership wasn't registered.'

Soneri shook his head. 'Do you know Iosif Milick?'

'No.'

'However, it seems you phoned him on at least two occasions. He worked for Bovino.'

'Possibly,' he stuttered, in obvious embarrassment. 'It could be, but I don't remember.'

Soneri pressed on. 'It also seems you are overextended. Could it be someone or other came forward to help you out financially?'

'I've been having problems in this crisis, like everyone else. That was one of the reasons I had to sell the vehicle.'

'You've been facing more than one crisis,' said Soneri, giving the impression of knowing more than he was letting on.

Andalò stared hard at him as he tried to work out how best to respond. 'I can guess who supplied you with all these details,' he replied bitterly, 'but I don't know why you're dragging me into it.'

'Your boat was stolen and found at Stagno with a hole in the hull at the same time that Caputo disappeared.'

'I don't know this Caputo,' he repeated.

'Your daughter went along to pick him up from a clinic,' said Soneri, raising his voice slightly.

'My daughter!'

'In fact it was your girlfriend, Erika, but she said she was your daughter.'

'Ah! That man!' he said, pretending to remember. 'I'm sorry but I've got it now. It was some time ago. Let's say it was a favour,' Andalò admitted, reluctantly.

'There are so many favours in this business,' Soneri remarked. 'Who was this one for?'

The man sighed. 'There's no point in me concealing anything, since you already know so much. A few years back, things weren't going particularly well for me, debts were piling up and the banks were unwilling to take risks with somebody like me. It was the bank that recommended who might be willing to give me some cash.'

'And they proposed Carmine Bovino?'

'No, they suggested some equity firms, but nothing came of it.'

'So then you got onto him?'

Andalò put on a serious expression. 'I asked my ex-wife for money. I offered her the majority stake in my business. When all's said and done, it was a business proposition. In order to keep the ship afloat, I was prepared to humiliate myself by becoming her employee.'

'And what did she say?'

'She said she'd not risk one euro on me.'

'And she advised you to get in touch with Bovino?'

'Not explicitly.'

'What does that mean?'

'That she'd try and work out some scheme to help me. She gave no guarantee she would come up with anything, but she did say she would think it over.'

'So she arranged the contact with Bovino?'

'I'm not entirely sure. The fact is that a couple of days later, he turned up.'

'So you think that...'

'No, no,' Andalò interrupted in a panic. 'Perhaps she had nothing to do with it. These people sniff out companies in trouble, so they know they're on firm ground. They have lists of actions for unpaid invoices. Did you know that?'

'Did you cede the entire property?'

'I kept hold of a small part so as to appear among the owners.'

'The front man,' Soneri summed up, witheringly.

Andalò turned nervously away, not denying the point.

'I imagine that Bovino came in as part of a company,' Soneri suggested.

'Yes, that's how it's done.'

'What was its name?'

Andalò thought for a while before saying, 'River Blues.'

It was Soneri's turn to be taken aback. 'Do you know the manager's name?'

The man nodded. 'Rinaldo Gallerani,' he muttered.

Soneri frowned. He was not sure how that information fitted in with the scenario he had been putting together. Andalò rescued him from embarrassment. 'What do you think? I'm the only one covered in shit?'

31

Half a dozen carabinieri officers in uniform were marching along the towpath as though on border patrol. Among them, Soneri picked out Maresciallo Motti with his slightly curved profile. The officers pulled up alongside the tree trunk house, and stood taking it in. With their binoculars over their shoulders and overcoats down to their knees, they looked like actors in a war film. On the riverbank a hundred metres ahead, their diver colleagues were manoeuvring a dingy in preparation for taking a plunge, while on the flood plain Casimiro was in animated conversation with one of the company who was already attired in wetsuit and mask. Soneri went up to the group and introduced himself.

He was greeted by the superior officer, who gave his name as Colonel Lucentini. 'So you're part of the action as well?'

'No, anything but! This is your enquiry!'

Lucentini looked with some bewilderment at Soneri's yellow waterproof jacket and at the boots halfway up his legs he had recently purchased.

'The prosecutor's office requested this operation,' the colonel went on sceptically, pointing to the divers. 'The problem is locating the wreckage.'

'Did you ask him,' Soneri said, pointing at Casimiro, who was making grand, disappointed gestures.

'They're talking to him right now, but he's mad.'

Soneri turned to Motti, who said, 'He's a bit odd, but there's nothing he doesn't know about the river.'

The colonel looked at his squad standing by in silence and shook his head. Meantime, the officer who had been talking to Casimiro clambered back up the embankment and was coming towards them.

'He was talking about monsters and creatures who live in the Po,' he whispered to his superior to confirm that he was not wrong in his judgement.

'He's an oddball. I don't think he has ever wandered further than ten kilometres from the flood plain,' said Soneri.

'They're not going to find anything there,' Casimiro protested, about a couple of metres from them. 'I told him they're wasting their time. The current flows in the opposite direction, and it will definitely have pushed it one metre at a time down to the San Vito bend in the river.'

Meanwhile, two divers had made their dive and two others were waiting on the dinghy. The Madman kept his eyes on them, all the while shaking his head. The Viking and Cefalú came along and people from the town who were curious, arrived as though in a procession. After a short time, the first diver came back to the surface.

'There's only sand down there,' he shouted, pulling off his mask and mouthpiece.

The other one re-emerged shortly afterwards. The man in the dinghy who was supposedly in command gave the order to search another stretch of water some twenty metres away.

'You proceed by quadrants,' Lucentini explained.

The rest of the party seemed to be in agreement and all nodded.

'We might want to take a sounding first in the zone Casimiro indicated, so as to eliminate all doubt,' suggested Motti timidly.

The colonel gave a wave of his hand as though telling him to be quiet.

'Let us proceed as per the agreed plan,' he ordered. 'Then we'll get there,' he said, alluding to the place Casimiro had indicated. After a quarter of an hour, the divers came back to the surface. One of them gave a shake of the head in the direction of the officer on the dinghy, who enquired, 'Nothing doing?'

The first diver once again shook his head.

'There are some monster fish down there,' shouted the second diver, either fascinated or terrified.

'It you carry on that way, it's going to end badly,' the Madman threatened.

'What do you mean?' bawled Lucentini.

'The river doesn't like people rummaging about on its bed. What's down there isn't our business.'

The colonel waved his hand in the air again indicating not to interfere and turned away. Casimiro walked brusquely towards the towpath, climbed down the other side and vanished into the poplar grove.

'What an idiot!' the colonel raged.

'Want to bet that we'll find the wreck where he said we would?' muttered Soneri, trying to remain calm.

'So what? We'd have got there anyway in our own time, in line with our schedule.'

'Of course you would! There's drag fishing and there's selective fishing, and everybody's free to choose between them,' replied Soneri, taking an instant dislike to Lucentini.

The feeling seemed to be mutual since the colonel walked off as if he was uninterested in the commissario's views. The Viking and Soneri exchanged glances, the Viking scowling.

The whole morning passed with one dive after another. The two divers making the first search were replaced a couple of hours later by another pair who arrived for the changeover. The original pair were numb with cold and made straight for the club to warm up. As he passed, one of them said that water was so dark at the bottom it was impossible to make anything out.

'That means they're extracting some sand upstream, possibly at the oil press at Stagno,' suggested Cefalú.

'Does that mean they might not see the ruins of the houseboat?' asked Soneri.

'Everything on the river bed is gradually covered by sand. The river is a great leveller of everything, like time. But it's still early. It's slow work, except when there's a flood,' replied Cefalú.

In the silence, it was possible to overhear the conversations between the divers and their colleagues in the dinghy every time they came to the surface. Finally, towards midday, one of the divers gripping the craft shouted: 'Found it! On the bottom, on its side.' It was exactly where Casimiro had indicated.

The divers were exhausted. They made a beeline for the club, frozen to the bone by the water. Soneri followed the carabinieri procession. He heard talk of currents, sands, oriverbeds and huge fish the size of catfish. He waited till they were all inside because he wanted to call Angela, but he was surprised by the sound of shuffling feet behind him. It was the hurried step of Casimiro, who from a distance had kept his eye on the detachment as it stood down.

'This lot don't understand a thing,' he blurted out.

Soneri made an attempt to soothe him. 'The carabinieri have their own ways.'

'Did you see how cloudy the water was?'

'No, I didn't go down to the water's edge.'

'Anyway, it's all very strange.'

'Why? It has never looked so transparent to me.'

'This morning it got cloudy in just a few hours, but it's hard to understand why when the river is flowing normally. There's no flooding. It's all calm.'

'So?' enquired Soneri, his curiosity aroused.

'It means that someone is working on the riverbed, removing sand.'

'Where?'

'It must be at the oil press at Stagno. If it were further upstream, it wouldn't get as far as this.'

'Maybe they're engaged in dragging operations or they're extracting some material.'

'That could be,' Casimiro admitted, 'but unlikely in this season, with no building work going on.'

'Are you saying that someone is deliberating muddying the waters?'

'Maybe it's a coincidence,' he shrugged.

'You don't sound convinced.'

'There are new people at the Stagno press. They're offering cut-throat prices to destroy the competition, and nobody knows how they manage. Ask the ones who've nearly been forced out of a job,' he said, indicating the piles of gravel and sand at the plant in Torricella.

Just then, Soneri's mobile rang, and Casimiro withdrew.

'He's disappeared again,' said Angela.

Soneri, still engrossed in thoughts of the Po and its muddy waters, was taken by surprise. 'Who's disappeared again?'

'Ragu. I was waiting for him this morning so we could go together to the notary's office, after assuring me he would come. Besides, he has to stay in the city to sign in every day at the police station.'

'He'll never manage to lead a normal life, that lad.'

'I swear he was convinced. He even seemed at peace when he was talking to me.'

'Maybe he'd just been smoking grass.'

'I'm tempted to give up on him. I can't trust him anymore.'

'When you've never known love, you either make yourself a victim because you're searching too desperately for it, or else you become a thug to get revenge on people who do have it.'

'And so Ragu is taking revenge?'

'I think so. He has a great need for love but as he's never received any, he despises it. Like when you fall in love with someone who doesn't return your feelings. It makes you hate them.'

'Perhaps Caputo too hated someone.'

'He stopped at the victim stage. I think he was only seeking the love of a mother who kept him hidden away and of an absent father.'

'Well then, who...?'

'I have a vague idea.'

'Are you playing the mystery man?'

'No, I'm just confused.'

As they said goodbye, he heard voices coming from inside the club. Soneri looked in and made a sign to Motti, who got to his feet and went over to him.

'Can I have a word with you?' They moved to a corner of the bar. 'What do you know about the oil press at Stagno?' asked Soneri.

'I understand that the anti-mafia squad is looking into it. It's aroused a lot of discussion.'

'The Neapolitan camorra or the Calabrian 'ndrangheta?'

'As I told you, they've divided the territory between them. The building sector has been farmed out, but the press seems to be managed by the 'ndrangheta through some front man. A couple of months ago, a block of flats in Sorbolo was sequestered and the magistrates on the trail of building material supplies got as far as here. Some lorries were followed. Sand and gravel are like gold.'

'It could be them that muddied the waters.' Soneri was thinking aloud.

'In what sense? They do that all the time,' laughed the maresciallo.

'No, I mean in a material sense. Casimiro was telling me that the Po is unusually cloudy, and that might be to obstruct the divers' work.'

The maresciallo signalled to an officer, who got up from his table to join them. 'Are there any activities underway on the river bed upstream from Torricella?' he asked.

'Up the valley towards Stagno they're extracting some material, but they have permission to do it. I've checked.'

'When did they start?'

'This morning.'

'Do you think there's some connection?' Motti asked when the officer left them.

'Your guess is as good as mine. In this whole business, there's nothing more than suspicions. A great many details waiting for something to make sense of them.'

Soneri took a seat beside the Viking. He deliberately kept his distance from Lucentini who was still pontificating in the formal style of the commanding officer. 'The search will continue tomorrow morning,' he announced. 'There's not much left of the afternoon, so we'd have no more than a couple of hours of light.'

Motti spoke up. 'Could I suggest we get an order to block the extractions upstream? It would facilitate our work.'

'You can hardly see anything under there,' one of the divers confirmed. 'It's as if there was an underwater fog.'

This observation produced a gale of laughter. The only one who remained serious was the colonel.

'Would you attend to this, maresciallo?' he said, turning to Motti, who nodded in reply.

Meantime, Marisa was serving *tortelli di zucca*, the only thing which seemed to mollify Lucentini.

'Did you see anything of the houseboat? What's it like? Is it all smashed up?' the Viking asked the divers.

They looked over at the colonel as though seeking permission to speak, an act which reignited Soneri's intolerance of hierarchy.

'No, it seemed intact,' one of the two replied laconically.

'Did you say it was on its side at the bottom?'

'It's resting against a little dune where the river curves round,' the man confirmed.

'The San Vito bend,' Soneri said, repeating what Casimiro had previously told him.

Lucentini looked askance at him and the table fell silent for a while until the colonel took advantage of the silence to begin speaking again.

'We will leave the material here for the night,' he ordered. 'You,' he said turning to Motti, 'will see to overnight surveillance.'

Immediately, Lucentini rose to his feet and left the table. The others in the company, while looking regretfully at the dessert which Marisa was about to serve, did likewise.

Motti was not pleased. 'There's a sleepless night ahead of me,' he grumbled. 'I've only got two men, and one is off sick. Now I've got to stand guard over the rubbish bins.'

'If only they'd listened to Casimiro, they'd have saved two hours and everything would be resolved by now. I work while I'm supposed to be on holiday so as not to have my superiors looking over my shoulder,' said Soneri.

'Good for you! But if I were in your shoes, I'd be off somewhere lying on my back.'

'This is a very special enquiry.'

'I know,' replied Motti, 'you've taken that poor bastard to heart, but what now? With Bovino's murder, both of us have been downgraded. Did you see that one?' he said alluding to Lucentini.

'The mafia leave dirt everywhere they go and don't tidy up,' said Soneri.

The maresciallo gave him a perplexed look, then turned and moved quickly away. 'The colonel can attend to it,' he said, making his way out of the club.

There were not many of them left. The Viking was on his own ruminating over what had occurred. Cefalú was teasing Marisa, and Ceriani, leaning over the windowsill, was watching Landini clean the deck of his launch. No-one was speaking, so the only sounds were Cefalú's cheeky remarks to Marisa and the occasional retorts from Marisa trying to make him shut up. Then the phone rang out, and Soneri heard Marisa become deferential. 'Ah, it's you, Reverend. What a pleasure. Who? Yes, he's here. What was that? You want to speak to him?'

She put her hand over the speaker and signalled to the commissario, who moved over to pick up the phone. 'It's Don Amilcare,' she announced.

Soneri put the phone to his ear, and heard a feeble voice, hardly more than whisper, say at the other end, 'Hello?'

'Don Amilcare, how are you? Are you better?'

'At my age, there's no getting better. It's the worst illness one can have.'

'Are you in Sissa?'

'No, I left the parish a couple of days ago. The doctor said I was no longer fit for all the duties of masses, catechism, confession and rosaries. You also need physical health to attend to souls.'

'So, where are you?'

'At the San Bernardo care home in Porporano, but it doesn't matter where I am,' he said, with slight annoyance. 'I really want to unburden myself before moving to the house of God.'

'You're not asking me to hear your confession, are you?' Soneri joked, before lowering his voice when he became aware of Cefalú and Marisa eavesdropping while pretending to chat between themselves. 'The confessions I hear are of a quite different order.'

'It's nothing to do with confession, but with a piece of information

I want to pass on to you. In fact Monsignor Gorini, whom I spoke to you about, will give it to you.'

'Should I go to him?'

'Yes, go there. I understood you were deeply interested in the events involving that man. I'm calling you because I detected some compassion in you, something that's very rare nowadays.'

'Do you know what it's all about?'

'I know quite a lot, but Monsignor Gorini will talk to you. I've passed everything on to him.'

'Why didn't you talk before now?'

'A priest is neither a police officer nor a magistrate. He follows a different law.'

'But if it's a question of justice, that's a matter for priests as well.'

'We have different courts.'

'Why are you delegating this to Monsignor Gorini? Couldn't you and I meet face to face?'

'I'm elderly and unwell. I'm taking leave of this world, and I want to discharge the one outstanding account that remains. I want it to be paid in full, and I want it done by someone who isn't personally involved. I'm too deeply tied up with it all, and my heart is very weak. It might not stand it.'

'Will Monsignor Gorini tell me everything?'

'He will,' replied Don Amilcare.

There was a momentary silence, like during mass, before Soneri heard a deep sigh. 'Goodbye,' said the priest hanging up.

32

Soneri woke at around three o'clock in the morning in an agitated state, as though it was the night before an examination. There were still some smouldering ashes in the stove, so he raked them with a poker to rekindle the fire. He had overindulged with the *Gutturnio* the night before in the company of Landini, the Viking and Cefalú, and now the alcohol was getting its own back, waking him up in the dark despite the efforts of the current to lull him. He wandered about for a while in an attempt to quieten his anxiety. The room felt like a cage and to escape that feeling he peered out through the tiny window, leaning on the sill in search of a horizon, but in vain. All that came looming towards him were the nighttime spectres which had just woken him up. He imagined them breaking through the flooring of the boat without giving him time to escape. His agitation took such a hold that he was tempted to throw on some clothes and leap onto the jetty before everything fell apart. A heave in the current made him afraid he was about to sink inside a prison of freezing water. Fearful visions played inside his head, as though he were running a temperature. Perhaps he really had contracted some illness and that might be why he could not credit what had been unfolding before his eyes: strange darting figures, shadows in the darkness – contortions of the blackness itself or vortices of the night. For a second it seemed that a shining light appeared on the river surface. He watched the water change colour and turn phosphorescent, as though struck by a moon ray. All this was happening a hundred metres away, on the Lombardy bank, at the San Vito curve.

He tried to work out if it was some trick of the eyes, a hallucination, or the last trace of one of the spectres he had seen in his dreams. He switched off the light in the room to see better, and it was then that he glimpsed once again that rapid movement on the surface of the water, as fleeting as a shudder. He got dressed and went out onto the jetty, only to be hit by the heavy night chill. He hurried to the club where he saw Motti on his feet in a state of some alarm.

'Did you hear it as well?'

'I saw something,' Soneri replied, confused.

'Rather than see anything, you feel the water move.'

Soneri stood listening. In the deep silence, a battering sound could be heard intermittently above the river lapping against the banks.

'What could it be?' Motti wondered.

'You know as much as me. You can imagine what it is,' Soneri said.

'That's why I got in touch with my colleagues at Motta Baluffi. The San Vito curve is on their side of the river.'

Casimiro emerged from the darkness. 'The river is agitated and the water is alight,' he said in some excitement.

'And you believe it's your beast wallowing about?' said Motti, annoyed at this intrusion.

'No, I don't believe that at all. He prefers the hour before dawn.'

The maresciallo turned his back on him and focused on the water.

'There's no beast there, but there is someone in the middle,' Casimiro went on.

A light began to shine in the dark and the rising mist was coming down like a stage curtain.

'There's no doubt about it. Did you both see that?' asked Motti.

The officer then pulled out his phone and once again intermittent lights could be made out, this time more distinctly, followed by a hum or muffled hiss coming and going, like a mosquito circling around. The lights were now moving more quickly in a straight line: it was a vehicle on the towpath. The droning sound could be heard more clearly, and the maresciallo said, 'An electric craft.'

Two shots one after the other shattered the silence of the night.

'Shit!' bawled the maresciallo. 'It's a real battle.'

'Was that your colleagues firing?'

'Yes, the sound came from one of our Berettas.'

'It's not going to be easy to stop them. There're no checkpoints on the river,' said Soneri.

'If the person who's fleeing has a speedboat and you're in a car, you've no chance.'

The lights faded into the distance, as did the rustling sound. Everything disappeared from view, hidden by the poplar grove.

'There's something underneath all this involving a whole lot of people,' Motti said.

'Your colleagues will let us into it tomorrow.'

'If they haven't already carried away what interests us.'

'It was a mistake not to complete the inspection yesterday.'

'It was a mistake to rummage about on the bed of the Po,' was Casimiro's judgement.

Motti decided to make a phone call. 'You say there are four of them? They've made their escape up the river? They can't get past the dam at Isola Serafini. Did they come down here?'

Soneri picked up half-phrases before the maresciallo gave him a full summary. 'They lost them because they came over towards this bank. In any case, it was impossible to pursue them from the towpath.'

They stood unmoving and silent in the night, caressed by the wisps of mist accompanying the current. The maresciallo resumed his communication with colleagues who had set up road blocks on the surrounding streets. Casimiro wandered about, appearing and disappearing in the darkness like a stray dog. Soneri felt tired and cold. He was haunted again by the memory of those spectres he had imagined in his sleep, and by a desire for intimacy now that he was faced by the great expanse of the river, unseen but present. He found refuge in his boat and threw himself on the bed without undressing.

He was awakened some hours later by the din. Through the window he saw the divers already preparing to make their first plunge. He felt annoyed and out of place. Everything seemed to be slipping away from him just when he thought he was on the point of clearing things up. He lit a cigar trying to placate his anxiety.

He hurried out, late for an appointment he had not made but which nonetheless he felt obliged to keep. This time the divers had been directed to the San Vito bend. Soneri watched their manoeuvres as they continued to go down and up again, bringing to the surface objects he could not identify. They continued for about an hour before they returned to the harbour with a loaded dinghy. The moment they moored, Motti turned up. Soneri nodded to him and then turned his attention to the boat, watching one of the divers pull back the canvas over the cargo removed from the submerged houseboat. He noted sub-machine guns, rifles, pistols, packages of explosives sealed inside foil, detonators and cables.

'There's enough there to wage a war,' said the maresciallo.

'They were at war.'

'Your intuitions were right. Who'd ever have guessed they had such an arsenal?'

'It's because it's the last place anyone would've thought of looking for such a thing.'

Motti seemed upset. 'I'm sorry,' he said.

'For what?'

'That now that colonel will get the credit even though he's done nothing.'

Soneri shrugged his shoulders. 'I've learned not to give a damn. You can score a goal and still lose the match.'

'Don't tell me you're about to take a penalty.'

'I've placed the ball on the penalty spot, but I might shoot wide.'

The maresciallo smiled. 'I hope you do score.'

They said goodbye to each other and Soneri got into his car. The irregularity of last night left him feeling odd. He seemed to be stumbling about. As he drew near to Parma, he phoned ahead to Monsignor Gorini to say he was arriving.

'I was expecting you,' said the priest to Soneri's surprise when he introduced himself.

This too appeared odd. Everything seemed to fit into an unknown script, but he felt this was a good sign. Events were speeding along, whirling about like water near its outlet. He parked his car some way away as he wanted to walk a little in his own city, incognito. He smiled at the thought of feeling like Odysseus at Ithaca. From Via Cavour, he turned into Strada Duomo. The first sight of the Piazza with its combined Gothic and the Romanesque styles always moved him. He left behind the stone and marble vista to climb the steps of the Episcopal Offices where he was greeted by the silence in the sacristy and the faint scent of candles. The building seemed to bear the weight of centuries, and even Gorini's office had a certain timelessness. The monsignor gave the impression of being a provisional resident. Thousands had sat on that seat before him, and a thousand others would rest there after him.

The prelate pulled out a file. 'Don Amilcare is a humble priest, a gentle, innocent soul,' he explained. 'He's had an extremely important role in this whole affair. He may even have seen himself in that child.'

'Which child?'

'Giovanni Caputo. Aren't you here on his account?'

'Yes, of course, but...'

'He's the one we're dealing with. The Church is close to the humble, to those who come last. Don Amilcare has spoken to me about you, of your determination to give a name to the dead man.'

Soneri moved uncomfortably but had no time to speak before Gorini went on. 'You are, in your own way, a good Christian.'

'Do you mean I'll be saved because of my work?'

'That I can't say,' he replied in that gentle, solemn tone that priests acquire. 'Even if Giovanni was buried unknown to men, he couldn't be to God. That doesn't alter the fact you have done a good, human and civil deed.'

Soneri could not conceal his embarrassment and with a wave of his hand invited Gorini to move beyond that. The priest smiled and opened the folder.

'You know who Gualtiero Gallerani is, don't you?'

Soneri nodded.

'A man who led a somewhat colourful and troubled life in all ways, including, shall we say, the emotional.'

'I know. Carmela was one of his women,' Soneri butted in, in an attempt to hurry the story along.

Gorini looked hard at him, peering over his thick lenses.

'There we are. That's the point I wanted to get to. Giovanni is Gualtiero's son. Did you realise that?'

'It was one of the possibilities I was considering. In fact the most probable.'

'It was kept under wraps for a long time until the opportunity arose. Carmela was being stalked by the family she had fled, while Gualtiero, even if he was a widower, wasn't keen to reveal his paternity, which would've upset the family equilibrium. So Giovanni was brought up by both parents almost in hiding. In fact, quite unseen because that's how it had to be. Do you understand what happened to him?'

Soneri shook his head. 'A life sacrificed at the altar of fear, image and self-interest.'

'Gualtiero, perhaps repentant, wanted to confess before God that he was Giovanni's father.'

'That doesn't show up in the registry,' Soneri noted.

'He wanted to assume responsibility in the eyes of the Church.'

'When the damage was already done. When he was already old and time for bum-clenching anxiety.'

'Don't undervalue an act of repentance,' Gorini exhorted him.

'What repentance!' Soneri snorted. 'It's sheer cowardice confessing only to you, to avoid harming the family interests. Don't you think he should've made a man's life easier rather than deny him his dignity? That would have required real courage. As well as going to Don Amilcare, he should've gone to the Registry Office. Do you think one single, late act of contrition is enough to absolve a man?'

'Gualtiero always loved that son. He never forgot him. Do you know they used to meet each other?'

'Love is never abstract, nor can it be measured in hours.'

'That too is correct, but feelings, even when unexpressed, carry some weight.'

'I prefer those who do good out of a sense of duty rather than those who would like to but do nothing.'

Monsignor Gorini seemed lost in meditation. 'Gualtiero met his son regularly. In the early years, Carmela lived in a house which belonged to the Gallerani family.'

'Via Bassa dei Folli?' Soneri asked.

'I think that's the one,' replied Gorini, flicking through documents without finding what he was looking for. 'Gualtiero often ate with them. They might have looked like a family.'

'It might also have been the only time they were a family.'

'Don Amilcare believed they were. Perhaps Giovanni couldn't remember this. At some point, everything stopped, like the enchantment of childhood itself,' murmured Monsignor Gorini.

'With the boarding school? Was it then?'

Gorini nodded. 'The relationship didn't end but it changed. They saw each other when Carmela picked up her son to keep him with her in the shop before returning him to the boarding school for the night. An hour to talk to each other about various things.'

'One precarious hour, perhaps in the back of a haberdashery,' said Soneri scornfully.

'I know.' Gorini sighed. 'You see what sin leads to? Never mind what we teach at catechism classes. I'm talking about moral, secular sin, something which is true even for non-believers.'

'The real sin is to choose your own self-interest,' said Soneri trenchantly.

Gorini smiled. 'You too are a good Christian.'

Soneri waved the comment aside. 'Why didn't Don Amilcare report all this to me himself?'

'He's a priest of the old school. He would've preferred to tell you, but he learned many details in confession, and you know that in confession...'

'But you are telling me everything.'

'I'm not Don Amilcare. I assume responsibility for the sin of disobedience. The Church overlooks failures if the intention is good. St. Augustine would have forgiven me,' he smiled seraphically.

33

It was early afternoon when Soneri pulled up in Pizzo opposite the Gallerani house. He kept pressing the bell until a wary-looking maid appeared. He asked for Fabio and Rinaldo.

'They're at the slaughterhouse,' she shouted from the doorway, before dashing back in without so much as a greeting.

Ten minutes later Soneri turned into the factory yard where a couple of lorries packed with pigs about to be turned into salami were parked. The stench of blood and butchered flesh which Soneri knew well emanated through the doors. Inside a glass-fronted office which looked like an aquarium, the two brothers were engrossed in a discussion with another man. When the man left, Soneri introduced himself. Fabio gave him a dark look, while Rinaldo timidly stretched out a hand which was as damp and soft as an octopus tentacle. The two brothers put their papers down on the desk, leaned back in their chairs and waited in silence.

'Your houseboat hosted bad company,' were Soneri's opening words.

'We were surprised ourselves. We've just found out,' replied Fabio.

'Don't take me for an idiot,' Soneri roared.

'We'd brought in Boschi, the Viking, to manage the houseboat. Ask him how the weapons ended up there. He had the keys and our full trust. We're in here all day.'

Rinaldo said nothing, but his silence seemed full of anxiety.

Soneri shook his head and smiled as if he did not believe a word. He then turned to Rinaldo. 'The company of which you're sole director rents out places to the camorra.'

'The camorra!' Fabio butted in, seeing his brother's embarrassment.

'River Blues rented a houseboat from Battioni and it was Iosif Milick who went to pick up the keys. He was working for Gennaro

Bovino, a *camorrista* from Portici who was murdered yesterday by a rival gang.'

The two men remained silent. Fabio was perhaps trying to get out of a tight spot and pretend he knew nothing about it. He turned to question his brother. 'Did you know that?' he asked, with phoney surprise.

Rinaldo looked on the point of losing control.

'I was threatened. These are dangerous people.' He struggled with the words, looking painfully and resentfully at Fabio.

'What kind of threat?' asked Soneri.

'They could attack us on many fronts.'

'And you knew nothing about all this?' Soneri said to Fabio.

'I knew nothing about the rental,' he replied in a whisper.

'And the threats?'

'We receive so many, like everyone else who has property.'

'Ah, property,' Soneri sneered. 'There's even a case about that. Your cousin...'

'She's been given her share,' Fabio grunted.

'But there is an unresolved issue.'

Rinaldo looked over at his brother, who remained impassive. 'Our cousin is a jackal. She'd sell her mother down the river for money,' he said.

'I doubt if you can take the moral high ground. Did you know about your father's somewhat eventful life?'

'We couldn't do anything about it. That's the way he was.'

'And you did know he had a son by Carmela Caputo?'

'We knew that he was seeing that woman, but not that her son was his.'

'Did you know the other one, the older one, a bit better?'

Rinaldo turned away tensely, while Fabio reacted with affrontery. 'Who?'

'Gennaro Bovino,' replied Soneri. 'You see how we're back at the starting point.'

'Go on. You explain to him,' said Fabio, drawing back and addressing his brother.

Soneri noticed a growing resentment in Rinaldo's alarmed expression, even if he did not dare rebel. Soneri intervened, not giving him time to speak: 'Maybe you could explain it to me better,' he said to Fabio.

Soneri's confident tone struck home like a burst of rifle fire.

'Me?' he stuttered.

'You knew him well.'

Fabio stayed silent, waiting to see what cards the commissario had in his hand.

'The evening of the bank robbery in Sissa, you were seen with Bovino himself. Really bad luck for you. The carabinieri acquired the footage from the CCTV outside the branch and spotted you in that man's company. The two of you are seen going into the bar under the portico and coming out half an hour later. Bovino then heads off and you walk into the bank shortly before it was robbed by Milick.'

Silence fell once more, but this time it seemed like an admission. Soneri waited patiently until Rinaldo could stand it no longer. 'It's no good,' he said to his brother.

'It's no good denying it,' Soneri went on. 'You've already spouted enough bullshit.'

'What do you want to know? My brother's already told you about the threats,' Fabio burst out.

'Why were they threatening you?'

'Don't you know what these people do? They ask you for money and guarantee they won't touch you, so what do you do? We own houses, fields, factories. Who's going to run the risk? So you give them a few euros so they won't make things a hundred times worse for you.'

'I don't believe they were asking you for protection money,' said Soneri coldly.

'Ah you don't! Nobody is going to protect us here. Bovino had enlisted the catfish fishermen from Eastern Europe. They're ruthless ex-military men. Have you seen the faces on them?'

'Why didn't you report them?'

'What good would it have done? The maresciallo has a

detachment of two, while there are many of them. We'd just have upset them even more.'

'There's a charge already facing you over those weapons. It's a serious matter,' Soneri threatened.

'They've already sunk the houseboat,' Rinaldo moaned.

'There's no reasoning with that lot,' added Fabio.

'Did you just hand over the houseboat and let them get on with their business?'

'They asked if they could use it,' admitted Fabio.

'Bovino, or someone else?'

'It was him. After that I've no idea what went on. In fact, we never set foot on it again.'

'Was that your way of paying them off?'

The two brothers looked at each other, lost and indecisive, before Rinaldo nodded.

'What's going to happen now?' he asked, his voice shaking.

'You'll have to deal with the carabinieri. It's their case,' said Soneri, as he took his leave.

As soon as he got into his car, he took a call from Signora Falchieri. 'I do take chances with you, but I'm not wrong. Colonel Lucentini has reported everything to me. I told him that it was your hunch to search the houseboat under water, but you know what he's like.'

'It doesn't matter.'

'Are you thinking of something else?'

'Of how life must have been for Caputo, a man rejected by everybody. An unseen man.'

'You're obsessed by him.'

'I'd like permission to hear from his partner, that Lorette who lived with him in Rue Maupassant in Toulouse.'

'What good would it do?'

'It would be interesting to find out what contact Caputo had with the Gallerani family, and if they spoke to each other from France.'

'I don't understand. What's Caputo got to do with the Galleranis?'

'Caputo was Gualtiero's son.'

'Ah,' said Falchieri, clearly taken aback. 'That opens up a new scenario.'

'And above all it reveals a web of different interests.'

'And also possible motives. You always did believe there was more to it.'

'Yes, ever since I saw a shattered skull.'

'Which one? Another one?'

'It was part of a crime committed thousands of years ago.'

'I'm never going to understand you! But I will seek authorisation for you to speak to this Lorette.'

Soneri then called Juvara and asked him to find the number of Lorette Martignon. He spelt out the address, Rue Maupassant 11, Toulouse, and guaranteed that he would shortly receive final authorisation. A quarter of an hour later, the inspector got back to him with what he wanted. Soneri wrote it all down in a notebook and set off for Angela's office in Via delle Fonderie. She was surprised to see him.

'Do you have some urgent need of a female lawyer?' she asked.

'Extremely urgent, specifically of one who speaks perfect French.'

Angela gave him a disappointed look. 'I'd hoped for something better.'

'Here in your office? Perhaps with a client in the waiting room?'

Angela's glowered at him. 'Alright, tell me what you want.'

'I would like you to call Lorette Martignon, Caputo's ex-partner,' he said, handing over the page with the number.

She sighed. 'What do I have to ask for this time?'

'Whether Caputo had dealings with people in Sissa or thereabouts. If possible, with whom exactly.'

'Do you think she'll tell me? I can handle men easily enough, but women aren't my strong point.'

Angela dialled the number and began talking. Soneri listened in without understanding very much but appreciating the musicality of the French, reminding him of some *chansons* by Georges Brassens. When Angela hung up, he waited quietly for her to speak.

'This Lorette is very nice. She says she knows Verdi's territory quite well.'

'So she's been to the Po valley as well?'

'Yes, three times with Caputo. He wanted to show her his part of the country.'

'Did they meet the Gallerani family?'

'On all three occasions, they stopped off in Parma to see Elvira. Later, however, Caputo went on his own.'

'Does she know who he saw?'

'She wasn't able to tell me, but she presumes Elvira. They phoned each other quite often. After Gualtiero Gallerani died, their relationship became more intense. Even though she and Caputo were no longer together, they kept in touch.'

'Did she say why Elvira in particular?'

'I did ask her but she didn't know. She said he was a bit vague about it. Once he'd alluded to something in common, perhaps something of mutual interest.'

Soneri thought this over. Might Caputo's last meeting before disappearing have been with Elvira? Might that be why he was told that a trustworthy person would pick him up at the clinic, instead it was Andalò's new girlfriend who turned up, perhaps to put people like Bosi who had seen them leave, off the track?

Angela looked at him in some perplexity, unsure whether he was deep in thought or had had a stroke. He shook himself and went over to give her a hug. Overcome by that unexpected show of affection, she kissed him and both were overcome by desire, all the keener because so sudden. They made love on the table, like two teenagers taking full advantage of their parents' absence, and afterwards laughed off that sudden impulse.

'The office door wasn't locked. Anyone could have just walked in,' Angela said.

'They would have seen you without your gown.'

'Rather, they would have seen you with your weapon unsheathed.'

'When are you coming back to the Po?' Soneri asked.

'I'm a bit busy these days. I could ask you the same question.'

'It won't be for much longer, but then the holidays are over.'

He left her office and walked along the Via delle Fonderie, looking down at the riverside where so many species coexisted in the urban zoo, and at the people congregated there, leaning their elbows on the parapets. He called Elvira Gallerani, observing as he did so old Parma on the far side with its pale yellow bell towers, turrets and cupolas. In the midst of the densely-packed houses, he imagined Elvira's apartment, where the phone continued ringing. He tried the Portuguese number, and this time had better luck.

'I think you need to hurry back to Parma,' he announced.

'What's happened?' she asked apprehensively.

'It's to do with Caputo's death.'

He heard a deep sigh, and then Elvira continued in a relieved tone of voice. 'I thought something had happened to my daughter.'

'Your daughter's involved as well, but I believe she's in good health.'

'Can you tell me what this is about?'

'Some matters need to be clarified.'

'Is that all?'

'As far as you're concerned, they can't be so easily dismissed.'

'I still don't understand. I was about to come back in any case. I have one or two things to attend to. We could meet tomorrow afternoon.'

'I think that you need to attend to your family's concerns first,' was Soneri's cryptic reply, hanging up without waiting for her to answer.

34

Anyone could see it was Saturday from the commotion at the jetty. Every weekend, the nautical port was in frenzied activity as people arrived from the city, and boats in the dry dock were lowered into the water either by little cranes or chutes. Those which had been moored went spluttering out. A tractor moved up and down dragging boats to the river while from the dock a chorus of tools struck up their own tuneless music. All around, there were scenes of rubbing, painting and hammering as if it were a ritual prelude to the feast when the river folk celebrated their union with the Po, or came down to its banks as though to meet a lover.

Soneri emerged for his breakfast. He had learned from Marisa that the Galleranis had been in the carabinieri offices for hours, well into the night and that they been accompanied by a lawyer. This was the sole topic of conversation at the club, but no-one had any idea what the two brothers had said. Extravagant and contradictory versions were bandied about, but they only produced a fog as thick as that on the river. The commissario was the object of curiosity for the bar's *habitués*, but once he replied he knew nothing about it, their questioning slowly gave way to disappointment. When Soneri realised that they suspected he knew more than he was letting on, he escaped to his car.

He set off in the direction of Parma, and half an hour later parked in Via Italo Pizzo. He went over what could have occurred: Gualtiero's death which had sparked a race for the inheritance, Elvira's aspirations, the threats, the blackmail with the DNA tests and finally the compromise. Was it possible Caputo too had wanted his share?

He rang the bell and Elvira spoke over the intercom in an imperious tone: 'Come on up!'

She greeted him in the drawing room. She maintained her

ferocious, catlike sensuality but was worried about her untidy appearance. 'I got back last night,' she said in apology.

Soneri scowled to convey it was of no importance, which seemed to disappoint her.

'Well then, do you want to tell me what's been going on?'

'You knew that Giovanni was Gualtiero Gallerani's son,' Soneri began, in a tone brooking no contradiction.

Elvira agreed but remained impassive.

'You discovered you were half brother and sister. Was that why you saw each other so frequently?'

'Not in the slightest! Why should we have cared about that?'

'Then why? He lived in France and you were travelling all over the world. However, he might have been a rival for the inheritance, maybe even with a stronger claim than you.'

'You underestimate me. You think I'm a cynical, cold-hearted woman. I don't deny it. We all have to fight our own corner, but a person can also show generosity and fellow-feeling. I felt sorry for Giovanni. He'd been badly treated, but so had I, to some extent. I thought it right that we get our revenge.'

'Do you mean the inheritance?'

'What else!' Elvira exploded. 'It's what would enrage him more than anything else.'

'You mean 'them,' don't you? There are two of them,' Soneri corrected her.

Elvira shrugged her shoulders. 'Rinaldo doesn't count. He's a pathetic soul with no balls. In his own way, he too is a victim.'

Soneri agreed. 'Fabio's in charge.'

'Like Gualtiero with my father!' shouted Elvira. 'You have no idea of the unhappiness that man created. My father died humiliated. He's replicated the same relationship between his sons.'

'If Gualtiero is your father, it seems he has transmitted something of his character to you.'

The woman glowered at him with hatred. 'I've learned that in this life you either dominate or are dominated, and I had no intention of ending up like Rinaldo. I don't know if I have Gualtiero's DNA but I wouldn't rule it out. I took the risk so as to scare Fabio, and knowing his father he really was scared. But when all's said and done, I hope it wasn't Gualtiero who got my mother pregnant.'

'So did you put Giovanni up to claiming a share of the inheritance?'

'Certainly. The Galleranis have to stop playing about at other people's expense, having children and then hiding them away in a boarding school.'

'Did he agree to file a claim?'

'At the outset, he didn't want to. Years of humiliation had left him with no self-esteem, and he always reacted by running away. He wanted to forget everything, but his childhood ghosts pursued him everywhere.'

'So he changed his mind?'

'Yes. I proposed a joint action, and in the end he was persuaded. He said that with me at his side, he felt more secure.'

'Had you already chosen the lawyer?'

'We had some idea, but then he... you know the rest.'

'Was it you who organised that strange journey from the clinic to Parma?'

For the first time, Elvira looked agitated. 'Well, the other time, when you asked me, I lied to you. Seeing how everything had gone, I wanted to keep out of it. I was tired of squabbles after months of law cases. I was about to get the money and Giovanni had disappeared.'

'Are you sure you're telling me the truth this time?'

'Do you believe I'm so devious?'

'I don't believe anything, but I take nothing for granted.'

'My ex-husband and I came to an agreement. We thought that our daughter would attract less attention. If I went, as I'd already accepted a compromise, I would have been bound to arouse suspicion and the clinic would have alerted the Galleranis. My husband didn't know Giovanni but he was well known in the town. On the other hand, my daughter had always lived in the city or down in the valley so nobody knew who she was.'

'But in the event it was your ex-husband's partner who went along.'

'At the end of the day, it was better that way. She has nothing to do with me.'

'What happened next, when Giovanni arrived in Parma?'

'We met up. It seemed more discreet to meet in a café near my old address. I brought Giovanni here to my house where there was a lawyer waiting for us. We drew up proposals to submit to Fabio to resolve the case.'

'Money, quotas, shares?'

'Exactly. We asked him for one half of the inheritance. I would have given up the money they had offered me not to take the DNA test, but together we would have obtained much more. I was desperate to see Fabio's reaction.'

'Did you really need all that subterfuge? Picking up Giovanni at the clinic, meeting in a bar...?'

'Giovanni had run out of money and didn't know where to go. After leaving France, he more or less lived like a tramp, and anyway, as I was saying, it was better if we weren't seen together. That claim came as a shock, even if Fabio had already been arranging things in his favour.'

'In what sense?'

'Gualtiero hadn't left a will, then out of nowhere two turned up!'

'And what did they say?'

'More or less the same thing. Fabio was to receive two thirds of the property with the rest going to Rinaldo. One was immediately discarded because it was a crude imitation of Gualtiero's handwriting. The other one required more time but finally it too was judged by an expert to be a forgery.'

'What happened after the meeting with your lawyer?'

'I got accommodation for Giovanni in a bed & breakfast run by a friend of mine not far from here. We agreed to meet the following day to decide on a strategy after we'd handed over our papers, but that morning my friend told me he'd left.'

'Without saying anything?'

'Yes.'

'What do you think happened?'

'All this took place on Tuesday. We were supposed to meet again with the lawyer on Thursday to confront the two brothers. We wanted to settle without having to go to court.'

'Did Caputo show up there?'

'Not there either. I found myself on my own, me with my lawyer on one side and Fabio with his on the other.'

'Wasn't Rinaldo there?'

'No, we were told he wasn't well.'

'How did your demands go down with Fabio?'

'He got into a rage. You can guess the words he said to me and what he said about my mother. He went so far as to threaten to make me pay for all this.'

'How long did it take you to come to an agreement?'

'A couple of months, I think. As soon as the judge fixed a date for the examination you know about.'

'So it was autumn.'

'Late November, if memory serves.'

'And in all that time, you never wondered what became of Giovanni?'

'I assumed he'd returned to France to arrange his affairs or to draw a line under the whole business. After all, right up till the last moment, he'd been hesitating and I'd had to drag him along. I was actually quite resentful about him disappearing like that. I considered it ungrateful.'

'You didn't suspect anything? When the body was pulled out of the water, didn't it occur to you that it might be him?'

'I have told you that I spend a large part of the year abroad. And they didn't exactly put up posters. It must have appeared in the newspapers when I was away.'

'You've already lied to me once about your time abroad,' Soneri pointed out to her. 'You told me you were in Portugal that August when Caputo disappeared.'

'I've already told you why I lied. I was sick of the whole business.'

Soneri fell silent. Once again he found himself facing a brick wall. 'Who is this friend who put Caputo up?'

'Her name is Olga Ricci, 11 Borgo Marodolo. Her bed & breakfast is called La Cuccia.'

Soneri took his leave. Borgo Marodolo was on the other side of the river, so he decided to walk along the Lungoparma until he reached Via Imbriani. Borgo Marodolo was then first on the right. Initially, Olga Ricci took him for a tourist, but when Soneri introduced himself she turned serious.

'Your friend Elvira Gallerani sent you a guest, Giovanni Caputo, the subject of my enquiries.'

She sat down at her computer and put her hand on the mouse. 'In recent weeks?' she asked as she started to click on entries.

'No, August three and a half years ago,' Soneri replied.

Olga turned to him in surprise, then resumed her search. After a few minutes, she came up with something. 'Ah, the Frenchman! Here we are: 11 Rue Maupassant, Toulouse. That was the night of 4th August three years ago.'

'You remember him?'

'Yes, a somewhat awkward character, who rolled his 'R' like the French. We chatted about the Po and the valley because I'm from those parts as well, Roccabianca.'

'Did he say where he'd be going the day he left?'

'No, nothing at all.'

'What do you remember about him?'

'I've just told you. We spoke about the Po and the places we come from.'

'Nothing else? Did he have breakfast before he set off? Did he say goodbye, or did he leave early?'

'It was so long ago,' Olga murmured as she searched her memory. She browsed her computer once more. 'No, it would appear he didn't have breakfast. I draw up a list every day, making a note of the guests. See,' she said, proudly showing him the screen on which dates and annotations came up. Olga then stopped, transfixed, as though she did not understand something. Soneri saw she was pointing with one finger at the 8th October. The 6th and 7th were not there. 'Ah! That's the year I came down with an intestinal virus,' she stuttered.

Soneri frowned. 'Well, it's passed now.'

'Yes but now I remember I had to close for two days and move bookings elsewhere, because I could hardly stand and that morning...'

'You didn't prepare breakfast for your guests,' Soneri completed the sentence.

'I remember being relieved when that man left quietly. I hadn't slept a wink that night. I heard him receive a phone call at about half past six, after which he got up and went out. You see, I live upstairs and I hear everything.'

'So he left at about seven o'clock.'

'More or less. I went over to the window to see if he wanted a *caffèlatte* but he was already halfway up the street. Shortly after, he got into a black car waiting for him at the junction with Via Imbriani.'

'Can you remember what make it was?'

'I don't know about these things, but some days later, joking with the barman in Via Imbriani about the virus that had struck us both the same day, it emerged that he'd noticed that car, and he knows about these things.'

'Did he tell you what kind of car it was?'

'A woman's name.'

'Mercedes?'

'That was it. Mercedes. Like Mercedes of Orleans, the unhappy queen of Spain who died when she was only eighteen. You see, I used to teach history.'

Soneri left and made for the bar. It had changed hands a year previously and there were screens on the walls and deafening music blaring out. The two young men who now ran it were unable to tell him where the previous owner could be found.

As he walked away, Soneri wondered where Caputo could have been heading for after receiving that call. Was it an unexpected call, or one he had been waiting for? He took out his mobile and dialled Falchieri's number. Without waiting for him to speak, she blurted out: 'The Galleranis have admitted something, but they are hard nuts to crack. Rinaldo is totally under his brother's thumb. He acts as the lackey.'

'Did Lucentini give you a briefing?'

'Yes. For now, it looks like we're only talking about aiding and abetting a crime. Do you think there's more to it?'

'Could be,' replied Soneri vaguely. 'I'll be clearer when I've seen the phone records.'

'In whose name?'

'Caputo and Gallerani.'

'Whenever you wish, I'm at your disposal.'

35

Signora Falchieri had left out a dossier for him containing the courtroom printouts reserved for the criminal division of the police force. The on-duty officers were taken aback when they saw him turn up but fortunately it was Saturday and the offices were about to close. The officers would shortly be off home, so Soneri was left in peace to get on with his work. He opened the dossier and began looking at the telephone records, concentrating on the 5th August, the day of the presumed disappearance. The call Olga had mentioned had come from a bar in Sissa, the Centrale in the Piazza. Of greatest interest was the route mapped out by the transmitter masts linked to Caputo's mobile. The last two were in the Sissa area, but that could cover a vast, perhaps partly overlapping, area. They might indicate Giovanni's last journey. That was where he had to look. Everything led back to that starting point, around the dark navel of the river.

He got back into his car and set off. As he drove along, he received a call from Adelaide. Milick was semi-conscious and she had got him to say something. From his somewhat confused utterances she had understood that once Fabio Gallerani heard about the legal action he asked Bovino to intimidate Caputo into renouncing his inheritance. His cousin had increased his fears when she told him she had got Caputo involved. Soneri connected that information with something the Prosecutor's Office had just passed on to him: Giovanni had received calls from phones using sim cards which turned out to be Romanian. According to Milick, Elvira too had been threatened, but she must have been too difficult even for a *camorrista*.

Adelaide said: 'He didn't manage to say it, but gave me to understand he thought it was Bovino who murdered that man.'

'Is he sure?'

'No, he lapsed into a state of unconsciousness. Unfortunately, that's the way it is. The doctor says there's no way of knowing when he would become more stable.'

The vagaries of Milick's memory paralleled the sequence of events surrounding Caputo: momentary light was followed by sudden darkness, like a mist hanging over the Po Valley, sometimes phosphorescent in the sunlight, at others dense and thick.

He stopped in Viarolo, at the *Cavalier Gelmino* restaurant sign. The moment he saw it, his stomach took control. He really had to prepare thoroughly for an afternoon which promised to be decisive. Motti had informed him the Galleranis' second interrogation would start at four o'clock in the carabinieri station, and better to go to that kind of appointment on a full stomach. He imagined the meal would be in the same order as the interrogation. *Culatello* in pastry as the tasty *hors d'oeuvre* where the clues were set out, then *tortelli di zucca* where the charges were laid and finally veal cheek with the evidence put on the table. The rest was unclear. Would there be a confession as dessert? Or would everything end with a *liquore* to deaden the bitterness of vanishing certainties? He rose from the table consumed by doubt. Back in his car, he wondered if Elvira had been lying again. Had she used Caputo as a battering-ram to demolish Fabio Gallerani's self-confidence, or had she genuinely pitied him, her possible half-brother? There was no way he could work it out.

He parked near the carabinieri station and took out his mobile. He had many calls to make: to the Viking, Marisa, Pezzani and Landini. He asked them all if the Galleranis owned or had ever owned a black Mercedes, but none of them was able to give him an answer, so in disappointment, he made his way into the carabinieri station. The officer at the desk informed him that the men under investigation were already in the maresciallo's office, and there he found Lucentini and one silent attendant. Fabio and Rinaldo were seated against the wall facing the window, the former looking angry and the latter seemingly staring through the window at the mist and the falling darkness. Alongside them sat a little, balding man with a thin moustache and a mousey face who was introduced as Leoni, their lawyer

'Well then,' Lucentini began, in a peremptory, official tone which irritated Soneri. 'You have already admitted to having contacts with Bovino and his gang. Now explain more clearly the nature of these contacts.'

Fabio shifted nervously. 'But we've already told you everything.'

The lawyer threw him a conciliatory glance, an invitation to stay calm and to collaborate.

'They made threats and asked for money. With all those foreigners taking over on the Po and elsewhere.'

'Did you pay up? And if so, when?'

'Not exactly. We did them some favours to keep them quiet. If you don't protect us...' Fabio protested.

'Such as renting houseboats through one of your companies and made available to the gang? Or even handing over the family houseboat for them to use as an arsenal?'

'They requested our place for the winter months to provide accommodation for the foreigners who weren't returning home. They could hardly stay in tents.'

'And you gave the boss more comfortable lodgings,' intervened Soneri.

It was only then that Rinaldo seemed shaken. He turned his eyes from the window and looked straight at the commissario.

Fabio tried to play the matter down. 'He only went there occasionally. It had been empty for a long time.'

'A house filled with memories,' Soneri emphasised, seeing the two brothers grow more nervous.

'What's this got to do with it?' jumped in the lawyer, as though addressing a jury.

Lucentini, who did not understand what was going on, raised his hand to restore calm. 'Let's move on. How long have you had these contacts?'

'A couple of years,' replied Fabio vaguely.

'You must realise it seems odd you didn't know what was being hidden in your houseboat. You used to go there, didn't you? We know you were often down on the Po.'

For the first time Fabio seemed embarrassed. He gave a hostile look at his brother as though he were an obstacle in his path.

'He was manager of the company which let out the houseboat,' he replied, pointing to him dismissively. 'It was him they told to keep away from it.'

Lucentini then turned to Rinaldo, trembling slightly as though a pistol was pointed at him. 'They did tell me to leave it to them for a while,' he confirmed.

'And you obeyed?'

He shrugged his shoulders in an eloquent gesture, while Fabio looked at him out of the corner of his eye.

'They had the keys. They told me they'd give them back once they fixed up certain things.'

'Ah, certainly, and we now know what these things were,' the colonel said, raising his voice. 'And you had no idea! You knew who Bovino was, didn't you?'

'What was I to do?' Rinaldo replied, with some candour.

Soneri intervened again to address Fabio: 'Your brother didn't have sole responsibility for the house in Bassa dei Folli, did he?'

'No, but so what?' Fabio replied defiantly.

'Then it's no good you trying to wriggle free.'

Leoni jumped in once again. 'That is a quite unnecessary insinuation.'

Soneri took no notice, and turned to Rinaldo. 'You realise the trouble you're in?'

'That's enough of these underhand methods,' Leoni said.

Soneri desisted, confident he had achieved his first objective of sowing anxiety and suspicion between the two brothers.

The lawyer said: 'My clients are here in good faith. They gave in to pressure and threats and were forced to allow the gang the use of one of their properties and to rent out a property to third parties via a shell company.'

'Is that your declaration?' Lucentini asked.

'I will make it formal in two days' time and make everything available to the magistrate,' Leoni replied.

'There's still the inheritance,' Soneri added. 'There was the legal case which Caputo was also involved in before he disappeard.'

'What do you mean?' the lawyer hissed.

'That there's more to it,' Soneri went on. 'And we can't say it had nothing to do with the relations between your clients and Bovino.'

Leoni cut him off angrily. 'For the last hour, you've done nothing but make insinuations. None of us here has any time to waste. If you have any proper questions, speak up, and if not I consider this discussion closed.'

'Don't pretend you don't know. You know perfectly well about the case between your clients and their cousin, which ended in agreement. Caputo was fully involved as Gualtiero Gallerani's son.'

The lawyer was taken aback. Perhaps he knew only one part of the story. The two brothers on the other hand remained silent, but Rinaldo seemed on the point of blurting out something.

After a theatrical pause, Soneri continued. 'And then Caputo disappeared.'

'And so?' said Leoni.

'Elvira Gallerani had only suspected he was Gualtiero's son, but Caputo was certain. You get it?' Soneri's voice was calm.

'He killed himself. There's no proof to the contrary.'

'But neither is there any proof of suicide. Quite the reverse. The amount of water in his lungs was not enough to confirm drowning, and the wound on his head was compatible with a previously inflicted blow as much as with a collision after a fall. Furthermore, your clients had taken on a man like Bovino as mediator with Caputo.'

Leoni tried to make a covert sign to the brothers but Soneri noticed.

'Did you think Bovino had great diplomatic skills, or maybe he could use other means?'

This time the lawyer turned openly to the brothers, inviting them to join in. 'I'm a criminal lawyer,' he stated in some embarrassment. 'I have a colleague who attended to these matters.'

'I think you're going to have to attend to this matter as well,' replied Soneri calmly.

A deep silence fell in the room. Motti and Lucentini exchanged puzzled glances. Leoni was looking for a way out but seemed in the dark. Fabio was boiling with rage and Rinaldo had started to shake as though struck by an electric bolt, but it was he who broke the tense silence.

'It was Bovino,' he said, speaking in a low voice. 'He murdered him.'

His brother looked at him askance, and for the first time seemed to approve. There was even a hint of admiration.

'Did you ask him to do it?' Soneri asked.

'No,' burst in Rinaldo. 'We only asked him to convince him to abandon the case,' he went on, using the plural.

'Convince him?' repeated Soneri with a provocative smile.

'Something like that.' Rinaldo was plainly embarrassed. 'Anyway, just convince him.'

'By beating him up?'

'He was a beast!' Rinaldo finally blurted out. 'All we wanted was him to put the frighteners on him.'

'You could have struck a deal, as you did with your cousin.'

'With her you could do things on the quiet,' he muttered.

'But not with Caputo,' said Soneri, returning to the attack. 'He reappeared, he came home and you knew everything.'

Fabio's voice rang out. 'It was that snake who convinced him. She turned him against us to force us to pay. We couldn't allow her to blacken our father's name after what she had done to her own mother. She used Caputo to put pressure on us.'

'And you,' said Soneri looking squarely at Fabio, 'really cared so deeply about your father's reputation?'

The tone was so insinuating that Fabio struggled to contain his anger, but his expression was one of hatred. He stared hard at him, his eyes aflame.

Leoni intervened. 'Leave their feelings out of it. You have no right to interfere.'

Rinaldo's hands were trembling like those of an old man. Fabio raised his voice. 'Of course I cared deeply about it.'

'Feelings!' Soneri replied sarcastically. 'I doubt if they have any part in this business.'

'My father had many defects,' said Fabio, who spoke as though his brother was not there, 'but he was an honest man. It's not right to defame him because of an error in bed.'

'Error?' repeated Soneri. 'When all's said and done, your mother was dead and he had every right to remake a life for himself. So had Carmela Caputo. Two widowed people who met each other. However, that affair with his sister-in-law...'

'Bovino was bitter about Caputo,' Rinaldo burst out, ignoring Soneri's last remark. 'He was outraged with his mother because she had left the family and he couldn't accept he had a half-brother.'

'Neither could you two,' said Soneri.

'That's why he murdered him,' Rinaldo murmured, as though trying to convince himself.

Fabio glanced again at his brother, as if to ensure he had not lost control.

'Or is that why you wanted him dead?' asked Soneri.

'Enough of these insinuations,' exclaimed Leoni. 'Statements without proof are mere slander.'

Soneri was afraid he had gone too far and tried to pull back. 'It's only a hypothesis.'

The lawyer was right. There was no proof of any kind.

That false step halted any headway in the interrogation. Like a train reaching its destination, Soneri felt the impact of the crash against the buffers. The lawyer rose to his feet, as did the two brothers. The three made their exit without saying a word. They nodded only to Motti and Lucentini, ignoring Soneri.

'You really got under their skin,' said the maresciallo when they were on their own. 'Do you really believe it was Bovino?'

'It's the most obvious solution, don't you think?'

Motti agreed.

'And I have never believed unduly in obvious solutions. Too often they're false, but this one is plausible. And even people who put across a false image are not always liars,' Soneri concluded, before going out into the evening mist.

36

Soneri drove into Torricella as dusk was falling. His mood was dark too, and as he got out of his car, he saw the club lights surrounded by an opaque halo. He had no wish to face the usual clientele, the questions and the often phoney tales, even if he did still relish the charming misty evenings in that bright little corner on the riverbanks. When he was outside his abode, something took shape in the stillness of the night. Soneri felt his heart skip until he recognised the moustache – it was Casimiro.

'I've been waiting for you for over an hour,' he said.

'Come in. It's cold.'

'No, I'd rather talk here. Don't switch on the light.'

'Are you afraid?'

'Prudent.'

'In regard to what?'

'This town is full of people you can't trust. They're not wicked people. It's just that they go along with whoever's in charge. You never know. Do you remember how my father met his end?'

'Bovino is dead.'

'Yes, he is, but the Galleranis are not.'

'What have you got to fear from them?'

'They're powerful and provide work for everybody.'

'And why should they bother you?'

'Because of what I'm going to tell you.'

'Go on.'

'That car, the one you phoned everybody about.'

'The Mercedes?'

'Yes, that one. The Viking called it that as well.'

'Did it really exist? Did it belong to someone?'

'It was Rinaldo's.'

'Doesn't he have it any more?'

'I haven't seen it for a while.'

'Are you sure?'

'I heard the Viking say he's traded it in. I was in the club when you called.'

'Did he say what's become of it?'

'I didn't understand, because shortly afterwards he lowered his voice. Anyway, that one will never say anything. He works for the Galleranis here on the Po. That's how he makes his living.'

Soneri started thinking, and Casimiro took advantage of the pause to take his leave. 'I'd better be getting back to my tree trunk house,' he said before vanishing into the dark.

He went into his house and took out his mobile. That revelation had set his mind spinning.

'Hello, Juvara?'

'Hello sir. Are you back from your holidays?'

'No, but I'll be back on duty again.'

'From Saturday?'

'No, from Monday, but it's just like I was already there. In any case, I need to know about a Mercedes, whose model and number plate I don't know but whose owner I do know. His name is Rinaldo Gallerani. It you don't find that name right away, try Fabio or Gualtiero.'

'I'll try with the national car register.'

'And listen, one other thing,' Soneri began after a pause, but he had waited too long and the inspector had already hung up.

It occurred to him that he should try and check Bovino's movements. If he'd killed Caputo, he might have left some trace. Perhaps the Romanian telephone records would have to be checked, or else go over the boat found smashed against the breakwater in Stagno with a fine comb.

He picked up his phone again and called Signora Falchieri.

'Any news?' she asked.

'I'll be more certain tomorrow,' was Soneri's uncertain reply.

He heard a peal of laughter at the other end of the line. 'Where have I heard that before?'

'We're getting closer all the time.'

'I hope so. I've got some news, and I was just about to call you. It's to do with those phone printouts.'

'What do you mean?'

'The transmitter mast Caputo's mobile was linked to that last time has been identified with greater precision.'

'And which one is it?'

'Here we are. The transmitter mast is the one at Bosco Piazza in Lombardy, just over the left bank. It's not the one at Sissa, although there's a partial overlap into the same zone.'

'So that means Caputo was closer to the river than to the town.'

'So it would seem.'

Soneri ran over in his mind the now well-defined geographical area in which everything had presumably unfolded. He thought of the registry in Sissa where they had lost all trace of that human who had ended in the Po, of Pizzo where the Gallerani family resided and of the house in Via Bassa dei Folli where Carmela had lived with the baby Giovanni, where Gualtiero made frequent visits and where, perhaps, they had been a family for a short time. Certainly it was the zone nearest the embankment and the only one which could have been linked to the transmitter mast at Bosco Piazza.

'This explains so many things,' Soneri said, as though in a dream.

'Which things?' the prosecutor asked.

'Where the murder took place,' he said without thinking.

'If I didn't know you, I'd say you were bragging, but experience has taught me to take you more seriously. Should I prepare an arrest warrant? But you'll need to tell me first in whose name.'

'The degree of accuracy is now almost certain, but I distrust reality too much to be totally sure.'

'You're quite right, but I feel we'll be in touch again soon.'

Soneri flopped down on a chair next to the table. He had not switched on the light and only a faint brightness came from the club. A boat sailed by, shaking the houseboat and projecting the light along its sides through the windows. He was about to sink into sleep when he saw the screen of his mobile light up. He read the name D'Onofrio and answered.

'What did I tell you?' He said crowing like a cock at dawn.

In a daze, Soneri mumbled, 'Tell me what?'

'What do you mean – tell you what? About the war between the camorra families! You've got the first death there. I told you they would eliminate Bovino. I know all about this lot.'

'The problem is whose weapons they were. Were they Bovino's? Was that the reason he wanted to hide them so they wouldn't fall into rival hands, or did these rivals act in reprisal to show everyone who was in command?'

'You need to get to the bottom of that,' replied D'Onofrio. 'In the first camorra war three years ago, it seemed that the Bovino side was losing.'

'Three years ago?'

'Yes, there was a shootout at Portici, and two people on the Bovino side were killed. That was the beginning. Then they got another four of them. A slaughter that wiped them out.'

'And Carmine was involved?'

'Your guess! They interrogated him but he's always denied it.'

'When did this happen? And when did they interrogate him?'

'I'd have to look up the records, but it was three years ago. All I can say is that it was summer.'

'Could you find the exact date when he was questioned?'

'Give me time to look it up.'

Soneri hung up. His mind was spinning again, all trace of torpor gone. He stood there for few minutes in the dark until his mobile started vibrating once more.

'I've got the information on that car, sir.'

'Whose is it now?'

'No-one's. It was scrapped three years ago. We're talking about a Mercedes 180 diesel.'

Soneri digested this information. A perfect fit, everything matching.

'Was it in Rinaldo's name?'

'He was sole owner.'

Soneri thanked the inspector but he had scarcely put the phone down when it began vibrating again.

'You're a lucky man to have a colleague like me in a police station free of fog,' D'Onofrio began jovially.

'But you send all your problems up here for us to deal with,' Soneri replied.

'You wanted to know when he was arrested and questioned. He was brought into the station the night of the 4th of August and was released in the afternoon of the following day.'

'You're sure?'

D'Onofrio reacted with a touch of annoyance. 'Listen, mate, what are you implying? That I'm just gibbering on?'

'I meant to say, this information is of great importance. Decisive, I might even say.'

'Glad to hear it. Next time you're in Naples, you owe me a dinner.'

He heard a knock on the door. He jumped to his feet in alarm and asked who it was. He heard Landini's voice and the next moment he was standing in front of him. He had a bottle in one hand and a bag in the other. 'I'm on my own, and so are you,' he said.

'There's nowhere you can be so alone as on the Po.'

'No-one's more alone than a man on the river,' Landini agreed. 'That's why I came. Nobody's keen on being left to himself all the time.'

He put the bottle down on the table and opened his bag to take out a salami, some bread and a jar of mushrooms in oil.

'It's a pity not to have company when you're eating,' he said, laying everything out.

They chatted about the river and navigation, about his past as a maritime pilot, about the risks of travelling at two hundred kilometres an hour on the surface of the water. 'I had behind me a twelve cylinder, six hundred horsepower Lamborghini engine,' he explained. 'If you capsize at that speed the water is like marble.'

Eventually the conversation turned to the events concerning the Galleranis and Bovino's murder.

'You know, when I saw that man's photo in the papers, I thought I recognised him.'

'Have you seen him around here?'

'On one of these houseboats. Remember me telling you that I'd accidentally witnessed a nasty encounter somewhere along the banks of the Polesine?'

Soneri nodded.

'Well, I think one of the men I caught sight of was him, the *camorrista*.'

'Could well be,' was all Soneri would say. 'That could be why they ripped the pages out of your logbook.'

They ate in silence. Landini had brought all manner of *salume* – *salami*, *culatello*, *prosciutto*, *culaccia*, *coppa*, *pancetta* and other delicacies.

'Nobody wants fat salami or fat women any more. Their loss,' he said stuffing a waxy, pink-striped slice into his mouth as though it were water from a fountain.

'In your opinion, what was Caputo doing on board the launch?' asked Soneri, referring to the remains of the ticket found in his waterproof jacket.

'How would I know?'

'Didn't you know him a bit?'

'Not in the slightest! I'm from Boretto. I know a lot of people, but I'd never seen him.'

'They think a lot of you in the club, as they do of everyone who knows about engines and navigation. When you speak, it's like you're the bishop.'

Landini turned defensive. 'Don't exaggerate. You know the way it is. Around here, engines are like divinity. There are some folk that go on the water and some that plough the fields.'

'Would you do me a favour?'

'If I can.'

'After dinner, drop into the club and tell them that you've been told that tomorrow morning the carabinieri are going to search the Gallerani house in Via Bassa dei Folli.'

'Is that true?'

Soneri shrugged his shoulders and leaned his head to one side. Landini looked down at the floor and seemed to be considering the matter.

'Come to think of it, there's no need for you to state it with certainty. It's enough to make them think it's a probability.' He seemed to be trying to convince himself. 'No, nothing certain.'

'But you might all be going?'

'We might. Not necessarily tomorrow morning.'

'Then when?'

'Maybe even sooner,' was Soneri's cryptic reply.

37

Landini closed the door and Soneri listened to his steps as he walked towards the jetty. He settled down to wait, like a hunter hiding in a shooting box. He turned off the light and tried to rest. Time slowed down and seemed to move in pace with the river. He was dropping off when once again the screen of his mobile lit up.

'It's been a while since I had to spend a weekend on my own,' Angela grumbled.

'If everything goes according to plan, we'll have dinner together tomorrow evening in Alceste's.'

She gave a groan, clearly disgruntled.

'Ragu has written to me. This time he's definitely gone.'

'Where to?'

'Abroad, but he didn't tell me where. I'll let you read the letter, a farewell note full of anger.'

'People of his age find it easier to make a getaway. They have less of everything.'

'They start to get cheated when they're still in the playground. And their parents don't even notice.'

'There's not much difference between Ragu and Caputo,' reflected Soneri, suddenly struck by the parallels.

'What do you have in mind?' asked Angela.

'The fact there's only one thing at the bottom of everything. Now I understand why that lad came to me.'

'Stop sounding like some astrology column.'

They share the same fate. Ragu and Caputo are linked by the same destiny. Rejected as children and rejected by society. Rage and indifference were their mother and father, but in spite of that they wanted to be loved.'

'But they couldn't manage to show love because they'd never received it,' she replied. 'Reading between the lines, Ragu tried to be grateful to me, but he lacked the means to express it.'

'They're wrecks left to go under. We're reduced to the primitive, survival without ideals.'

'You've given Caputo a name. It's only good for an inscription on a tombstone, but it's something.'

'It's the best thing I've done.'

'As well as understanding what became of him.'

'Sometimes human wrecks fight among themselves, and it all ends badly. A wreck is a wreck and it makes no difference if you're poor or rich.'

'What are you saying?'

'That Caputo was murdered.'

'How did you find that out?'

Soneri laughed. 'You won't believe it but it was from that Neanderthal's shattered skull.'

'You're kidding!'

'It's true. A blow like that is from a brawl. It's not a mafia crime. Can you see a *camorrrista* like Bovino lying in wait with a wrench, a club or an iron bar?'

'What are you going to do now?'

'Wait. If everything goes the way I think it will, I'm going to have a clear-the-air meeting.'

'The same old riddles.'

'As you know, I'm a bit superstitious. I'm afraid to say what I think is coming next,' Soneri concluded.

He lay down on the bed fully clothed without even taking off his shoes. He tried to sleep but without success, his imagination overwhelmed with all that had been unfolding. The events followed one after another in sequence, all neatly lined up and forming one fluid current like the river which was gently rocking his abode. His exhaustion evaporated with a rush of adrenaline. Before midnight, he saw the Viking come out of the club and get into his car. Then came Pezzani, Ceriani and finally Cefalú, who stood outside smoking, waiting for Marisa to make her exit. The two of them stood chatting while she turned off the lights and locked the door. The man made a pass but to keep him off she gave him an unconvincing push which was perhaps more an invitation. Then they went off together. Everything was as ambiguous as the mist. Soneri waited a little longer and then, around two o'clock, made his own way out. The silence and the dark were so absolute as to put daylight's arrival in doubt. He climbed into his car and made for Via Bassa dei Folli. There he hid the car in the bushes and continued his journey on foot. He had come equipped with some Parmesan and two rolls to keep him warm during his wait. He entered as before from the back and moved to the upper floor. He took a brief look through the blinds at the courtyard outside which gave onto the road, and sat down in the damp darkness of the kitchen. If everything went as he expected, the epilogue would not be long delayed. The hours before dawn are when the terrors of the night crowd in and inspire escape in search of hope.

From a far-off belltower it struck three, then four. Soneri was beginning to feel a flicker of disappointment when he saw a car approach and switch off its headlights before slowing down in front of the building and proceeding into the coach house. At that hour it could be no-one else but him, faithfully keeping an appointment which had never been agreed but which was pre-ordained. He heard the clink of the keys, one being inserted in the lock, turned three times and the door opening. Before the man had time to pull out his cell phone to switch on the light, Soneri shone his torch in his face. Rinaldo Gallerani took a step back and almost lost his balance. His back bumped into the door, which snapped shut with the sound of a trap.

'I've been waiting for you,' said Soneri, keeping the light on his face.

Gallerani began trembling as he had done during the interrogation. He must have had a nervous problem, a deeply ingrained insecurity.

'I have insomnia, and so I go out,' he said mechanically, twisting his hands as he tried to justify himself.

'And here you would find peace, when you didn't find Bovino here.'

'We gave him permission to come here from time to time.'

'Because he no longer trusted sleeping down at the river?'

'That might have been the reason.'

'He was afraid of being ambushed.'

'Probably.'

Rinaldo tried to take refuge in the darkness of the room, but Soneri kept the light trained on his face.

'Do you know what your showing up here means?'

Rinaldo's eyes opened wider, and his mouth fell open in stupefaction and fear.

'Don't you want to speak out? Shall I speak for you?' Soneri goaded him, his voice rising and sounding threatening.

The other seemed paralysed. The torch blinded him and fear left him dumb. After a little while, he gave way. Twisted and turning, he put his hands over his face, crumpled and a bundle of nerves before falling to his knees on the floor trying to escape the light. When Soneri turned the torchlight on him again, he spun round suddenly and in the beam of light a look of hatred and terror appeared. Foam formed at the edges of his mouth as he mumbled something incomprehensible and sounding like a lament.

'It must be a great weight on you,' said Soneri, suddenly understanding.

Rinaldo curled up even more tightly. He clasped his hands round his knees, pushed his back harder against the wall and turned his face away to escape the torchlight. He sought darkness like an animal seeking his den.

'You used to come here with your father, didn't you?' Soneri started up again.

The other turned slightly, in a gesture to signify assent.

'They were lovely times, I imagine, with the house on the Po, going fishing and the houseboat afloat on the river. In springtime, when the waters were in flood with the thaw, it must have been wonderful to spend time here with your father.'

Soneri gave his imagination free rein. His own reconstruction of the case was finally taking a distinct shape. He had a hunch that it must have all gone the way he had thought, and he now felt entitled to put these thoughts into words. Rinaldo, far from denying anything, listened in silence like a child enraptured by a fable of monsters and witches. At a certain point, Soneri stopped talking and the man turned round, giving the impression of wondering why he had fallen silent.

'Is that how it was?'

Rinaldo relaxed a little and said simply, 'Yes.'

'Then everything fell apart, the love, the happiness…'

Rinaldo once more curled up with a tremor, like a sudden spasm of pain.

Soneri resumed the questioning. 'When did this happen?'

'At secondary school.'

'Your father noticed that you weren't like your brother Fabio, unflinching, unscrupulous. You weren't cut out for a life in business. You were too sensitive, too delicate and insecure. Like your mother.'

Soneri heard him swallow hard several times, and then moved the light away, leaving him briefly in the dark. He was unsure if he was crying or if he was suffering tearlessly. He was aware of him breathing heavily in the effort to relive what had been taken away from him.

'And then the other one turned up,' Soneri continued relentlessly. 'Caputo came along to usurp not only your father but also your memories, the touching memories of happiness in this house. From that moment, the happy child was Giovanni, unconsciously taking on the role which had been yours. You and your mother were the losers, both replaced by others, but you were still alive!'

Rinaldo was no longer breathing heavily. He was quite still, not moving a muscle, like an animal pretending to be dead in order to ward off some danger.

'For a number of years you tried patiently to heal the wound, dragged along in Fabio's wake, leaving all the decision-making to him. When your father died, you dreamed of retiring here, the one place in the world where you had been happy, but the past came surging back in the form of your half-brother who had been lost and all of a sudden was refound. And then the wound started to bleed again.'

In the dark, Rinaldo gave a start.

'You really wanted this house, didn't you?'

'He wanted to take it away from me!' he screamed, jumping to his feet in a fury. All his rage exploded like time bomb. 'I offered him more money. I didn't give a damn about that, but he wanted the house.'

'You could have opposed him. You had no obligation to give it to him, and he couldn't claim it as of right.'

'My brother was quite prepared to sign it over,' he shouted, his eyes filled with hatred. 'Let's leave him that shack and we'll make a saving, that was his view. He already had more than me, but it was never enough for him. He might have sold off his part of the house and what was I to do then? All he ever thought about was money.'

'What happened the day you went to pick Caputo up at the bed & breakfast in Borgo Marodolo?'

Rinaldo seemed resigned and even relaxed as he began to speak. 'I phoned from a bar in Sissa and promised we would find a solution. Then I went to pick him up in the car. We came here, sat at that table and we both felt it was like speaking in front of a mirror. Do you understand that there was no possible solution? You can mediate between different people, but how do you proceed between two who are identical? We were squabbling inside the nest and one of us had to leap out.'

'What did you use?'

Rinaldo shook his head and gave a little, nervous giggle. 'My father's walking stick. It was big and heavy, carved of oak. '

'Did you get rid of the body yourself?'

'No, I called up Bovino, and he took care of it. He then set up that scene with the wrecked boat, but since he didn't understand the Po he chose the wrong boat and it was all ridiculous.'

'Where's the walking stick?'

'I threw it into the river, and the current carried it off. The river carries everything away. It'll carry off us as well, me and you, and all our useless strivings,' Rinaldo murmured, pulling out a chair from under the table, collapsing onto it like a dead body.

Soneri went outside, searching for some light, perhaps from a nearby lamppost. He phoned Signora Falchieri, his phone ringing fifteen times before it awakened her.

'You must have a good reason for phoning at this time,' she replied wearily.

Soneri grunted by way of agreement.

'Have we arrived at the terminus?' she asked.

'We have and I'm getting off.' He sounded exhausted. He summarised how things had gone and promised a report at the earliest opportunity. As he spoke, he could hear the river flowing by on the far side of the towpath, measuring out the time.

'You can't get off yet,' she admonished him. 'Not now, after solving the case.'

'I haven't solved a thing.'

'You just told me Rinaldo has...'

'He too is a victim.'

'So what should we do?'

'What could we have done, you mean?'

'I don't get it.'

'Oh, forget it. Discussions now are useless. Or maybe they always were.'

'We've played our part, and we've come out on top. That should be enough for you,' she said, cutting him off.

'You're wrong. Other people, the survivors, the cynics, the indifferent, they're the winners. We're the people who gather up the bodies after the battle.'

Acknowledgements

Thank you, Alex Borlenghi, Anna Galvani, Anna Johnson, Karen McAulay and Charlie Johnson.

Many thanks also to David Janes for the cover design and to Tobias Jones.

About the author and translator

Valerio Varesi was born in Turin. He became a journalist and is currently working at *La Repubblica* newspaper. He is the author of 16 crime novels starring Commissario Soneri. *River of shadows* was nominated for the prestigious Italian prize 'Strega' and also for the Gold Dagger award in Britain. The books about the gourmet Soneri have been translated into eight languages. Four of his novels, including *River of shadows*, have been dramatised for the Italian television series, *Nebbie e delitti*. The English editions of his books were previously published by MacLehose Press.

Joseph Farrell is Professor Emeritus in Italian at the University of Strathclyde, Glasgow. He has translated several Italian novels, including by Leonardo Sciascia, as well as other novels by Valerio Varesi. Theatre works include English editions of plays by Dario Fo, Eduardo De Filippo, Carlo Goldoni and Luigi Pirandello and translations of three film scripts by Giuseppe Tornatore. He is co-author with actor-author, Franca Rame, of *Non è tempo di nostalgia* (2013) and *La mia vita, le mie battaglie* (2015) with the novelist Dacia Maraini.

Lightning Source UK Ltd.
Milton Keynes UK
UKHW041302210622
404747UK00010B/212